THE YOUNG WIDOWER'S HANDBOOK

THE YOUNG WIDOWER'S HANDBOOK

a novel

TOM McALLISTER

ALGONQUIN BOOKS
OF CHAPEL HILL
2017

McAllister

Published by
Algonquin Books of Chapel Hill
Post Office Box 2225
Chapel Hill, North Carolina 27515-2225

a division of
Workman Publishing
225 Varick Street
New York, New York 10014

This is a work of fiction. While, as in all fiction, the literary perceptions and insights are based on experience, all names, characters, places, and incidents either are products of the author's imagination or are used fictitiously.

LIBRARY OF CONGRESS CATALOGING-IN-PUBLICATION DATA
Names: McAllister, Tom, author.
Title: The young widower's handbook / a novel by Tom McAllister.
Description: First edition. | Chapel Hill, North Carolina : Algonquin Books of Chapel Hill, 2017. | "Published simultaneously in Canada by Thomas Allen & Son Limited."
Identifiers: LCCN 2016016078 | ISBN 9781616204747
Subjects: LCSH: Man-woman relationships—Fiction. | Bereavement—Fiction. | Voyages and travels—Fiction.
Classification: LCC PS3613.C2653 Y68 2016 | DDC 813/.6—dc23
LC record available at https://lccn.loc.gov/2016016078

10 9 8 7 6 5 4 3 2 1
First Edition

For LauraBeth, as always

ONE

You don't fall in love at first sight, or first kiss even, but many months later, at that indelible moment when you awake in her bed before sunrise, her breath hot on your back, arm draped across your ribs, the contours of her hips flowing into you, and you feel like you're two interlocking puzzle pieces, built specifically to fit together with each other and no one else. The room is sound-less and still, and you're afraid to move because you don't want to disturb her, so you stay there, unblinking, unbreathing, for nearly an hour, until she finally shifts and grazes your shoulder with her lips, a kiss soft like the caress of a ghost.

When she wakes up you want to tell her you love her, but you don't say anything because you're terrified she doesn't feel the same way, and so you wait another month, all the while seeking the perfect way to make the grand announcement. Should you give her the same generic greeting cards that thousands of less deserving women will receive from men less devoted than you? A singing telegram? Skywriting? You're nearly drowning in love, unable to see her without feeling your heart quivering, and at night you cry in the shower while envisioning her inevitable rejection of you, because you're too awkward or too ugly or too boring for her to want you in the same way you want her. Still red-faced and puffy-eyed, you exit the bathroom with a towel wrapped around your suddenly embarrassing body, and she reads the angst in your expression, asks what's wrong. In your brain, the response sounds like this: *I love you and I don't ever want to lose you.* But somewhere between brain and mouth, the words mutate into this: "I want to spy on you," which you immediately acknowledge as being creepy, and she tells you, yes, it really is creepy, and you try to explain that you are not actually a creepy person. "What I mean is, I want to watch you," you say, and she says that's not much better. And, understanding that she has vaguely defined anxieties about invasion of privacy, understanding she's a more fearful person than she wants people to know, you tell her it's like this: you totally and completely trust her, and don't want to spy on her in that way, but rather you want to watch her because you love her so deeply and want to know every-thing possible about her, even the parts of her she feels compelled to hide from you; all you want is to be entrenched in the knowledge of her and to wrap yourself inside of her being. And she says, "Yeah, that's still creepy." At which point you think perhaps the only ratio-nal solution is to dive headfirst through her bedroom window and disappear forever, but then she adds: "I love you too."

You don't fall in love with breasts or legs or a smile—although you notice them too, can't help noticing them the first time you see her, wearing denim shorts and a white tank top on the roof of a college friend's apartment during a midsummer party—but you fall in love with something intangible, the hollowness like devastating hunger when she's gone, the sense of safety she engenders, as if her presence alone will protect you from the terrors of the real world. Still, you're groping at each other during every private moment, and you know for her it's not because of an intense physical attraction but because she loves something fundamental about your being. All the famous people she thinks are attractive look distinctly unlike you; they're powerful and tall and have permanent five o'clock shadows and tan faces and smiles made for billboards. On good days, you think you look a bit like a paler, less fit Paul Newman—it's the eyes, the hairline, the nose—so you make her watch *The Hustler* and *Hud* and *The Sting*, but she doesn't see the resemblance and she says he's not all that special anyway. "I like you much better than him," she says in such a way that you actually almost believe her. She does not quite look like the famous people you think are attractive, either, although you tell her she looks better than them, and you go out of your way to denigrate the appearances of celebrities who intimidate her, because the truth is, she is actually the most beautiful woman who will ever pay any attention to you and you want her to understand that she doesn't need to compete with movie people, because in your world movie people don't really exist.

You don't fall in love, like some people do, with the idea of being in love, but rather with her, specifically, and only her. Throughout high school and college, you were an extra in the movies of other people's lives, never better than the fourth most charismatic person in any group; your role was to be the designated driver and to occasionally deliver a sarcastic one-liner that your friends could later repeat and claim as their own. And yet when you speak, she listens. You begin telling her things you never thought you'd tell anyone, things none of your friends know and probably never cared to know—how, when you were very young, you used to hide inside household appliances, then laughed while hearing the panic in your parents' voices, although that all stopped when your father caught on to your game and ran the dishwasher with you inside, that's where that blotchy scar on your forearm comes from; how your grandmother bought you a telescope for your birthday, but you only used it to watch the neighbor girls, twins a few years older than you, spying on them for a solid three years until the day they both left for college; how you used to chew on your toenails when bored, bending your leg right up to your mouth and gnawing; how you once shoplifted seventy dollars worth of beef jerky from a convenience store and then fed the jerky one stick at a time to a neighbor's dog just to pass the time. The words spill out in torrents, begging to be heard by someone, and every time you think you're out of secrets, you find more and more and more and continually unload them, and even though you think you're talking too much, she asks follow-up questions, laughs when she's supposed to laugh, and says things like *that's interesting* and *you should be more confident*, and you find yourself, over time, slouching less, enunciating more clearly, projecting your voice, charming her friends and co-workers at dinner parties and in bowling alleys during company events. She thinks you're funny and you think she's clever and you retreat into conversation with her any time the rest of the world becomes too unwieldy. So you gradually discard your friends, sometimes making requisite appearances at grungy bars to check in with them and rehash embarrassing high school stories while asking questions like *what have you guys been up to?* so frequently that they begin calling you Sparky, short for Spark-Notes, because you're always seeking summaries and main ideas and character sketches rather than doing the real work of knowing them as people. They all say, "Where the hell you been at?" even though they already know the answer.

You live with your parents and she lives with her mother, both of you sleeping in your respective childhood bedrooms; post-college, it made the most sense to stay at home and save up to buy a house, rather than renting, and, except for the yawning distance between your home in Hartford, Connecticut, and hers in Philadelphia, this arrangement has been working out fine, even if some nights you don't feel like reciting the details of the day to your mother over dinner or explaining to her why your English degree hasn't helped you land a job, and the place is starting to suffocate you now that you've met this girl, and your shared love makes the possibilities of the universe seem truly limitless—in contrast to the realities of your current circumstances, which are in every way limiting. You tell your mother you're probably going to start looking for a place of your own soon, it's time for this bird to fly. She tells you to stop trying to sound poetic because you're not.

Your mother calls your bedroom the Shrine, and you tell her to get off your back, it's just some pictures and a few cards, no big deal. Your father says, "You're really into this girl, huh?" and you try to play it cool by shrugging and saying, "Yeah, she's pretty alright, don't you like her too?" And he says she seems nice enough, although she's not around much and he's beginning to wonder why you're hiding her. Your father adds, "I know how it feels to have your first girlfriend." You say she's not your first, there have been plenty of others, you just haven't brought them home; this is only about a quarter-truth, in that you have never brought another girl home, and you've spoken to many other girls in your life, and in college engaged in oral sex on five nonconsecutive occasions, and anyway, there have been girlfriends here and there, but never anyone serious, just people you took to the movies or accompanied to parties. But you don't say all of this to your father, because you're eyeing your laptop screen and scrolling through updates on the statuses of your friends' lives. Your father stands over you for a few minutes, breathing heavily due to his hypertension and his shallow lungs, and eventually he leaves. You send her a text message asking if you can visit this weekend, and she says *sure!* With an exclamation point, she says it.

You don't fall in love with her because she's like your mother, or because she's the kind of woman you're supposed to marry, but because there is no other choice but to fall in love. She says she feels safe with you, that when you're together she believes the world is a good and fair place; because you respect her and you make her laugh and you try harder at impressing her than you've ever tried at anything. You max out your credit card taking her on a Caribbean cruise to celebrate your nine-month anniversary, even though you know anniversaries, by definition, do not occur monthly, but as long as she commemorates monthly anniversaries, then you will too. Your father claims that a cruise is the ultimate test of a relationship; if you can deal with being stuck together at sea for a full week, then your love will last. Neighbors and friends seem over-eager to share with you their own love tests, all oddly specific and perhaps too revealing of their past failures. Your mother says the ultimate test is taking a road trip, which you also do, heading north from Hartford to Maine, and you return with three hundred photos and the trunk dragging under the weight of several cases of maple syrup. A co-worker at the rental car agency tells you the ultimate test is looking through childhood photo albums and still liking each other, and so you arrange an album-viewing night, the pictures only deepening your appreciation of her because even in her least flattering moments she still looks like exactly the person you love. Your elderly neighbor says the real test is living together, and after a year of dating, you tell her you want to buy a house with her.

She says, "I'm not moving anywhere until I get a ring," and you say modern marriage is just an expensive scam perpetrated by mendacious vendors, all of whom are expecting handouts in exchange for validating your love via the ornate decoration of pastries or the prompt delivery of calla lilies. You tell her the marriage industry preys on the naïve dreams of girls who have been raised under the delusion that they are all princesses destined for royal weddings, and that a failure to stage the most elaborate party possible will result in the failure of a marriage and therefore the manifestation of a woman's eternal unhappiness, because they, the vendors and the wholesalers of love, want women to believe they can't be happy or self-actualized if they're unmarried. She says she doesn't care about all that, she wants to be married—married to you, specifically—and would you stop dragging your feet already, you're twenty-four and it's time to start growing up, and although she's right, you're still not thrilled about the idea of spending thirty thousand dollars you don't have on a lavish party that you yourself won't get to enjoy because you'll be too busy attending to everyone else's needs to even eat your own cake. But a few weeks later, there's the proposal—down on your knee in Rittenhouse Square in Philly, a trite and unimaginative proposal, probably there have been fifteen thousand proposals made in the same spot, and you apologize later for the triteness of the proposal, but you truly couldn't think of any other proposal that wasn't prohibitively expensive, and still now, there's the regret for not doing it right, and not giving her the sweet and memorable proposal story to tell all of her marriage-obsessed friends when they ask her to re-create the moment for them.

And then the next year whirs past with planning and house buying and congratulations and gifts and party after party after party and the wedding and heartfelt declarations of love for each other on a Pocono mountaintop, where you go for your honeymoon because the wedding and the new home have wiped out your savings, but you'll have a real honeymoon soon, as long as you're responsible and you save.

You promise her someday you'll be able to afford a make-up honeymoon, you will get rich and embark on a perpetual vacation, and you'll be like people in the movies, the way your lives will always play out in front of the most remarkable backdrops. You insist you'll both be very worldly, the type of people who can say, with authority, *you don't want to go to Belize in May,* or *it's remarkable how different Irish cuisine is from Scottish* or *Doha was pleasant but I very much preferred Dubai.* She says she doesn't need all that, but you know that's not true, and you see the wistful look in her eye when she watches travel programs on cable, the way she relishes nitpicking and insulting the reality TV families who get to experience the things she cannot.

You open a joint bank account and take out exorbitant life insurance policies, and you buy one car, to share, and a king-size bed because she thrashes in her sleep, and get a new roof installed, and talk about building a fireplace and installing laminate floors in the bedrooms, and start repainting the kitchen, and host potluck dinners and cocktail parties for her friends and family. Nights you spend naming places you'll visit, the landmarks you will see and the memories you will create, the photo albums you will fill so you can circulate them among envious friends and family and later pass them on to your children and grandchildren. She drafts a spreadsheet with potential dates and costs and locations, and you notify your families not to schedule anything for June 2020, because you'll be on the Trans-Siberian railroad then, but July that year will be fine. You buy new luggage and new wardrobes. You get passports, international drivers' licenses, and translation dictionaries. You research the relative strength of foreign currencies. Life becomes an obsession of planning and consolidation. You're clipping coupons and studying travel restrictions, and she's working extra hours, and on exhausted miserable nights when she can barely open her eyes because of the migraine that keeps kicking her in the head, you tell her *I know you're unhappy now, but it will all be worth it later,* because you're laying the groundwork for a lifetime of happiness, but none of that matters anymore because she's dead and she's dead and she's dead and she's dead and she's dead and she's never coming back.

TWO

On Monday Kaitlyn Cady went for a five-mile run, on Tuesday night she experienced severe stomach pains, by Wednesday morning she was dead, on Thursday she was burned down to ashes and poured into a stainless steel cube, and on Friday she was delivered by a stranger to her husband, Hunter.

To describe her death as *sudden* is to reduce it to cliché, to not do justice to the swiftness with which she stopped existing. Suddenness refers to the honking of a car horn, or the dropping of a dish on ceramic tile, or the crack of lightning in a fast-moving summer storm. It does not, should not, refer to people dying, and yet that's the word everyone keeps saying to Hunter. They pat him on the shoulder and shake their heads earnestly and say *damn, it was so sudden.* They blow their noses and they squeeze his hand and they say *I can't believe how sudden it was*. They hug him, tears wet against his chest, and they say *it's so sudden; I feel like I was just talking to her yesterday.*

ON THE DRIVE TO the hospital that Tuesday night, he laughed. Made an ill-advised joke about menstrual cramps. Thought it would lighten the mood, make her feel better. She did not laugh, and so he turned up the radio and pretended he'd never said anything.

IN THE LAST MOMENTS, there were two people in the room besides Hunter and Kait: a tech fiddling with a malfunctioning IV pump, and a young resident palpating Kait's abdomen, asking if she was pregnant, if she had any food allergies, if she still had her appendix, and so on. While the doctor continued poking at her, Kait reached out to grab Hunter's hand and squeeze. It wasn't until this moment—feeling the military force of her grip, the strange coldness of her palms, the palpable fear—that he realized quite how serious this situation was. He gave her his other hand and let her squeeze, wanted her to crush all the tiny bones in his hands so he could absorb the pain for her. The resident said she wanted to talk to the gastroenterologist, but in the meantime they should run some tests. She told Hunter to go out and get something to eat because the tests would probably take a couple hours. And even though he was beginning to worry that this would end in some kind of surgery, Hunter believed her when she said, "We'll have her back to you soon." He didn't once think that this would be their last moment together. He barely thought at all. He leaned down and kissed Kait on the forehead and told her he would be waiting for her when she got back. "I don't want to go," she said, still squeezing his hand. A minute later, they were wheeling her away. Hunter followed her into the hall and watched her pass through the double doors and then get swallowed by the elevator and then digested by the building.

A NURSE TOLD HUNTER he could see the body if he wanted to. Not only did he not want to, but it seemed like the worst possible thing anyone could do at that moment was to look at Kait's corpse, and so he said no, but still the nurse hooked him by the elbow and led him through a series of doors and curtains until he was standing over the body, and he swore he could see her breathing, not just the up-down of the chest, but the actual breath, as if they were outdoors in winter. He wanted to capture the breath in a jar and carry it with him, uncap the lid during times of crisis and inhale her essence. He couldn't force himself to touch her, was afraid to move beyond the doorframe, and the nurse said she understood, it's very difficult to lose a loved one. Hunter nodded, said, "Please don't leave me," and the nurse, thinking he was talking to Kait, left.

HE WAS THE ONE who had to break the news. To everyone. He hadn't even told anyone she was feeling sick, his mild form of protest against the tyranny of her family's constant feed of updates, via every network imaginable: phones, Twitter, Facebook, photo-sharing websites, e-mails, text messages, especially text messages, every time anything allegedly noteworthy happened to anyone in the Dixon family, the definition of *noteworthy* being broad enough to include updates on a nephew's suspension from school and a cousin's recent battle with indigestion, so that every day demanded the filtering of reams of unnecessary information, which is why, when Kait wanted to call her brother to complain about her stomach pains, Hunter said, "Let's just wait, there's no need to tell everyone everything all the time." Not that their knowing about it would likely have changed the end result. But maybe.

He knew the first call should be to Kait's mother, Sherry, but didn't think he could endure that agonizing conversation, and was afraid that when he told her brothers, they would blame him and want to fight him, and so the first person he called upon learning that his wife was dead was Linda, one of Kait's co-workers at the bank, a casual acquaintance who nonetheless howled with grief, weeping so fiercely that Hunter's phone became waterlogged with her tears.

He made twelve phone calls before contacting anyone in the family, by which point he was already so numb from having repeated the story that he was doing it by rote, and expected to be able to break hearts without any hesitation. And yet, when he heard Sherry wailing on the other end of the line, he lost his voice, couldn't answer any of her questions, and passed the phone off to a nearby nurse.

THE OFFICIAL CAUSE OF death was listed as massive internal bleeding caused by a ruptured fallopian tube, the result of an ectopic pregnancy, a condition fraught with this reality: they had conceived a child together, and that child had killed her, or, more accurately, Hunter himself was the murder weapon, the one who had implanted the destructive thing inside her. If he had mixed anthrax into her oatmeal, he would be in prison, but now people are commiserating with him, as if he had nothing to do with it. As if it wasn't his fault.

THEY ARE ALL AT his house—her extended family, not his, he has no family beyond his parents—by the time he returns from the hospital, the brothers lining up empty beer cans on the window sill in the kitchen, Sherry flopped facedown on the couch, a nephew, obsessed with death like so many little boys, running aimlessly around the kitchen table firing imaginary pistols at everyone. Brutus, the oldest brother, grabs Hunter roughly by the shoulders and engulfs him in a bear hug. Billy, the middle brother, pats Hunter on the back while this is happening. Brutus releases Hunter and wipes a tear off his cheek. "It's okay to cry," he says, perhaps to himself. He digs into a cooler and tosses Hunter a can of Bud, which Hunter opens and holds in his lap for the next three hours, sitting on the floor in front of the couch while the brothers tell the same stories about Kait that they've told on every holiday and at every family gathering before this, a litany of palliative anecdotes so familiar they could all fill in the details without even listening: when she and her friends in sixth grade had been picked up by the cops for throwing rocks through a rival girl's bedroom window; when Billy, the middle brother, had paid a friend to hide in Kait's closet and spy on her, how she didn't speak to Billy for a week after that; how she had spent a whole summer secretly visiting a speech therapist to lose her Philly accent, but it always resurfaced when she was excited; how eager she had been to help Max, the youngest brother, get dressed for the prom, the way she cried when she saw him in his bow tie and his cummerbund, how angry she'd been when he got drunk and lost the tux after the dance, came stumbling home in his underwear.

Sherry, still lying on the couch, sometimes seems to vibrate, and they hear her muffled laughter mixed with her tears. She rests her hand on Hunter's shoulder, as if trying to keep herself from falling. He stays there, leaning into her touch and keeping her afloat, but says nothing all night, has nothing to say.

WHEN SOMEONE DIES, THE people around the bereaved become dramatically and disconcertingly helpful, to the point that no one will allow Hunter to do anything for himself, not even simple tasks like filling a glass of water or standing under his own power. They answer questions for him. They cook and they clean, and they would chew his food if they could. Hunter spends two full days being ushered about his own home by Kait's friends and family, carried like an oversized puppet, becoming a prop in a play about his own grief.

WILLOW, HIS MOTHER, ARRIVES the second morning, yoga mat tucked under her arm, a canvas bag slung over her shoulder, the squealing front door announcing her entrance. Kait's brothers, sprawled on the couches and the floor, groan and stretch and unleash boozy yawns. Hunter stayed downstairs with them, lay on the floor all night, didn't want to face his empty bed yet. He barely slept, wishes he hadn't slept at all; nobody should be able to sink into sleep the night their wife dies, no matter how tired they are.

Willow flows into the room, unstoppable, and kneels next to Hunter, engulfs him in a hug. "I'm staying here as long as you need me," she says, and she begins collecting the empty cans, hauling them outside to the recycling bin.

JUST A COUPLE WEEKS before Kait's death, she and Hunter were sitting in the living room watching a reality show called *Spirit Quest*, which chronicled four men who somehow made a living hunting ghosts. They traveled to rural towns with a variety of science-adjacent instruments and tried to communicate with the dead. Most scenes were shot in old mills and abandoned warehouses. The show seemed to posit that ghosts primarily congregate in sites of failed industry, rather than in the more intimate settings of bedrooms and family burial plots. Everything was filmed in a greenish night-vision tint and underscored with an unearned gravity, especially during the moments when they claimed to have made contact with ghosts. Kait liked watching reruns while they ate leftovers for dinner, a mindless entertainment for weekday evenings when they were both too tired to engage in anything intellectually, when all they wanted was noise and lights to distract them. She had looked particularly burned out that evening when she got home, dragging herself through the door.

One of the ghost hunters strapped a cranial spectrometer—essentially a miner's helmet with flashing lights on the sides—to his head and was lowered into a mineshaft. Kait absentmindedly ran her hand along Hunter's thigh. "I know this is ridiculous," she said, "and they're never going to find anything. But it's kind of hopeful, isn't it? The idea that there's something else waiting for us." As long as Hunter had known her, Kait hadn't been interested in heaven or hell, but she had always believed in the existence of ghosts.

"You do have to admire their earnestness," Hunter said.

"Do you think it's easier when you're a ghost?" she said. "Like, do you think you just get to be whatever you want, or do you think they still have jobs and bills and everything else?"

"I'm sure you're expected to put in a certain number of haunting hours. Thirty a week, maybe," Hunter said. "Middle managers die and turn into ghosts too. And there's no way they let you get away with just doing *nothing*."

"And then every six months there's a performance evaluation?" Kait transitioned into her Boss Voice, the self-important fat-jowled baritone she used when imitating men in power. "Dixon, your chain clanking and light flickering exceed expectations but your overall spookiness quotient needs some work."

"We'd like to send you to a professional development seminar this weekend on how to enhance your Internal Scare Factor," Hunter added.

She laughed with him. "What a bunch of assholes," she said. On TV, a guy named Wyatt looked at his instruments and said the ghostly activity in the room was off the charts. He called for the spirits to show themselves. Kait dropped her fork and it clattered on her plate. "Would it kill them to sometimes just leave the fucking ghosts alone?" Hunter reached over to squeeze her hand. As always, it was ice cold, seemingly bloodless. "Did I tell you I had a meeting with Jefferson today?"

She had told him that morning, and he'd been waiting to hear how it went, but he'd learned early in their relationship that it was best to let her talk about her work day at her own pace. If he'd started grilling her when she walked in the door, she would have just said it had been fine and left it at that. Jefferson was the regional manager. He had hair like a young Travolta and he kept an acoustic guitar in his office for impromptu jam sessions. He'd been accused of sexual harassment by three different women and gotten transferred to new regions each time. His father was Somebody Important. "So I went in to see him, and of course he was a half hour late to his own office, but I was there on time. But okay, whatever, that's how it is when you're the boss." She stared at the floor and her words came out too fast, like she was afraid of what would happen if she stopped talking. "I handed him everything he asked for—customer satisfaction surveys, quarterly reports, everything. And he didn't even look at them. You know what he said to me? He said, 'I've been watching you. You really ought to start smiling more.'"

"Christ."

"You're so pretty but think how much prettier you'd be if you smiled," he said. "Think how much happier the customers would be."

"He didn't even *pretend* to care about your work?"

"You know the worst thing? I smiled at him. I thanked him for his feedback." She picked up her fork and threw it down, stood up and walked a lap around the coffee table, fussed with the blinds on a window across the room.

"You have to report him."

"What if I don't want to fucking smile? You know? What if what I want is to be sad? Why isn't that allowed?"

"It is," Hunter said, standing and catching her in the middle of another lap. He pulled her into him and wrapped his arms around her; her shoulders were vibrating with adrenaline. "That guy . . . that motherfucker. He's not allowed to do that to you. He's not allowed to—"

"But he is. That's the problem. He can do whatever he wants." She buried her face in his chest and he felt the full weight of her pressing into him. She was right. There was no easy fix, no magic sequence of words that would solve the problem.

On TV, foreboding music suggested that a ghostly encounter was imminent. Hunter fantasized about marching into Jefferson's office, grabbing him by the tie, and pulling him close, eye-to-eye, issuing a terse threat about what would happen next time he disrespected a woman—real Clint Eastwood stuff. It wouldn't happen, he knew, and anyway Kait would be enraged with him if he did something like that. But for a moment, the fantasy made him feel less powerless.

"Thanks for letting me be crazy," Kait said.

"You are not crazy," he said. "I'm sorry I can't do anything to help you."

She leaned up and kissed him. "Thanks for trying," she said.

There is romance and then there is love and although they're related to each other, they are not the same thing. Romance is temporary, predicated on countless variables working synchronously to create something memorable that vaguely recalls a scene from a familiar movie; it's perhaps a step on the way to love, or a reaffir-mation of love, or maybe it's just a single beautiful moment with no other meaning beyond itself. Love, it's this other thing, a thing that manifests itself in the most unremarkable moments. It's there without having to assert itself. To be able to sit next to Kait in a T-shirt and ragged jeans, watching bad TV and eating leftovers, that was a gift.

Kait had once confessed to Hunter that before he came along no one in her life had ever accepted her as herself. Her brothers had mocked her for not being quite like them, for being "too fancy," for acting like she was too good for them and their neighborhood. They loved her, but they didn't understand her. Her mother had first neglected her and later spent years trying to convince her that the way she felt wasn't actually the way she felt. Her friends were friends to the extent that they had fun evenings together, but lately they called only when they needed something. The culture at large had exerted the same pressure on her that it exerts on all women, namely to feel insecure about herself regardless of what she was doing, to feel that simply by being a woman in the world she was necessarily doing something wrong and could only correct her wrongness via endless consumerism and an array of contradictory neuroses. She'd been socialized to always apologize, to smile when a man told her to smile, to believe men who told her she was doing something wrong.

Before Kait, Hunter sometimes worried that through some cata-strophic mix-up he'd ended up on the wrong planet, a place where he felt both like and unlike everyone else at the same time. Despite whatever euphemisms Willow used to describe young Hunter—he was *independent* or *eccentric* or *an old soul*—the truth is that he was a weird kid. He was uncomfortable and shy and twitchy, and even though he can't remember many specific incidents of bullying or rejection, the overriding emotion he associates with adolescence is a loneliness so heavy it pinned him to his bed most mornings and threatened to suffocate him. He'd tried—been forced by his parents to try—to assimilate, attending school events and joining the bowling team and calling girls to ask them on dates. But even when things were ostensibly going well, when he made the guys laugh at the lunch table or danced with a girl at a mixer, he felt that distance between him and his peers, an understanding that although he'd forged a connection, it was only temporary. Mostly he read books and smoked pot and watched endless hours of TV. By the time he met Kait, he'd accepted isolation as his fate, as a punishment for whatever part of him had gone bad at birth. Willow had assured him college would help him to open up and find himself, but he spent most of his time there wondering how everyone else felt so comfortable and confident. Wondering how everyone else *knew what to do.* It seemed like there was some secret handshake you were taught at birth by the Illuminati or the Freemasons or someone, and some people just weren't allowed to learn it. So he rejected the world in advance and erected a series of defense mechanisms that would exacerbate his problems. By this point, his every thought and action was a reaction to a perceived or expected slight. He was a prodigy at bitterness and cynicism. But when Kait made eye contact with him, the fear dissipated. When she held his hand, she anchored him to the world. When she spoke, he felt like a stranger in a strange land who finally hears a fellow countryman speaking his own language. For the first time, he felt that his birth hadn't been a terrible accident.

He wrote all of this down for her once, the way she'd saved him, because every time he tried to articulate his feelings, he stuttered and fumbled and got too frustrated to continue. He wrote about what a great fortune it is to be able to be in a room with another person who gives you permission to be yourself. He wrote that when they were together he felt the tumblers falling into place as she turned the key in his soul. One night, they were sitting in her car in a movie theater parking lot, and he handed her a letter. "These are a lot of things I've been trying to say, but couldn't figure out how," he said, only later realizing that her first instinct was to assume this was a breakup letter. While she read he couldn't tell from her expression whether she was weirded out or thrilled or what, and so he let himself out of the car and paced nervous circles around it. A minute later, she lowered the window and said, "I wrote you something too." She passed the letter to him. On the back, she'd left a single sentence: *Loving you is the easiest thing I've ever done.*

Willow makes him drive her to Old City Philadelphia, ostensibly so she can see Independence Hall and the Liberty Bell and the nation's first post office, but also so she can distract him. She says it is a beautiful day, which it is, the kind of day that inspires poetry and folk songs and that, at any other time, Hunter would call *life-affirming*, but instead it seems mocking and inappropriate. People lounge on every spare patch of grass, sunbathing, sprawled like corpses on a battlefield. Willow leads him to a restaurant that serves farm-fresh organic food and asks the server to seat them outside. While Hunter picks at his salad, she tells him about her college softball team's trip to Philadelphia for a tournament. The coach had tried to take the team on a tour of the historic sites, but she'd sneaked away to a South Philly bar and got herself kicked off the team. "I was so bad then," she says, laughing, nudging his leg beneath the table with her foot, until he forces a smile. "This was before your father, of course."

"I'm sure Jack would have been a real blast if he'd been there," Hunter says.

"He was different then. You've seen the pictures." She's referring specifically to her favorite photo: his father, Jack, sitting in the grass near a line of train tracks, beard unkempt, denim jacket torn at the elbows, red bandana pulling his hair back from his face, blowing cigarette smoke up at the sky and looking like an extra in *Easy Rider*. She has showed Hunter photos of college-aged Jack dozens of times, always narrating with comments like *you might not believe it but your father was a real free spirit*.

"A man like your father," Willow says, "he doesn't do well with this sort of thing."

"Your whole life you've been making excuses for him."

"Don't tell me what I've been doing my whole life," Willow says. "I've known your father since I was twenty years old. You want to think you two are so different but you have no idea."

Hunter flicks a crouton off his plate and into the street. He watches and listens for the crunch of a car tire destroying it. Willow swipes a finger through the condensation on her water glass and leans across the table. With her damp finger, she draws a cross on his forehead as if anointing him. "I hoped you would learn to practice forgiveness by now."

HIS HOUSE IS INFESTED: there are co-workers and college friends, neighbors and ex-boyfriends, and there are so many Dixons, many of whom he has not seen since the wedding. They are streaming through his house, eating the sandwiches and fruit platters that seem to be delivered hourly, as if people think the problem isn't that Kait is dead, but simply that she is hungry. The doorbell never stops ringing, because there are always more sandwiches and flowers to be delivered, and he feels obligated to tip every deliveryman, and by the way, how are flowers supposed to make him feel better in any way? Hunter sits on the end of the couch while little nieces and nephews and cousins scramble underfoot and throw chunks of fruit at one another. Kait's aunts are sorting her belongings into various boxes, some marked DONATE and some marked KEEPERS, and even though they are helping him, even though they are *tying up loose ends*, he is disturbed to see how easily a life can be categorized and boxed and bagged and disposed of, all of its loose ends tied up and all of its meaning suddenly stripped away. Everyone in the room fights encroaching silences, filling the gaps with jokes and loud laughter, no matter how unfunny the joke, as if volume alone can drown out the unhappiness. In the kitchen, a committee of Dixons has taken on the responsibility of planning the memorial service—which he is certain she would not have wanted—and others are calling credit card companies and utilities and cell phone providers to report the death. It's helpful, sure, but he does not want to be helped, he wants to be allowed to wallow, to let the bills pile up around him, to allow the food to rot, be allowed to stay motionless until he atrophies and develops legendary pressure sores, while his neglected house is swallowed by the earth itself.

"Where's your compost pile, Hun?" Willow calls from the kitchen, as if that has any relevance to his current life.

The next time the doorbell rings, Hunter announces, "Good news guys! More fucking sandwiches!" But it isn't sandwiches; what it is is the ashes, inside the container he must have chosen at some point but cannot remember choosing—blue-gray, like a cloudy fall day, her full name etched in gold on top of the cube. The cube is cinched inside a velvet sack and is accompanied by simple instructions for opening, *for when the time is right*. After Hunter tips him five dollars, the courier returns to his car and rumbles away, his trunk presumably full of similar containers, ferrying souls across the Greater Philadelphia area. Everyone behind Hunter stops talking and moving, closing in on him while he holds Kait's remains; many of them seem unaware that she was to be cremated, even though he had told them all before that she would be cremated, and so now they're coming to terms with the fact that they will not be able to view the body one last time. He feels like he should be making a speech, but what is there to say, besides *here she is!*? Thinks about, maybe, *Kait's Home!*—the kind of thing that would have made her laugh (the sound of her laughter already difficult to remember), but also the kind of thing that would probably get him punched by Brutus, who doesn't appreciate humor that is subtler than a fart.

He passes her around the room, the way one would share a newborn baby.

ON THE THIRD NIGHT, he finally enters his bedroom, lies on the floor, can't bring himself to touch the bed, doesn't want to disturb the physical impression she left in the sheets. The Dixons are all sleeping in their own homes now, and so it is just him and Willow and not Kait. Willow knocks on his door in the middle of the night—Hunter still lying awake, tracking his heart beats and treating them as a countdown to his own expiration—and lets herself in. She sits on the floor beneath his window and removes a joint from her pocket. She lights it and summons him to join her. They sit together, blowing the smoke through the open window like teenagers hiding from their parents. "This is not going to work," she says. She takes a deep drag and then exhales slowly, the smoke framing her face so that she looks like an apparition. "This stoic thing you're doing, just swallowing all the sadness and hoping it disappears. You don't have the constitution for it."

"This isn't a *thing* I'm doing," he says.

While Hunter works on the joint, she pulls out a small baggie of pot and some rolling papers, begins expertly rolling another. "When your grandfather died, your father completely broke down. For months, he'd just start crying spontaneously. Once, we were on the highway and he had to pull over because he couldn't see through the tears. He lost twenty pounds. He stopped reading, and every night he would lie on the couch listening to the same Elvis Costello record over and over. He sometimes didn't shower for a week." She runs her tongue over the joint and seals it, takes the lighter from Hunter. "I'd been with him for four years, and I thought I knew everything about him. But he became a new person."

"I thought Jack didn't even like his dad."

"His version of the story is very practiced. He needs to insulate himself."

"So you're saying I should have some kind of breakdown like he did? Then I can turn myself into him?"

"I tried to help him, but I didn't know what to do. I was too young. I'd lived a safe life. I'd never even had anyone die." She lights the joint and studies it in her hand before pressing it to her lips. "This is terrible, but I thought about leaving him. I couldn't handle it anymore."

"What stopped you?"

"I don't know. I had bags packed, I was going to move in with some college friends in Boston. They'd found a job for me. But something kept me there." She looks out the window somewhere beyond the clouds and the moon, toward some version of her un-lived past. "It took him six months to come back to life, and then it was because he had no choice. I got pregnant and we had to start planning."

"So maybe I should get someone pregnant, is what you're saying?"

"After that he was a different man. He's been afraid of his own emotions for three decades."

Hunter rests the back of his head against the windowsill and stares up at the ceiling, tries to focus on a small spot of water damage to keep himself grounded. He imagines the edges of the stain rippling and expanding until the entire ceiling is swallowed by decay. "I know there's some other way I'm supposed to be right now, but I don't know how to start being it."

"The deeper you retreat into yourself, the more it's going to damage you."

He sees in her glassy, bloodshot gaze that she is trying to save him, but she looks so far away, like he's looking up at her from the bottom of the ocean. "The only time in my life when I felt like the world made any sense was when I was with her," he says.

Willow finishes this joint and then opens the baggie to begin rolling another one. Hunter waves her off. She repeatedly zips and unzips the bag in the silence, and then says, "If you need to speak to her, maybe we should try a séance? I've only done it once, but—"

"No. Absolutely not." He rubs his eyes as if trying to dig them out of his skull. "Man, I am really fucking high," he says and they both laugh long enough that by the time they catch their breath and the room is quiet they've forgotten why they started laughing.

"Do you want to know the hardest part about being a parent?" Willow says. " It's not the diapers, the late nights, the parent-teacher conferences. It's knowing that no matter what advice you give your son, he's not going to understand it until it's too late. You have to watch while he makes the exact mistakes you're worried about and then hope he comes out okay on the other side."

Hunter buries his head in his hands and takes several deep breaths, trying to summon the courage to continue living. He tries to swallow, but his throat is so dry, it hurts to even think about swallowing. "How are you supposed to survive?" he says. "How does anybody get through life?" Willow wraps her arm around his shoulder and holds on to him until he falls asleep.

Hunter tells Willow he does not want to attend the memorial service. What good does it do him to put himself on display just to offer some closure to the community? He does not want to perform for them so they can say *oh, I feel so bad for Hunter, but he looks like he's handling it well* or *I'm glad I get to at least pass my respects on to her husband.* They want him there so they can ask *are you okay?* because they want him to say yes, and then they can all pat themselves on the back for being so compassionate, then move on, pretend this chapter of his life is over. Since when does he owe it to anyone to go out and pretend everything is okay, particularly when everything is decidedly, starkly, and painfully *not* okay?

But still he goes. Because Willow says, "It may not feel like it, but this is not all about you." Because Kait would have demanded that he go for her family's sake. Because Sherry—frail and very clearly not eating or sleeping—shows up at his door the morning of the service and says, "We all need to be in this together."

A week after Kait's death, Hunter's boss at the rental car agency calls and tells him it's time to come back. According to corporate policy, grievance leave only lasts four business days, so they'd done him a favor by allowing him a fifth day without officially writing him up. Hunter hangs up, tells Willow he has to go to work, and then spends the next six hours sitting with Kait's cube in his car in a strip-mall parking lot. The cube is easy to open; a simple snap lock on the top panel. At first, he only clicks it open just to see how it works, then closes it. But then he continues practicing, pushing down, unlatching, twisting, the sound unlike the vacuum-sealed pop he anticipated. It's a mechanical click, a quiet scraping of metal on metal upon the turn. Inside, she's like fine soil, like silt washed up on shore. He looks down at her, tries to picture her face within the urn, but cannot. Dipping his index finger down to the second knuckle, he feels her cool against his skin, but she does not feel like herself. After wiping his finger clean, pushing every grain of her back into the cube, he seals it shut. Over the next six hours, he becomes an expert at opening and closing, compulsively twisting and clicking and opening, but he does not look inside again.

When he returns home, Willow has her bags packed. She tells him she's glad he went back to work; he has to stay busy or he might crack up. She says, "Looks like you're getting back on track, and I have to get home." She says Jack is lost without her, and besides, people need her back home too. "Your father and I are planning to come down and check on you in a couple weeks," she adds. She says she loves him. Ten minutes later she leaves, and the house feels cavernous.

THAT EVENING, LYING IN bed with the urn on the nightstand next to him, he thinks about Willow's suggestion of a séance and even though he does not understand the mechanics of séancing nor does he believe in the general practice, he also thinks: maybe? He arranges candles around the perimeter of the room, watches their flickering shadows dance on the wall. He's not stoned now, because Willow didn't leave any pot behind and anyway he suspects that being stoned probably results in false positives vis-à-vis communications with the spirit world. He sits on the carpet in the middle of the room, holding the urn in his lap and trying to will Kait to emerge from within. A proper call to the spirt world almost certainly requires a soundtrack, so he sets Lou Reed's "Perfect Day" on a loop and sings along with it, telling Kait she made him forget himself, made him think he was someone else, someone good. By the fifth cycle through the song, the singing has taken on the tone of a chant. He pauses and follows the lead of the *Spirit Quest* ghost hunters, calling on Kait to show herself. He awaits some cosmic sign, the rattling of the house, the opening of a portal, the whooshing of a spirit through the room, but nothing happens. "I promise I'll leave you alone," he says, "but I just need to see you one more time." He closes his eyes and lies back on the carpet, hoping that if he concentrates hard enough, she will be there again.

When he opens his eyes, he sees thousands of ghosts in his home, each one a vision of Kait at a different stage of their shared life; they crowd into the house shoulder-to-shoulder and some are cooking and some are sleeping and some are dancing and some are hanging pictures and everywhere around him there are Kaits. Kait in motion. Kait in the wallpaper and bubbling in the water supply and buzzing in the wiring in the walls. He calls out to her but she doesn't respond. His voice sounds like it is underwater. He reaches out to touch her, but his arms feel like they've been tied down. His legs have grown roots and he is stuck to the floor, watching as she swirls around him. This is a dream, it must be, and he is torn between the desire to escape and the temptation to live in it forever. Floating just above him, she stops, looks down, and her lips move, but no sounds emerge. She dissolves, all manifestations of her dissolve, and the condensation from her spirit rests on his skin like dew.

In the morning, he is still on the carpet. The candles have burned out, but the song is still playing. Again and again, Lou Reed tells Hunter he's going to reap just what he sows.

THREE

You spend a week after her death so busy and overwhelmed that you don't even have time to grieve properly. Once everyone else has disappeared, you find yourself rooted to the couch and considering the feasibility of surviving if you never move again.

Everybody seems to think the best thing for you is getting out of the house, keeping busy. Keeping busy will distract you, they tell you via phone and text message and e-mail, it will make you feel productive and boost your self-esteem, it will keep you busy, which is good because when you're busy it means you're busy, but what they're forgetting is that even when Kait was alive you didn't like being busy, and so it's hardly a salve to do something you dislike in order to overcome a calamitous loss. As if, what, you'll go outside and chop some firewood, and you'll forget? You'll take a pottery class and learn how to paint ceramics, and someday wake up and think, oh, right, I'm a widower, no big deal anymore, I've always got my Hummels.

The thing you don't want to admit is that they're right, at least partly, because there is no worse place for you at the moment than in this house, wherein literally everything is a nagging reminder that she's still *almost* there, a psychic indent on your life: the afghan crumpled at the foot of the couch, awaiting her return; the clocks all nine minutes fast because if she wasn't early for work then she thought she was late; tomorrow morning's work outfit— pinstriped slacks, a black cardigan, and a ruffled blouse—piled on top of her dresser, waiting for her to fill and bring to life; her scrubby slippers tucked beneath the bed, the heels peeking out at you; the stray ink slashes she made on the comforter while she sat up in bed scrawling on documents for work, wielding the pen like a composer's baton; the chocolates she stashed throughout the house like a squirrel does nuts, just in case of a chocolate emergency; the DVR choked with episodes of TV shows she'd been saving to watch on a rainy day; the leftover chicken noodle soup in the refrigerator, poured into a container the night her stomach pains struck, the night you should have realized something was seriously wrong, rather than telling her to "stop faking it" (you'd meant it as a joke, but what if those were actually your last words to her? The last ones she heard?).

The day after Kait died, Brutus said, "You must feel pretty bad about this, huh?" but since then no one else has voiced what they've all been thinking: *this is your fault*. In public, people whisper your story to one another when you pass, afraid to look you in the eyes, and although Kait's death is a clear testament to the randomness of catastrophe, everyone wants to ascribe some meaning to it, so despite no one having said it to you, you know they've all been trying to determine exactly what you did to deserve losing your wife in this way. But what sort of transgressions can one commit for which the fair and reasonable punishment is the immediate death of one's wife? The primary characteristic of this situation is that it doesn't make sense and has no cause, aside from the fact that this is what happens to the living—they die—but everyone else needs to try to make it make sense in order to cope with their own mortality. Randomness is terrifying; the need for assigning blame is universal. That's the key to this whole ordeal—your culpability—the ensuing guilt that makes the atmosphere in the house toxic, clogs your drains, streaks your foggy mirror when you step out of the shower, drips from your walls like sweat.

You sift through neglected e-mails, texts, and Facebook messages, nearly two hundred of them, from acquaintances and college friends. Nobody is willing or able to use the word *death* or any variation of it; to all of these distant well-wishers, Kait is not dead, but rather she has passed on, or is no longer with us, or has reached her final resting place, or is at peace, or is at the pearly gates and is reuniting with the Lord. Many of these people haven't spoken to you in months, even years, and so you find little comfort in their promises to keep you in their thoughts or to pray for you, because it has become abundantly clear that they do not have space reserved for you in their thoughts and prayers, just like you haven't made time or mental space for them. A few extend vague offers of help, telling you to call if you need anything, saying *just tell me what I can do for you*. So you call them, but they do not answer; they look at their phones and turn to their living spouses and say something like *I don't think I can talk to him right now, too depressing*, and their spouse gives them tacit permission to ignore your call.

Brutus calls you a week after the memorial. The brothers propose a weekly barbecue, a new tradition, a way to keep everyone together and in touch. They feel obligated to be cordial now, might even feel guilty about never having been nice to you when Kait was alive, but you know it's not going to work, and you tell Brutus there's no point in trying. "Neither of us wants to do this," you say, and Brutus says they need to do it for Sherry. She's falling apart, and you all have to come together as a family. "Kait would have wanted us to take care of each other," Brutus says.

Now that she's dead, people are suddenly very concerned about *what she would have wanted*, and every time they say it, you feel the implication that you're dishonoring her memory by failing to do all the things she would have wanted.

EVEN THOUGH YOU'RE A night person naturally, have often referred to yourself as nocturnal and stayed up until four a.m. watching movies when you lived with your parents, you got in the habit of going to bed when Kait did, tucking her in, sitting beside her, a book open on your lap while you watched her body rise and fall with each breath, but now you don't even know when to sleep. You eat out of boredom, out of biological necessity. The phone doesn't ring. The doorbell is silent.

Most of your free time is spent gazing at your laptop screen, browsing from one website to the next, not out of any particular interest in what you're reading, but because following the infinite pathways online is a perfect distraction; it's a way to keep busy without actually being busy. You challenge yourself to go as long as possible without blinking. You read news articles and encyclopedia entries and research the histories of sitcoms and bands. You check Kait's Facebook page—still active, now a monument, messages pouring in from shocked friends and acquaintances—just in case she is posting from beyond the grave. She barely updated the site when she was alive, though; there are just a handful of updates, a few pictures, all the same old ones you have on your phone and have already viewed enough times to have them memorized. You move on to exploring other people's pages and are inundated with mostly useless information regarding the lives of your friends and famous people alike, everyone rushing to fill the void with an endless stream of banal details about themselves, and even though you know it's a waste of time, and even though your head throbs and your eyes are bloodshot and your wrist creaks and your back screams at the thought of slouching on the couch any longer, and the consumption of thousands of empty mental calories makes you feel physically ill and you hate yourself for not being able to stop, you don't hate yourself quite enough to actually stop.

KAIT HAD THIS THERAPIST for years—she claimed doctor-patient privilege trumped husband-wife privilege and wouldn't say why, exactly, but she occasionally was beset with a depression that could shut her down for days, turn her into a different person entirely, and so it was good for her to have someone else to talk to. The therapist was into new-agey type stuff, some of which struck you as absurd, an opinion you long-ago learned not to voice—every time you criticized some goofy new technique, Kait said, "You're too cynical sometimes." One thing the therapist suggested was that when Kait's self-esteem was low, you should lift her arm, like a referee raising the arm of the winning boxer, and declare her Champion of Something, as in *good morning to the World Champion of Waking Up!* or *thank you to the World Waffle-Making Champion!* Something about adrenaline and endorphins, physiological responses to receiving praise. It seemed to work, actually, gave her enough of a boost to face a stressful day at work or to cope with a fight with her mother. You try raising your own arm, now, and it doesn't feel the same. It feels like masturbation, except more hollow.

KAIT WAS SMART. YOU'RE smart too, but while you know a lot of trivia and have a good vocabulary, she was useful-smart; you would have beaten her on *Jeopardy!* because you know who Vasco da Gama was and you know all the abbreviations on the periodic table, but she knew how to read a map and pay bills on time and balance a budget. All your intelligence got you was a job at the front desk of a rental car agency, while she was a financial advisor at TrustUs Bank. It was her idea to get life insurance policies when you were both young and healthy. Low premiums, high payouts. Just in case, she said. You never know, she said. Your premiums were higher and the payout lower due to the congenital heart defect you'd had corrected via surgery as a child, and you remember saying to her, "You're worth more dead than I am," and she said, "Yeah, hopefully you're not the one who dies first." You remember, vaguely, laughing. And so it's because of her that you find yourself opening a check from Allright Insurance for three-quarters of a million dollars, accompanied by a letter offering sincerest condolences from Allright's CEO. It's because of her that the bank teller appears to have a minor stroke when she sees the amount you've written on the deposit slip.

IF IT'S POSSIBLE FOR Kait to see you, you know she sees a man incapable of living on his own, a parasite that has lost its host, a rudderless ship content to drift from the beginning of life to the end without doing anything noteworthy or even trying to maximize a depleted existence, and you know she is deeply, deeply disappointed in you, and yet she still loves you anyway, which somehow makes the whole situation even more pitiful.

SAY YOU'RE TWENTY-NINE. A white, college-educated, home-owning male in the prime of his life. And say you've spent roughly half of those twenty-nine years doing nothing, or talking about what you're going to do later, which makes you actually about fifteen when it comes to real life experience. Say you waste whole days as if there is unlimited time on Earth, despite all evidence to the contrary, and you can't explain why, not even when your wife pushes you to show more gumption and "just try it for once," not even when you have squandered several days nearly immobile in your house and your body and your brain are demanding an explanation. Say you claim to your wife you don't even know what she means by *it*, although the truth is, the specific etymology of *it* is irrelevant compared to the idea *it* represents. Say then your wife decides to die on you without any warning and you're now an ostensible fifteen-year-old with no experience and no idea how to take care of yourself.

What do you do now?

FOUR

Three things happen that force Hunter to do something. First, he begins receiving phone calls from the people at the bank, not because they want to offer sympathy anymore, but because they want his money. That is, they already have his money, but they want it in a different way. They want permission to remove it from the checking account, play around with it for a while, share it with their friends with vague promises of riches and all the risk on Hunter's end. They suddenly find him much more appealing and valuable, and they convey this revised estimation of his value via constant contact, via warnings about the depreciation of currency in a standard checking account. No matter how many times he tells them to leave him alone, they will not, because that is not what banks do—leave people alone. What they do is they push and push until people give them what they want, and then they ignore phone calls from people who desperately need answers. *Too cynical,* Kait would say.

Second thing that happens: Sherry appears at the house, demands the ashes. She looks like the "Before" picture in an ad for miracle sleeping pills. She says she's worried about Hunter's state of mind, can't trust him with Kait; she wants to dump the ashes in some park somewhere because supposedly Kait always loved this park even though Hunter never heard her mention it even once. Hunter refuses, says they need to wait for the perfect time and place, and Sherry says, "We need to get this over with so we can move on." She holds her palm out and says, "This isn't a negotiation." Hunter tells her she has to go, and closes the door. The next day, she returns with the brothers. Brutus, acting as their spokesman, says, "We deserve to be there when you do the ashes."

Blocking the doorway, knowing if they breach the threshold they will take Kait and he will never see her again, he tries to explain that, in case they all didn't notice, he's her husband, and he's the legal guardian of the ashes, so while they may have known her first, that doesn't mean they knew her better. For example, how could any of them think she'd want to be plopped in the grass at some nondescript park in Northeast Philly just because she'd *been there* before? In fact, her having been there is enough of a reason not to bring her back, considering her dreams of world travel, and besides, how could they have failed to notice that she hated Northeast Philly, ran away from it as soon as she could? Max doesn't like when people talk bad about the Northeast, because it's the best fuckin' neighborhood in the city, he says with conviction, even though he's never been anywhere else in his life, and now he lunges at Hunter. Hunter steps back and slams the door on Max's foot. Max leaps back, yowling in pain, and Hunter pushes the door shut, locks it, barricades it with a bookcase. They come back the next day expecting an apology, and Sherry shouts through the window that she wants Hunter to undergo a psychological evaluation to determine whether he's the appropriate caretaker of her daughter's ashes. She's hired a lawyer, she says.

Third catalyst to change: rummaging around the basement looking for nothing specific but feeling like he needs to unearth *something*, Hunter finds, buried beneath layers of Christmas decorations, a wrapped gift with his name on it. Three months in advance of their anniversary. (What else has she hidden here? Are there gifts for his fortieth birthday? A watch for his retirement?) A card, inside of which she has scribbled a note—her handwriting was always shockingly poor, loopy and stout, like a parade of jaunty fat men—that says how excited she is to have spent another year with him, how much she loves Hunter and appreciates his support even on days when she's not as nice as she wants to be, has come to rely on seeing him every day, wants him to know he is the most important thing in her life. The card says, "You're a better man than you think, and I can't wait to see what happens when you finally believe that." She'd always had greater faith in him than he had in himself, always seemed to believe he was capable of making meaningful contributions to his community and his family. She never specified what those contributions would be or how they would happen, whether they would be career-related or otherwise, but she repeated her vision to him with such conviction that it seemed more prophecy than fantasy. The note ends like this: "I love the man you are, but I can't wait to see the man you become. Four years is not enough; I want another forty." The gift, it's a globe, a nice one, classy, handcrafted in Malaysia. The sort of thing aristocrats keep in their study. She has taped a note to the globe. It says, "Tell me where you want to go, and I'll follow you."

It doesn't seem right, at first, to accept his anniversary gift three months early, or at all, given that this upcoming anniversary technically will be invalid, but Hunter figures why not treat these as her true last words and honor what amounts to her dying wish? He can use her insurance money to pay off the mortgage completely and to fund their first great vacation together. She died before he'd fulfilled many of his promises, but this is a goal he can still achieve.

He spins the globe and jabs his index finger blindly at it. Lands on the United States, East Coast. Spins again, jabs again, US again. Five times this happens, until he thinks perhaps the point is that one needs to explore one's own country before gallivanting around the rest of the world, speaking pidgin French and crowding onto tour buses in order to push past strangers to glimpse the Eiffel Tower. Perhaps what the globe is telling him is that what a mature traveler does is he takes his wife with him on a tour of his own country, learns about his roots before he imposes himself upon other nations.

The plan is this: the plan is to go west. What other direction is necessary? He's seen the Atlantic, frolicked in it briefly with

Kait, doesn't necessarily need to see it again. So why not aim west and keep going until they have to stop? Details are best figured out later, Hunter says to Kait as they pass through a tollbooth. The key isn't the destination so much as the act of moving away from where he is. It's something he's always talked about doing anyway, late nights in college with roommates, passing a makeshift bong around the room, wistfully diagramming their hypothetical cross-country journey. He's listened to Dylan. He's skimmed Kerouac. He knows that if you're a disaffected young American and you're looking to find yourself, then the place to look is somewhere between your current location and the other side of the country.

NORMALLY KAIT WAS THE driver, but that's not an option anymore, so now she's strapped into the passenger seat, Hunter cruising in the right lane behind a convoy of freight trucks. He got his license at sixteen like everyone else, but only because he wanted to keep up with his friends, and because Jack made him take the driver's test, said it would be his first step into the world of self-reliance. At the time, the idea of driving, in theory, seemed deeply appealing due to the freedom and the speed and the potential for picking up girls, but the reality of driving is that three-quarters of the cars on the road are piloted by lunatics and incompetents, a succession of blazing two-ton missiles weaving dumbly toward their targets. When Hunter tells people about his anxiety about driving, they generally assume he's been in a bad accident, a PTSD situation, but the truth is, no, that's not it at all. What happened is he took driver's ed classes, which consisted almost entirely of watching graphic videos of gruesome car wrecks, and by the time he got behind the wheel he knew not to trust anybody or anything, and this skittishness has only intensified over the past decade, since moving into the city and forsaking his car and generally relying on Kait to chauffeur him everywhere.

So, then—he stays in the right lane, moving at exactly the speed limit, a line of trucks a force field between him and screaming sports cars.

He pulls into a rest stop in central PA, needs a coffee. He started drinking coffee after college, when he was unemployed but also inexplicably drowsy every day, told Kait the drowsiness was probably due to *the ol' ticker*, which despite having been healed when he was an infant would never be quite as strong as one with a properly formed ventricular septum, and although he has never liked the taste of coffee, he likes the way a coffee cup looks in his hands. Passing through the rest stop with disheveled hair and carrying a warm cup o' Joe, he feels like a true adult male, almost fatherly, nods at a pair of passing truckers, tugs on the brim of his cap, implying centuries worth of accrued masculine knowledge. Cradled in his other arm is Kait, who sure as hell cannot be left unattended in the car, because one does not just leave one's most valuable asset sitting unattended in the car, no matter how badly one needs a cup of coffee.

He carries her into the bathroom. The men in there are clad in chainmail, feathered Elizabethan caps, cloaks, knee-high boots. The line at the urinal moves slowly, everyone clanking and grunting to maneuver in their complex outfits. In his jeans and T-shirt, he is the only one dressed for life in twenty-first-century America.

He looks down at Kait, rolls his eyes. Whispers, "You ought to see these guys," and points her toward the man at the sink, whose striped tights are several sizes too small and clinging to his groin so snugly that his testicles bulge out like a frog's eyes. He mutters to Kait, "This is like that time we went to the ballet," and imagines her smiling at the memory of that night, when they'd agreed to give ballet a try because they wanted to support the local arts and be more cultured. They had dinner at the trendy Moroccan fusion restaurant downtown, he in his suit and she in her cocktail dress, took a moonlit walk to the theater, sat respectfully through the two-hour performance, and afterward she admitted she'd kind of hated it, which was a relief because as much as he wished he'd enjoyed the show, didn't want to feel like a generic guy being bored by ballet, he had to admit he just did not get it. "That one guy's junk really stole the show," she said, and it was true, the lead was hung like a porn star, and neither of them had been able to look away from the impressive bulge when he was on stage. In their continuing effort to become more sophisticated, they'd also bought a season pass at the city's oldest theater, attended two plays, both of which they'd found intolerably turgid, and then never went again. Kait said they still deserved credit because they'd given it a shot. "It's not our fault if we don't like it," she said. "We don't have to apologize to anyone for liking sitcoms more than plays." The moment she said it, he realized he'd felt this way all along but was either not smart enough to figure it out himself or not courageous enough to own the feeling. Her gift: to see inside him and to understand him better than he ever understood himself.

In the rest stop's food court, he sees dozens of women dressed in corsets, surcoats, and headscarves. Even though they're wearing meticulous period dress, they have no problem with the anachronistic image of gulping from a bottle of soda and devouring plates of fast-food pizza. Many of the men are carrying weapons, broadswords and daggers sheathed in their waistbands, but the rest stop employees don't seem concerned at all. Maybe, he thinks, he has driven through an interdimensional portal and ended up in a world in which medieval norms are intermingled with modern technology. Maybe in a new dimension he'll have better luck, will learn that there is a magic potion to reanimate his deceased wife, and then, aside from the ogres and the dragons and the disreputable feudal lords, they can get on with the happily-ever-after portion of their lives.

In the parking lot, he sees a banner welcoming Renaissance Faire patrons, a reasonable, if unexciting, explanation for the weirdness inside. Still, he sits in his car with Kait and imagines the alternate dimension, envisions how they would adapt to their new lives. If Kait could talk—if she could see and hear and she could touch him on the arm—she would say something like *if we were in another dimension, we'd have to buy all new wardrobes*, and he would wonder where to get fitted for chain mail, which joke she would top with something about how hard it is to find a good blacksmith anymore, and they would continue for twenty minutes, digressing and layering jokes on top of one another until they'd exhausted the thread. Some of his favorite times with her were these preposterous conversations that would never be funny to anyone else in the world; their frivolity only made them more valuable, made him feel like he and Kait were inventing a secret shared language. Once, when they were cooking dinner together—she was always his sous chef, reading him recipes and prepping ingredients—she said she loved meatballs more than anything in the world. He responded, "If I were a meatball, would you eat me?" While many women he'd known would look at him quizzically then, or ignore him, or tell him that's a dumb question and he should stop being weird, she enjoyed indulging him in these hypotheticals and said, "It really depends how hungry I am." They traded jokes until they'd developed an entire *Metamorphosis* scenario in which Hunter Cady awoke one morning from uneasy dreams and found himself transformed in his bed into a savory meatball, and then his wife was faced with the difficult decisions of whether to eat him and, if so, how best to eat him. From that point forward, she occasionally addressed him as Meatball, even in front of confused friends and family, and each time he loved her a little more.

HUNTER TELLS KAIT THEY'RE taking a detour on the way to Pittsburgh to see medieval England. The Renaissance Faire, he says, will probably be their only chance on the trip to watch a live joust, so it's worth at least thirty bucks.

Fifteen years ago, Hunter would have loved this place. Falconry displays, replicas of guillotines, the promise of semireliable historical information, the general sense of low-level spectacle, the underlying sexual tension inherent in any setting that involves so many people in costume.

He spends the morning attending various performances scattered throughout the fairgrounds, and when watching the joust, or the staging of the witch dunking, or the Court Jester's variety show, he can't help noticing that these people are terrible actors. Which is not to say they're not *trying*; the palpable effort may be the most depressing aspect of their shows, in that Hunter can tell they care deeply about this performance, but mostly they're just spouting non sequiturs in faux-British accents. They're teenagers reenacting Monty Python routines, and surely some of them have spouses who are embarrassed to admit they're married to a Renaissance Faire person. Maybe they thought it was cute ten years ago but were also hoping their husband or wife would grow out of it and move on, and when asked *what does your husband do*, the wives will say, *oh, he's a historian*, hoping people will not ask any follow-ups and will instead be content to believe he is Very Deep and does Important Work.

After a few hours of experiencing the Renaissance, Hunter decides he has had enough. There is no benefit to staying here if he's not going to enjoy the performances, and even though he and Kait have nowhere specific to be, he feels like he is already behind schedule. The park's layout is intentionally labyrinthine, like a casino's gambling floor. He wanders down a pathway lined with a number of small mercantile huts—some selling semi-authentic medieval souvenirs, others hawking T-shirts that feature vaguely sexualized illustrations of heroic knights and distressed damsels and say things like I GOT LANCED AT THE PA REN FAIRE!

The merchant at the last hut calls out to him: "Halloo, Sah!" Hunter nods, keeps walking. "What be the rush, m'lord?" the merchant says. He is an immense person, made larger by his powerful beard and padded tunic. His belt holds his prominent gut aloft, makes him look like a woman in her third trimester of carrying triplets. He performs with the enthusiasm and relative talents of a community theater actor.

"I just, I have to get on the road," Hunter says.

"Ye be not from around here, I see," the merchant says, appraising Hunter's outfit. "You'll need an ally in these parts. They call me Mordecai." He extends a gloved hand toward Hunter.

Hunter shakes his hand, shares his name.

"A hunter! Will ye be accompanying us on the grouse hunt anon?"

"It's just a name, really. I don't know—"

"But surely you've come to regale us with tales of the hunt!"

"Look, I just came here because I was at the rest stop down the road and—"

Mordecai, still gripping his hand, pulls Hunter into the store. He leans in close, so that from a distance they probably look like they're embracing: "Listen, kid, you'll make my life a lot easier if you just play along." His breath smells like boiled potatoes. "Don't look, but I've got supervisors watching me, and I can't afford another write-up."

"Why are they watching you?"

"Just help me out," Mordecai says, and then his voice thunders again: "Please, m'lord, peruse my wares and spare a few shillings for an honest peasant."

"Um, sure, okay," Hunter says, looks over his shoulder for the supervisor. "It shall be done!" he says, and Mordecai's bellowing laugh rattles the hut.

What Mordecai sells is an amazing variety of heraldry-related products; anything that can be emblazoned with a coat of arms is so emblazoned, from traditional items like shields and cloaks to modern goods like lighters and lunchboxes. "What be your surname?" Mordecai asks, and Hunter tells him. "A fine name—fit for a Duke!" As Hunter rustles through the merchandise, trying to devise an exit strategy, Mordecai explains that the family crest is a window into the heart of a man, an illustration of his character, the perfect symbol of what he stands for. "When ye carry it into battle, 'tis the first thing your enemy shall see," he says.

Hunter can't find his name on anything, not even a keychain. Among thousands of surnames, his is not accounted for. "What if one doesn't know one's insignia?"

"The young Cady must look inside himself and allow the crest to reveal itself to him." Hunter searches inside himself for the symbol that would represent him. He thinks about Willow, whose crest—a weeping tree—would be almost too obvious. Jack's symbol would be a factory; for three consecutive years as a child, Hunter had to waste days of his summer vacation accompanying Jack on a Factories of Connecticut tour. Jack said he was trying to teach Hunter industriousness, didn't want him to end up wasting his prime years on frivolous pursuits like Jack himself had. Kait is not quite as easy to pin down; it would take a hundred crests to include all the images Hunter would want included, and the only fair way to represent her would be through something more complex than a coat of arms—a wall-sized mural, or a mosaic made of twenty thousand tiles. Hunter imagines himself charging into battle wielding an unmarked shield, his slain body left in the field while a victorious general steps over him.

Mordecai summons him behind the counter. "Perhaps I possess

the solution to the young man's quandary!" he shouts. He produces a binder from beneath his desk and leans over Hunter as they flip through it in search of his name. Hunter runs his finger along the *Ca-* page mouthing each name, but his name is unlisted. He checks surrounding pages just in case there was an error in alphabetizing. If he can find his name and his insignia, a little description of its meaning, then the book can give him a sense of what kind of man he is supposed to be. It wouldn't be perfect, but it would give him a concrete goal; in Kait's absence, Hunter needs whatever guidance he can find.

Mordecai slips back into his stage whisper: "Hey, can you do me another favor?" he says.

Every one of Hunter's instincts tells him that a sentence like that, spoken by a stranger, always leads to trouble. But he is trying to suppress his negative nature. He's trying to be fun. Fighting the urge to ask fifteen follow-up questions, he says, "What do you need?"

"You see the girl over there? Past the turkey leg stand? Looks kind of like the lady who does the weather on channel six?" Hunter nods. "That's the Queen. You'd be doing me a huge solid if you just play along when she comes by."

"Sure," Hunter says. "But, like, what am I supposed to do?"

"We do these skits, kind of. All through the park, we pick regular people out and it's a fun little thing. Makes people feel special and keeps the regulars coming back." The Queen is approaching, trailed by her retinue. She carries herself with the haughty posture of actual royalty. One of her hangers-on holds a turkey leg for her and occasionally hand-feeds her a small chunk as if giving a treat to a trained falcon. "You ready? Get ready."

Already, Hunter regrets being involved, regrets his failure to ask why Mordecai is in such dire need of scoring points with the Queen, regrets agreeing to engage in what is essentially an improv routine in front of a sun-baked and day-drunk audience.

Mordecai shouts, "Hail, Your Majesty!" He bows, and Hunter follows his lead. " 'Tis a true honor to be graced by your divine presence!"

"Yes," she says, the words slithering out the corner of her mouth. "I am certain that it is." She is a pallid and waifish woman with dead eyes and lips like earthworms.

"Your Majesty, we have been granted a visit today by the honorable Hunter Cady."

"Hey," Hunter says. "Nice turkey leg."

The Queen is silent.

"The young man is a stranger in these parts, Your Majesty," Mordecai says. "Surely he does not recognize the impropriety of his speech!" He nudges Hunter. The crowd grows around them.

"Oh, yeah, no. Certainly I wouldn't wish to offend royalty," Hunter says and reaches out to shake her hand. He pumps her arm limply once before realizing he has compounded the offense with an even greater breach of protocol.

A lightning flash of rage crackles in the Queen's eyes. "Peasant, has your insolent friend any business here?"

"Your Majesty, I owe you eternal apologies for our visitor's lack of social graces. But he has brought you an offering of peace." Mordecai reaches for the cube and Hunter tightens his grip. It takes all of his strength to hold on.

"I think there's been some confusion," Hunter says.

The Queen's assistant passes the turkey leg off to another lackey and then steps forward to help Mordecai wrest the ashes away. There are now six hands on the box and only two are Hunter's. He feels all the blood in his body pooling up in his stomach and his limbs going cold. The assistant leans in so close his lips graze against Hunter's ear, and he whispers: "We'll give it back, man. Just roll with us for one minute."

While this is a reasonable enough request, and there's no reason to believe these men would steal his wife's ashes, the idea of letting her go and trusting them to return her is too much for Hunter to handle. He wants to play along, wants to practice being more agreeable and spontaneous, but this is not possible.

"I'm done playing Harry Potter with you, dude," he says. He digs his heels in and tugs back. Hunter feels like Samson calling on god for one more moment of great strength so he can pull down the pillars and destroy the temple. His grip loosens and then he is holding nothing and he tumbles backward to the shop's floor.

Lying on the floor of the shop, he looks up at Mordecai and says, "Come on. Help me out here." But they have already passed the point of no return; there's an audience to appease, and it is clear that Mordecai and the others are working under a strict mandate to never break character, no matter what. Mordecai hands the cube to the Queen's assistant, and the Queen orders it be opened on the spot. "Let us see if this interloper's gift is generous enough to justify his abhorrent behavior," she says.

Hunter scrambles to his feet, but Mordecai holds him back with one arm, and now the eager crowd closes in on them like a hand wrapping around Hunter's throat. The box clicks open and the assistant lifts the lid, and suddenly everyone is silent. In a panic, he nearly drops it into the dirt and sends Kait sprawling through the park, but he regains his composure just in time to avoid disaster.

"It's my wife," Hunter says. "My wife is dead." Mordecai goes limp and allows Hunter to reclaim the cube. Hunter snaps the lid shut and then inspects the edges to see if there has been any leakage or other damage.

The crowd now realizes what they're seeing and they begin murmuring. The Queen has a crisis on her hands, and she acts quickly to control the damage. Mordecai towers over her, but with each step she takes toward him, he shrinks until he's so small he can fit in her palm and be stuffed into her pocket. He tries to offer a defense for this disastrous moment, but she cuts him off. She banishes him into exile, effective immediately. "Now—off with you before I decide to be off with your head!" she says. The crowd cheers as the security guards (disappointingly not dressed as knights, but rather wearing standard-issue mailman's shorts and blue polos, stretched over beginners bellies) escort Mordecai off the premises. Next, the Queen announces, "This most honorable young man will be knighted by my hand at the end of our festivities today." The crowd applauds. She waves the people away and tells Hunter to follow her. He does not want to stay, but a hundred people are staring at him, expecting him to follow the queen, and last time he failed to play along, he nearly lost everything.

Their procession takes them through the heart of the village, bystanders photographing them while others shout declarations of love for the Queen; she does not respond to them, does not even turn to look at them, sometimes mutters to her guards that she cannot stand these peasants. Their destination is a gray office building hidden behind the jousting stage. Some of the park's employees are here, on break but still costumed, sitting in what looks like a doctor's waiting room, gobbling up homemade lunches, playing games on their cell phones, and watching daytime talk shows on wall-mounted TVs. The Queen introduces herself formally to Hunter: "Everyone here calls me Your Majesty, but you can just call me Queen Margaret."

"I just want to get out of here, can I just get out of here?" Hunter says, and he can tell by the gasping of her followers that this sort of insubordination would be a fireable offense for them.

She inhales sharply and then apologizes for his maltreatment at the hands of a disorderly merchant. In addition to firing Mordecai, they're willing to compensate Hunter with two season passes to the Ren Faire, a fifty-dollar voucher for the gift shop, a free meal, and a personalized signed photo of the Queen. "Also," she asks, "were you planning to spread your beloved's ashes here? Because I think it's a violation of health codes and—"

"No. I mean, no way. That's not what I want. At all. Why don't I just pour her ashes in the dumpster out back?"

"Why would you bring them here in the first place?"

"Don't talk to me like I'm the weird one," Hunter says.

"This is my *job*," she says.

"Well anyway," Hunter says, leaving the gifts on the desk, and carrying Kait through the waiting room. The Queen shouts that he has to stay in order to be knighted, but does not follow him through the exit.

Approaching the parking lot, he passes the two security guards. One of them says, "Hey man, sorry. About. You know."

The other says, "You ought to be careful. Mordecai is still out there, and he's pretty pissed."

Hunter crouches behind a parked car and weaves through the lot, like a SEAL maneuvering behind enemy lines. He feels like he's sixteen again, sneaking out of the house overnight and tiptoeing past the creaky floorboards outside Jack's office. Jack caught him once when he was sneaking back into the house at dusk; he was waiting in the darkened living room and said, "Kid, you cannot do this to us," while Willow descended the stairs, phone in hand, ready to call the police to report her son missing. "You drove us half crazy," Jack said. They grounded him for three weeks and Jack got in the habit of performing random bed checks, fining him ten dollars for every time he was caught out of place. Hiding in the parking lot now only intensifies Hunter's anxiety; every footstep could be Mordecai closing in on him. His heart tap dancing, he darts through the final stretch to his car and has shifted into drive before even closing the door.

THE ADRENALINE RUSH OF his escape wears off quickly, and by the time he's safely on the interstate, Hunter's anger has largely subsided, replaced by a sense of envy he can't quite articulate. Despite the bad acting and the anachronisms, the overpriced merchandise and the hokey décor, the employees and attendees all seemed to love that park. After perhaps years of searching, they'd finally found a place where they could be comfortable acting strangely without *feeling* strange. He'd assumed at first that they were unhappy, simply because he was unhappy there. But it would be liberating to find a place where you could be whoever you wanted to be and feel okay about it. That, he thinks, is what this whole drive is really about: figuring out who he's supposed to be now, and where he can best be that person.

THAT NIGHT, IN A central PA motel, he leaves the bathroom light on, the door cracked to allow a thin bar of light passage into the room; Kait doesn't like sleeping in total darkness. The first time they slept in the same room, in a hotel in New York City, roughly halfway between their respective homes, he had assumed she was making some kind of joke when she plugged in a night-light and so he laughed, and he knew immediately that he'd done something wrong, the way her smile caved in and her posture sagged like gravity had doubled on her. She told him she was afraid of the dark, and he asked what's so scary about a little darkness? "Why *wouldn't* you be afraid? "she said, and then she stopped speaking, curled tightly inside the blankets as if trying to vacuum seal herself, and scooted to the edge of the bed against the wall. Over the course of the night, he caressed her side a few times, hoping she would awake and they could make up and forget the ugly business of him laughing at her fears, but it was as if she'd already left him. In the morning, she told him the light isn't funny, it comforts her, and he shouldn't laugh at someone for trying to make herself comfortable. All of which seemed fair enough, especially since she didn't mock him for his fear of driving. They never discussed it again, but he bought a night-light for the guest room in Jack and Willow's home, and when they purchased their own house, he made sure to plug in lights in every room, in case she found herself wandering the house at night.

He sets her on the nightstand on the right side of the bed, which has become her usual place, and then lies on top of the covers because the room's air conditioner is malfunctioning. Sometimes on hot nights, he used to take his wedding ring off, said it made his finger too sweaty while he slept, and even though right now he wouldn't mind having a less sweaty finger, he refuses to remove the ring. He will not move all night, feels greedy taking her side of the bed away. Staring up at the ceiling, he tries to force himself to sleep, but can't even close his eyes.

FIVE

You don't cry much when you think about her. It's not that you're afraid to cry or consider it a sign of weakness; you've been trying, squinching your face up and pushing behind the eyes, making animal sobbing sounds, but your eyes are dry as ever. It's as if the ducts have closed up. You can feel the swelling of tears in your sinuses, your whole head soggy with grief. It would be an incredible relief to puncture yourself and let it all leak out. Before bedtime, you litter the floor in your motel room with debris, hoping to stub your toe while stumbling to the bathroom in the middle of the night, thus sparking a spontaneous crying session, but all that happens is you bash your toe and you become enraged, begin throwing things, punching walls. The next day, you check out early and are twenty miles down the highway before management will have seen the damage you've done to the room.

YOU BEGIN TO MISS even the annoying things about her. Especially the annoying things. A proper road trip should be fraught with underlying tension and frayed nerves, sustained frictive stretches punctuated by occasional cathartic stops at memorable landmarks and delirious nights along the roadside. Without the tension, the frivolity of vacation seems less justified. So you find yourself wishing she were sitting in bed next to you, clipping her toenails and scattering the shards in the sheets, leaving them where they will prick your legs. You find yourself wishing she were here to wake you up in the middle of the night in order to say something like, "Did you know you were snoring?"

You miss her awful taste in music—she liked the *She Loves You* Beatles but hated the *Rubber Soul* Beatles, considered reality TV singers real artists on par with Dylan and Ray Charles. You miss her tendency to mispronounce common words like *nuclear* and *library*. You miss the fact that she was pathologically incapable of finishing packaged foods, she always left the last chip or the last cracker or last whatever *in case you wanted it*, which meant your cupboard overflowed with cereal boxes containing one cornflake, year-old packages of stale graham crackers (you even miss the ant infestations, and the subsequent complaining to the exterminator about your wife in that socially acceptable way married men do). You miss the fact that she was so uncomfortable blowing her nose in public—it was the honking noise she hated—that she would rather walk sniffling from one end of the mall to the other with mucus pooling up in her philtrum. You miss making dinner reservations for Friday night and then having them scrapped when she fell asleep on the couch at eight p.m., her head pressed against your chest, trapping you into watching TV quietly for several hours until she woke up and slogged upstairs. You miss the nagging (and you hate calling it nagging because it makes you feel too much like a stereotypical put-upon sitcom husband, but that's what it was, it was nagging) about your career prospects and your inadequate levels of motivation. You miss the arguments, from the monumental (i.e., here's why we need to stop spending time with your awful brothers) to the minuscule (i.e., how hard is it to close a drawer when you're done with it?). It's the arguments that breathed life into the relationship. It's in the arguments that you ultimately felt the love. It's the passion inculcated by such dramas that makes you wish you could just one more time hear her say, "Of course it's pronounced *liberry*," a smirk lurking beneath her defensive façade, letting you know that soon you can smile and she can smile and you can kiss her and she can kiss you and everything will be fine.

WHAT YOU MISS MOST is her eyes. Seeing them across the dinner table when you look up from your plate, the eyes of your wife like polished jade, watching over you.

WHAT YOU MISS MOST, actually, is the way she walked, the comically proper posture, as if she were always carrying a stack of books on her head. The rigidity of the spine, the shoulders thrown backward, chest thrust forward. Knowing you were the only one who could fold her into your arms, make her relax.

OR MAYBE THE THING you miss most is the thing everyone misses most about her, which is her generosity. Volunteering at blood drives and at walks to benefit children with heart disease, while you stayed home playing video games. Cold-calling people to raise funds for women's shelters in the city. Maintaining a meticulous record of birthdays and anniversaries for every one of your acquaintances, sending cards and gifts, however nominal. Giving money to beggars even when it was obvious they just wanted booze, saying, "Who am I to keep him from getting drunk?" or, "What if he's had a really bad day?" finding someone's digital camera and then spending the next two days sleuthing through the pictures for clues to find her and return it. Sneaking out of bed on Sundays to make you breakfast. Stopping by work during your lunch break to bring you a bottle of lemonade you'd left at home.

IT COULD BE HER legs you miss most. The way they gleamed. Calves taut like guitar strings, muscled like she was always wearing high heels. The way they felt when they were wrapped around your waist pulling you into her.

YOU MISS THE MOLE on the back of her neck, a tiny dot almost indiscernible from a distance. The odd pale patch of skin between her shoulder blades, a splotch like bleach spilled on a T-shirt. The scar from her appendectomy, stretched like an uneasy pink smile above her hip. The way her knees bent at perfect forty-five-degree angles when she was painting the wood trim in your new home. The way she laid the next day's clothes out on the dresser every night before bed. The single incisor that flashed between her lips when she grinned, a detail you never mentioned to her because you knew it would only make her more self-conscious about being photographed. The inward curve of her toes, as if they'd been bound together when she was a child. The way she always missed the same spot on the top of her left knee when she shaved.

WHAT YOU MISS MOST, really, is being able to say anything you wanted to her and getting a response. Being able to tell her how afraid you are and having her validate your fears, having her tell you she's scared too, mutually reassuring each other whether you believed yourselves or not. Having someone to affirm your rightness even when you're obviously not right, someone who knows the correct time and manner to tell you you're wrong. Having someone off of whom you can bounce your most ludicrous dreams, someone who knows to pretend they're attainable.

You talk to her still. You talk and talk, more than you ever did, but she never says anything, which makes it all as empty and useless as prayer.

SIX

What is there to see in the middle of America? There is nothing and there is everything. Unless one knows where to find the action, the world seems barren. The attractions are hidden here, and Hunter has wasted full days without seeing anything noteworthy. He has no guidebooks, and although he vaguely recalls the names and identities of some mid-American landmarks, he has no concept of where they are or what they represent.

He is taking I-76 west through PA, will eventually connect with I-80, headed in an impossibly straight line alongside impossibly dull scenery. The primary goal is to leave Pennsylvania and to decide later if he ever wants to come back. The only definite stop he has in mind is Chicago—Kait went to college at DePaul, and

Hunter thinks he might find some answers there, even though he's not sure what questions he wants to ask.

At first, when he passes a field full of cows, it is a little bit interesting, in that he rarely sees cows in his daily life. But by the fifteenth dairy farm, there is no reason to look anymore, because they are all essentially the same.

Mostly, he sees power lines, wood fences, and endless rows of crops. He sees convoys of freight trucks barreling past him, a runaway herd of rumbling monsters rattling his hatchback. After sunset, the trucks are illuminated by colored Christmas lights, a surprisingly festive way to remain visible. The rural highway at nighttime is as lonely and foreboding as the deep sea. He drives for miles without anything changing in front of him; he feels sometimes as if he is driving into a black hole.

Hunter thinks about the pioneers, how helpless they must have felt on the frontier, taking whole days to move twenty miles, which he covers in twenty minutes, staring at vast stretches of uninterrupted land with absolutely no reason to believe. How could they have had faith that there even *was* another ocean? What did it take to convince them that the journey was worthwhile, despite their family members succumbing to dysentery, the persistent threats of wild animals and native tribes? In such bleak circumstances, what gives someone hope? And why is it that with all the many advantages he has over them—a motor, paved roads, a smartphone and a radio, easy access to penicillin if necessary, empirical evidence that something exists on the other side—he still feels underprepared and ill-equipped? Maybe, he says to Kait, humans weren't meant for this kind of travel, not even with the benefit of modern technology.

Maybe there is no reason to keep going at all, he says. But he drives past the next series of exits, resists the temptation to pull over and turn back toward home. He imagines Kait asking where they're going, and all he can say for sure is that he's staying in motion because what else is there to do?

THE FIRST THING HE ever said to Kait, standing on his friend Joel's South Philly rooftop, was, "How do you know Joel?" She sipped from her plastic cup and said she didn't know Joel, she didn't know anyone at the party, but her co-worker had made her come and then her co-worker had ditched her the moment she ran into an ex.

"Do you think it's bad I took a whole bottle of wine from downstairs?" Kait said, dumping the remainder of the bottle into her cup.

He'd seen her the moment he walked stoned and weightless up to the rooftop, her arms crossed over her chest, jagged skyline behind her like an EKG reading of a racing heart. She chain-smoked then; between the cigarettes and the wine, her hands were always full, always in motion, and one or the other was pressed against her lips. She looked simultaneously vulnerable and unapproachable.

She offered Hunter a sip of wine, which he took, because he didn't want to seem standoffish. "That's good wine," he said, his own cup filled with lemonade.

"No it's not." She sipped it anyway. "I'm sorry I'm smoking, I don't know why I'm smoking," she said, but she did not stop smoking. "Who do you know here?"

Joel was one of his college roommates. He started to tell her about the day he and Joel had moved in together, but felt her getting bored when she became fixated on swirling the wine in her cup, and so he shifted gears. "Truth is, I kind of hate parties. But I haven't seen these guys in a while."

"Parties are the *worst*," she said. "I've been up since five o'clock. I just want to go to bed."

He knew a different kind of guy would seize on that last comment, say something like *I've got a really comfortable bed if you want to try it out*, but he was not that kind of guy. So instead he asked her what she'd rather be doing right now if she could be doing anything in the world. Which is when she told him she'd love to go backpacking through Europe someday, and he shrugged, said, "It's kinda cool, but it's not that great." By which he meant he'd heard somewhere that it wasn't great, had read comments on an online message board about how the hostels are dirty and unsafe, had watched most of a documentary about a college kid who was abducted by Albanians while backpacking. What she said was, "Oh my god, you've done that? I would LOVE to do that," and so he said, "Sure, I travel all the time," because what else could he say in that situation? The smoky scent of dozens of charcoal grills was overtaking the neighborhood, and the waxing moon glowed on them like a spotlight, and she was glistening in the summer heat, sweat beaded on her collarbones and dripping down into the valley between her breasts, so he had no choice but to say whatever she wanted to hear. Besides, the secret of seeming smart, he had learned from Jack, is not in studying any particular subject intensely, but in knowing just a little bit about as many subjects as possible, so one can fake expertise and let others carry the conversation, after which they will tell their friends *Hunter is a really smart guy*, and the friends will nod because, yes, they think so too. Not that Jack had consciously taught him any of this. In fact, Jack might not understand it himself, because not only is Jack's office lined with dense reference books but he seems to have actually *read* them cover to cover. Having watched his father conduct conference calls from home, or eavesdropping on him at company luncheons, Hunter knows everyone considers Jack a sharp guy, really sharp, but he never says anything of substance; he just has a natural ability to make people outside his family feel comfortable while speaking. What Jack is is a mirror for others' intelligence. The difference between himself and Jack, Hunter has always thought, is that Jack does not know he's fooling people, whereas Hunter knows exactly what he's doing, which is embracing our new cyber culture (Hunter recently picked this phrase up from a *New Yorker* article, and has been trying to weave it into daily conversation) in which it is much less important to have interests and expertise than it is to have opinions and know trivia answers.

All of which served him well that night on the rooftop with that glistening girl, as he talked about the landmarks he'd visited, passed authoritative judgment on various cities (Brussels was luminous and Amsterdam was effervescent, but Majorca was too pedestrian), described the shimmering canals in Venice. He told her the women were beautiful over there, and she said, "Guess I wouldn't fit in," and to his credit he actually said the right thing here, which has never been his strength, usually he thinks of the perfect thing to say an hour too late, when he's by himself and rehashing the conversations he *should* have had. What he said then was this: "You would put all of them to shame."

It is rare that one can browse through one's personal history and pinpoint an individual moment that can change everything about one's life—it's a fantasy perpetuated by video games and bad films that our lives are littered with such moments, when in reality most of our circumstances have been triggered by a *series* of moments, a chain of decisions—but Hunter has always considered that response to have been the foundation of their entire relationship. Had he said something stupid like *yeah, but tourists aren't supposed to fit in anyway* or *seriously, those women over there are uh-MAY-zing*, it's likely that conversation would have ended, and when he tracked down Joel the next day and demanded the glistening girl's e-mail address, the girl never would have responded to his e-mail asking her to go out for lunch, and she would have started dating someone else, would currently be married, not dead, the mother of two children and the owner of a passport heavy with stamps. Hunter wonders if it's selfish of him to think he prefers the current timeline still. Would she have preferred this way too, if she had known how it would work out?

She found out later that he'd lied to her about backpacking, because he had no pictures, no passport, no specific details. He confessed that he was just trying to impress her, and by then they were so deep into their relationship that she thought it was cute. Just Hunter being Hunter, another game they could play, in which she named a foreign city and asked him to tell her all about it, the people he'd met, the sights he'd seen, the cuisine he'd sampled.

But everyone else, they still think he's seen the world. His co-workers used to solicit vacation advice from him. Her family considers him a real globe-trotter, not that it matters much to them.

(Max once asked, "What's the point in going other places when you've already got good places here?") Even Jack and Willow, who know he's never visited Europe, think he has traveled throughout the southeastern U.S. But he's never been anywhere. Or at least not anywhere worth documenting. As he drives into Ohio, it is the farthest he's ever been. He pushes forward in the blind hope that, sooner than later, he will find himself in the place where he has always belonged, and that when he arrives he'll have the good sense to recognize it.

IN SANDUSKY, OHIO, HUNTER finds himself unable to resist the allure of a billboard hyping Cedar Point, the world's largest amusement park. He owes it to Kait to stop here, because she loved roller coasters more than anyone he'd ever known, forced him to go to carnivals and ride the coasters despite his insistence that it is actually insane behavior to put oneself on a rickety carnival ride for the express purpose of cheating death. He pays admission and carries Kait to a frontier-themed coaster, chosen because it is advertised as family friendly; the more daring coasters with their huge, gravity-defying loops could cause him to drop Kait, and a fall from that height would be sure to crack her in half, allow her to escape from him again, this time forever.

The coaster is modeled after a freight train and is filled primarily by fathers and their young sons. It whistles and rolls them through a series of gentle hills and mild slopes before whipping them around a tight turn and then chugging up a twenty-foot incline in anticipation of the big finish. During the final descent, he raises Kait above his head, and he screams along with everyone else.

After disembarking, he passes a table offering souvenir photos snapped of each passenger during the ride. He buys three copies of his, and in the morning, he mails them to Sherry, Brutus, and his parents, a note scrawled on the back of each: *Headed west with Kait. Tried to make her wear her seatbelt, but couldn't convince her. She's always been stubborn! Having a blast. XOXO.* As soon as the jaws of the mailbox squeal shut and swallow the envelopes, he feels a choleric constriction of his gut, a piercing moment of regret that doubles him over. He wishes his arms were long enough to snake inside and wrap themselves around the envelopes, pull them back out and then destroy them, but they are already out of reach, may as well already be loaded onto trucks and rumbling toward the East Coast, may as well already be in the hands of his concerned parents, his heartbroken in-laws.

ONE THING HUNTER FORGOT to do before leaving the house was to tell anyone where he was going. He departed only a few hours after making his decision; during that interval, he downloaded a mortgage payoff form and then mailed the largest check he will ever write, stuffed a bag full of clothes, and cooked himself several grilled cheese sandwiches, because he was suddenly beset by a ravenous hunger. There was no time to call Willow and Jack, and anyway, Willow would have wanted to tag along with him, and Jack would have tried to talk him out of it, told him there are more fruitful ways to invest his money. Kait's family didn't deserve to know where she was, not after the scene they'd made at his house, and besides, they would have tried to hold him back, either via some kind of legal injunction or, more likely, Sherry sending her meathead sons to his house to pound the desire to travel out of him. He considered e-mailing friends, but realized most of them would be glad to have him gone, didn't want the specter of premature grief hanging over their heads. They are all busy getting married and buying homes and making babies, and they don't need him lurking along the periphery of their lives, reminding them what happens to the best laid plans. Hunter is the first among his peers to have had a marriage end, Kait is the first person their age to die without warning, and it is easier for them all to look away, denying that it could ever happen to them. And so their inevitable quiet rejection of him is enough to revoke their right to know his or Kait's whereabouts.

So, okay, he didn't forget, exactly. But that's what he tells Willow when she calls him two days later. He's in Somewhere, Indiana, parked along the roadside and having a picnic with Kait in the grass beside a pasture. There are birds and there are mooing cows, and there is a very unwelcoming border collie on the opposite side of a fence, but there is also him and there is Kait. What Willow says first is, "You cannot outrun your grief." Hunter shrugs but does not reply. Chews. "You need to be surrounded by people with positive energies," she continues.

"Do you realize I've failed at everything I've ever done?"

"Oh, my son. Your soul is so damaged right now."

"If I can't even finish this, then what good am I?"

"Your value does not derive from a list of completed tasks," she says.

"But maybe it does," he says. Maybe that's exactly how one's value is defined, by tasks completed and not completed, by promises kept and not. Their marriage was built on a promise of some brighter future, of a lifetime of travel, of him learning to love himself the way that she loved him. But she died before he could ever reward her faith in him. If he is ever going to redeem himself as a person, he needs to keep the promises he made to her; he needs to somehow discover that person she believed he would be.

Willow offers to fly out and meet him, drive him home to Hartford, where he can live with her and Jack again, at least until he's feeling more like himself. She says, "You need to be encircled by love. You need to be immersed in it."

"I have a new home now," he says. "I belong to the road."

"Poetry doesn't become you. You know that," she says.

"Have you ever heard how loud an actual farm is? It's ridiculous."

"Your father says he's okay with you coming home. He'll move his office out of your old room. You can stay here as long as you need to."

"I mean, like, cows and chickens. And donkeys! Have you ever heard a real donkey?"

"Please don't reject my spiritual embrace. Your mother wants to heal you, Hunter."

"And the tractors and the birds and everything else. There's so many things."

HUNTER MOVED TO PHILADELPHIA for college because he wanted to get away from home and because Temple University was one of the only schools that had accepted him; he'd overshot with most of his applications, tried for too many Ivies and selective private schools, hoping his strong SAT scores would overshadow mediocre grades. During his first semester in the dorms, he received occasional e-mails from Willow asking about his transition, and occasional e-mails from Jack telling him he really ought to respond to his mother's e-mails, but otherwise he spent those first four months effectively disconnected from his parents. This was before social media. It was a time when it was possible to be physically separated from other people and not know the intimate details of their lives.

If he'd read the e-mails more carefully, he would have been more prepared for the dramatic change in his home. He would have seen Willow referencing things like "uncovering my spiritual side," and Jack writing, "I want to warn you your mother might be losing it." But he didn't read the e-mails carefully, and so he was disconcerted when he saw Willow in the airport terminal dressed like a wood nymph in a flowing white gown and a necklace that looked like it was made from thistles. When she flounced over to him and grabbed him by the cheeks, planted a loud, performative kiss on his forehead, and announced, "My beautiful boy has returned to the nest!" Hunter worried that perhaps she'd had a stroke just before arriving at the airport, or she'd been replaced by a clone who looked like her but was definitely not her.

"I've had a spiritual awakening," she told him on the drive home. "I know who I am now, and I've discovered the way to express the self I have always been."

"Did Jack have an awakening too?"

"Your father doesn't have time for self-discovery anymore."

"Well, they say the self is always in the last place you look."

"I know you're making fun of me," she said. "But I don't care."

Jack was waiting for them at the front door. He took Hunter's suitcase and shook his hand, then said, "Just wait till you see what she did to my house."

In only four months, she had transformed their unremarkable suburban home into a place that looked like it would sell moonstone crafts and house a fortune teller in the back. She had hung a beaded curtain between the living room and dining room. There was incense burning somewhere. Willow inhaled deeply before announcing, "Welcome to your new home."

"What the hell happened here?" Hunter asked.

"The house has always been like this, but its identity hadn't manifested itself before," Willow said.

"So you see what I've been dealing with," Jack said. "You were gone a few weeks, and all of a sudden we're living in fantasyland."

"As you might expect, your father doesn't understand," Willow said.

"And now you're all caught up on the last four months," Jack said. He carried Hunter's suitcase upstairs and led him to his bedroom. "I didn't let her touch your room. Well, almost." There was a small stone carving of Buddha sitting on his bookshelf, but otherwise the place was as he'd remembered it, right down to the rumpled sheets and the Nietzsche he'd never read but had dog-eared and left on his bedside table in case a girl ever came over. "Listen," Jack said, laying a hand on his shoulder like a bishop conferring a blessing. "I know you're busy at school, but you really have to call your mother sometimes. This has not been good for her."

"Yeah, it's pretty intense downstairs," Hunter said. "Sorry I left you hanging."

Jack smirked, gave Hunter's shoulders a squeeze, holding him at an awkward distance with outstretched arms, like a boy at his first middle school dance. His hands lingered on Hunter a beat longer than they should have, and Hunter saw a loneliness in Jack's eyes that he'd never seen before, the vulnerability of a man who felt disassociated from his own life. "It's good to have you back," Jack said, and left the room, shutting the door behind him.

Although the scope of Willow's commitment was grander than usual, she had experienced many awakenings in Hunter's lifetime. Before his birth, she was a Realtor specializing in high-end homes. She'd had a breakthrough early in her career selling a few large properties to pro athletes—she was, in her words, still a jock then, and could relate to them. At that time, Jack was working two jobs but Willow was the breadwinner. He doesn't mention it now, but the seed money for his first business—a manufacturer of parts for high-end appliances—came from Willow, and these days Willow doesn't mention it either, only makes vague references to her past lives. She lost her realty job when she asked to extend her maternity leave an extra month; the postpartum depression had hit her hard and she knew she wasn't yet capable of returning to work. Jack's success cushioned them from the blow of her firing, and so that extra month stretched into a year and then two years, and Jack found he liked the idea of being the provider while his wife (rather than some college-dropout nanny) stayed at home to care for his child day to day. By the time Hunter started school, she was so far removed from the workplace that the world had redefined her not as Willow or as a Realtor but only as Hunter's mother. Since then, as Hunter has become more independent and her daily responsibilities have dwindled, she's been chasing one identity after another, including but not limited to:

painting, first in watercolors, then in oils; community theater, both acting and directing; knitting, which only got as far as a few half-finished scarves; volunteering for nonprofits, first delivering meals to shut-ins and later as an organizer at an abused women's shelter; a few semesters teaching real estate basics at the adult learning annex; canvassing for local Democrats, often against Jack's business interests; a brief foray into day trading; online poker player; a year as a devoted Catholic, including a full baptism ceremony; and a failed attempt at becoming an alcoholic, which didn't work out because some days she just couldn't bring herself to drink any more gin. Jack had encouraged some of the early awakenings, but after they didn't stick he had declared Willow incapable of following through on anything, a lost cause. During her summer of gardening, Hunter, then fourteen, and Jack sat in the kitchen together while she tended to her cucumbers, and Hunter asked Jack why it bothered him so much to see Willow trying new things. Jack said, "Your mother doesn't realize there's a difference between being happy and being not-unhappy. But we have to let her figure it out for herself." Willow has told Hunter how long it took Jack to settle down—he was thirty before he'd ever gotten an actual paycheck rather than working odd jobs that paid under the table—but once he determined to become Business Jack, he fully embraced the role and, in Willow's words, "stopped evolving." For reasons both practical and personal, he's eliminated all traces of young Jack, hiding old photographs and rarely speaking about the time before his reinvention.

When Hunter left for college and Willow was alone most days, it was no surprise she embraced yet another new life path. And while the intensity of her commitment has waned since then—she no longer seems like an overzealous college sophomore who just discovered the Dead—she has remained on that path for a decade, so that Hunter is convinced it's no phase anymore, but actually the person his mother wants to be. "It's not so weird," Kait said once, when he suggested she would eventually grow out of it. "It takes women a long time to be comfortable with who they are. Everyone says you have to get to at least forty and then you stop caring what other people think." It was important to Kait to believe in the magic of forty, the confidence it would bestow upon her. "I think it's cool she finally gets to be who she wants. Just you wait till I'm forty and you'll see."

JACK CALLS IN THE evening. Hunter pulls over, uses the call as an excuse to stretch his legs. This area of the road is as desolate as any other, indistinguishable from the previous two hundred miles. He sets Kait on the roof, circles his car while talking. Jack wants to know who is taking care of the house. No one is. Why should they?

"Because the house is an asset and the contents of the house are assets, and you should protect your assets," Jack says. "Someone needs to mow the lawn, run the water, open and close windows. This is basic stuff, kid."

"You want to take care of the place? Willow has a key."

"I have a job, Hunter. I can't just disappear whenever life becomes inconvenient for me."

"You think you always have to remind everyone you have a job."

"Sometimes I think you forget what adults are supposed to do during the day."

"I had a job, but then my wife died. I don't know if you heard." Hunter sees shadows along the roadside in the distance. He's certain there are serial killers on this road; in every story about murderous drifters, these are the kinds of places to which drifters will drift.

"Someone had to stay here. The company can't just shut down for a weekend."

"Priorities."

"Responsibilities. There's a difference." Hunter imagines Jack closing his eyes and inhaling deeply in his exaggerated gesture that announces *I am trying to be patient with you.*

"I've got responsibilities too," Hunter says. "I made promises to my wife that I didn't keep. You of all people should appreciate that. I'm trying not to fail at something for once."

"What I need you to understand is: this is not the way I wanted things to be."

"No? Because this is *exactly* how I wanted things to be," Hunter says, and he wants to hang up but has never actually hung up on anyone, and besides, he knows Jack will keep calling until he feels like he has made his point.

"I'm not trying to fight with you," Jack says.

"Then what the hell are you trying to do?"

"I don't know. What am I supposed to do here? You tell me what I'm supposed to do." He sighs, slow and long, like a balloon with a pinhole leak. Hunter thinks it would be a grand, impressive gesture to hurl his phone into the field, but knows he can't afford to lose his one remaining connection to the world. Besides, is it still an effective act if nobody sees it? "Bad things happen to everyone," Jack says. Hunter mentally hangs up, holds his breath so Jack can't even hear the air expelling from his lungs, wants him to know what it feels like to speak into a void. "This might even turn out to be a good thing for you. It's about time you learn how to take care of yourself—"

"Hey, Jack, if they find me dead out here, don't worry about taking off of work for the funeral."

Surviving Pennsylvania is a heavyweight grudge match, fifteen rounds of being bludgeoned by dullness. Ohio welcomes bedraggled and unhappy drivers; its rest stops are sparkling and its atmosphere sleepy, the people disconcertingly polite. Indiana passes like a camera flash, and Illinois slaps drivers in the face with bitter winds and row after row after row of cornfields.

Hunter checks himself into an Eastern Illinois hotel room, tells the desk clerk he'll need a wake-up call at six a.m. Says he has to get an early start. Says he's already behind schedule. The clerk asks where he's going, and Hunter tells him he's headed to Chicago. "For research," he says. "I'm doing research."

In the room, he and Kait watch TV, and he picks the bacon off his grilled cheese sandwich; already, he is learning that in some parts of America, everything comes with bacon, whether you want it or not. A few months ago, he watched a documentary on the meat industry, skimmed a handful of articles on the topic online, and told Kait he'd reached a momentous life decision: he was going to become a vegetarian. February would be the Month of the Vegetarian Transition. He marked it on the calendar, gave his frozen meats away to his brothers-in-law, purchased vegan substitutes for all of those foods. What amazed him was learning how skilled the vegan food industry is at shaping the essential protein-based nonmeats into the form of actual meats, as in the cases of tofurkey and vegan bacon, even if he didn't understand why vegetarians needed their foods to still resemble the meats they were rejecting. He worried that the meatlike appearance undermined the gravity of his decision; how would people know he was consciously rejecting the corrupt and inhumane meat industry if everything he ate looked like everything everyone else ate? It's not like carnivores molded their meats into the shape of vegetables; there is no such thing as pork apples or beef on the cob.

He lasted as a full-on vegetarian for more than two weeks, and Kait did too, a sympathy conversion. She didn't believe he could do it, never said so directly, but it was obvious when she applauded his every meatless evening the way one praises a child for completing simple tasks like cleaning up his toys. Kait had seen him fail at implementing sweeping changes in his life before. She claimed he had a *quick-fix mentality*, while Hunter insisted, "I strive to improve myself, there's a difference." His first effort at improving himself occurred when he was twelve, and his teacher showed the class a video about pollution; he couldn't shake the image of the Texas-sized garbage island floating in the ocean, and so he embarked on the Month of Recycling, collecting cans and papers and exchanging them at a local plant for two dollars a pound. Jack said it was good to see him finally taking initiative, bragged to friends about how his son had already become an entrepreneur, but the recycling ended abruptly when Hunter was stung on the lips by a pair of bees attracted to the soda cans he was hauling. Later, there was the Month of Fitness, which consisted of doing fifty pushups and sit-ups every morning and night, until one day he felt a sharp pain in his shoulder and decided to take a week off, never got back in the habit. There was the Month of No Hot Dogs. The Month of Maturation. The Month of Being More Reliable. The Month of Reading Books. The Month of No Bad Feelings.

He relapsed on his vegetarianism before Kait did, ordering a Meat-Tastic pizza from Padre's Paradise of Pizza, arguing that it can't hurt to indulge now and then. A couple weeks later, he found himself eating a hamburger and hot wings for lunch. He may as well have been drinking a glass of lard, he realized, so he converted back briefly. He would have forgiven himself for those slip-ups if not for Kait's insistence on maintaining her own vegetarianism. She called it commitment, he called it stubbornness, but regardless, when she died, she was still a vegetarian, completely free of meat-based toxins, and yet she still died. It made the whole veggie/meat distinction seem so insignificant on one hand, but on the other it also seems particularly important in the sense that if he dies today, he will have died having failed at even the most fundamental elements of self-control, which is why he's trying again to stick with grilled cheese (cheese admittedly being a bit of a gray area, ethically) and French fries, despite the world's best efforts to entrap him into carnivorousness.

He flicks the soggy bacon into the trash can. Tells Kait he's sorry this trip is so boring, but he didn't think he could feel so foreign within his own country. The whole point of a road trip isn't the getting from point A to point B, it's the stuff that happens between, the people you meet and the sites you see; he may as well have spent the past week sitting on his couch at home, because he knows no more about these places now than he did before leaving. Without any connections or prior knowledge of an area, how is he supposed to infiltrate it? He can check tourism websites online, but it's hard to know which ones to trust, and anyway he forgot his laptop, somehow, before leaving, which means he can only use the unreliable and tedious web browser on his phone. Besides all that, he's ostensibly a self-reliant adult male; shouldn't he be able to figure things out without the help of a handheld GPS and access to a comprehensive collection of the world's atlases and encyclopedias? But how is he supposed to learn anything about the places he's visiting or find the answers he's looking for if he stays isolated within his car at all times? How do other people do it, develop that courage to talk to strangers and expose themselves to potential harm (emotional, physical) via impromptu interaction? "That was your job," he says to Kait, who had learned how to fake confidence from years of meetings at work. He does okay in social settings when he has time to rehearse, to hone his one-liners and filter his conversation topics, but when it came to extemporaneous dialogue, he deferred to Kait. She was the one who had to call plumbers and electricians, had to make dinner reservations and complaints to the credit card companies. She was the one who asked for directions and told rude people, "Excuse me, but my husband and I were actually in line before you."

Here's what else she was good at: ironing clothes, minor repairs like fixing squeaky stairs or patching drywall, maintaining relationships with the neighbors, paying bills on time, organizing family gatherings. Hunter had jobs in the relationship, although he feels divorced from them now. He knew better than anyone how to make her laugh. He cleaned the bathroom, because the sight of dirty bathrooms stressed her beyond all reason. He went grocery shopping every week, and even though she sometimes wished he wouldn't make so many impulse purchases, she hated going to the supermarket herself. He was a better cook than she was. He was much better than her at using the Internet, a skill that ate away at his concentration and free time, but also made him a valuable teammate at bar trivia tournaments and always gave him something to say, even if he was unsure when to say it.

He logs on to his Facebook account via his phone. Checks her page again. A distant relative has written on his wall: *Much love 2 u n urs Cant believe shes dead, smh.* He scrolls through thousands of updates from friends, former classmates, and others whose connection to him is untraceable. Their updates generally alternate between complaints about how hard life is and passive-aggressive bragging about how great life is. A shocking number of people think their responsibility as the curator of a social media page is to report the news after they hear it on TV or to tell everyone what the weather conditions are in their city. A disappointingly large number of people think it is okay to discuss the contents and function of their bowels on the Internet. Everybody is posting pictures of everything, even if the pictures are unremarkable, but the accumulation of useless news and updates creates a social pressure on everyone else to spew out their own stream of updates. If one is not constantly telling the Internet what he or she is thinking, it seems entirely possible that one no longer exists. Hunter does not want to check but he continues checking, captivated despite the insipidness of it all.

Even though there is nothing he wants to watch on TV, he

keeps the set on so there is some noise in the room. While flipping through the channels, he sees a rerun of a show called *Happy Home-comings?* in which couples search for their dream homes and a host offers them unsolicited advice on their relationship. Normally, this is the type of show he'd ignore, but he and Kait were once featured on an episode of *HH?* In the twenty-first century, anyone who lives long enough will end up on TV at some point. Fame is a fluke and it is unrelated to merit or value. Hunter and Kait had their turns during their engagement, when they were house hunting and found themselves, through a series of complicated circumstances, roped into being one of two featured couples. Cameras followed them for three weeks just to produce about twenty minutes of content on what is an objectively terrible television show, and although it seemed exciting at the time, it quickly became an afterthought; it was just a weird thing they'd done, with no tangible benefits or consequences except for the rare stranger who recognized them and was excited to meet someone from TV. He has never seen their episode; contractual conditions imposed by the parent company prevented the production company from giving copies to partici-pants, and the night it aired, a massive thunderstorm knocked the power out in their neighborhood. Friends and family had either lost their power or had failed to record it. Soon after, the show was canceled. For Kait, this was a relief, as she'd never wanted to see herself on the screen anyway, and had only agreed to film the show because Hunter thought it would make for a good story and they were paid five hundred dollars each. He has tried many times—be-fore and since the death—to find video clips online, but has come up empty-handed. This episode currently airing does not feature them, and none of the upcoming show descriptions match their episode. So he tries again to find it online, digging through hundreds of pages of search results in the vain hope of seeing her in motion one more time, of hearing her voice.

Near midnight, the phone buzzes in his hand, jolts him from his trance. He expects it to be Sherry, who has been calling nearly every night and leaving angry voicemails. This time it's Brutus. He's drunk and wants to know where the fuck is his sister.

"She's on vacation," Hunter says, hoping that if he keeps repeating this, it will eventually be true, eventually she'll just come home and everything will go back to normal.

"Where the fuck are you going with her?" Hunter hears the chaos of a bar in the background.

"Anywhere we feel like."

"You think this is funny?"

"How could it possibly be funny?"

"I like how you're all the sudden a real tough guy when you're hiding," Brutus says. "You try and get tough up around me, I'll stomp your dumbfuck head in."

"She didn't even like you, you know that?"

"No respect for nobody, that's your problem."

"The whole family. She wanted nothing to do with you." Hunter feels himself clenching an involuntary fist.

"Think you're better than us because why? You got rich parents? You read some books before?"

"She called you all white trash. Didn't even want me to meet you." This is barely a half-truth; she loved them, even though they often embarrassed her. His rational brain tells him he's being cruel and Kait would disapprove of his lashing out, but his rational brain is powerless when pitted against his grief, which tells him the only thing that will make him feel better is to make Brutus feel worse.

"If it wasn't for her you'd of gotten beat already."

"Tell your mom to stop calling me too."

"You keep fucking with my mom, and—"

"You just pretend I'm already dead," Hunter says. "Pretend we're both gone forever." Brutus unleashes a torrent of curses and semi-coherent threats; rather than hanging up, Hunter sets the phone on the table next to Kait and allows the insults to wash over him like an aggressive white noise. He imagines what it would be like to actually fight Brutus, the swiftness with which he'd be knocked out, the taste of blood on his tongue, his brain rattling against his skull. He would deserve it, but would it make anything better? Could the physical pain at least distract him for a while? Would it somehow help her family understand that he's not doing any of this for pleasure but to punish himself for his failure as a husband?

He didn't meet her brothers until he and Kait had been dating for about six months, and she rarely talked about them. On her twenty-fourth birthday, she semi-invited Hunter to a party at her mother's house. "You can come if you want," she'd said. "I mean, you don't have to, it probably won't be that fun." Things were getting serious between them, and Hunter figured now would be a perfect time to finally see the place where she'd been raised, and to meet the whole family in one shot. He'd never said it to Kait, and he'd never realized it himself until the moment was upon him, but he wanted her family to become his family, he wanted to be assimilated into the group and to have something more than the strained love of Jack and Willow.

On the drive to Kait's house the day of the party—she drove, he passengered—she bombarded him with warnings and disclaimers. Told him the uncles might give him a hard time, but they're okay, mostly, except for Uncle Bobby, but he won't stay long because he doesn't like the way everyone stares at him when he drinks. The brothers, she said, are nice, you just have to give them a chance. Her preferred euphemism for describing unpleasant relatives was *they're not like you and me*. Gripping the emergency brake as if trying to choke it, she turned to him and said, "It's okay if you don't want to go in, I can tell them you got sick or something."

The first one to greet them was Uncle Bobby, who hugged Kait and picked her up, passed her to Uncle Somebody, who passed her on to Uncle Somebody Else, who nuzzled her with his goatee as if greeting an infant, and within seconds, Hunter was standing alone in the doorway.

"You the boyfriend?" Uncle Bobby said.

"I prefer the term *lover*," Hunter said, smirking, expecting a laugh.

"What kinda gay shit is that? You hear that?" Uncle Bobby said, smacking a cousin on the shoulder. He flicked his wrist and adopted a lisp, "Oh, pleath let me thee my *lov-ah*," he said, while the cousins and uncles and aunts laughed.

"Just a joke," Hunter said.

"Oh good, she's dating a comedian," Bobby said. "You want a beer, Seinfeld?" He put his arm around Hunter and led him toward a keg in the kitchen. Brutus—who Hunter recognized from Kait's pictures—was standing next to it.

Hunter said, "Do you have any lemonade? I'm not really a beer guy."

"Jesus, now I *know* he's gay," Uncle Bobby said. "Fucking lemonade!"

"It's good for preventing kidney stones." Jack had a history of kidney stones. Hunter had seen his tears after passing a stone, heard him try to suppress his groaning by shoving his face into a bath towel, felt his bedroom walls shake as Jack pounded his fist against them from inside the bathroom.

Uncle Bobby shook his head and walked away, looking as disappointed as if Hunter had just said he doesn't like America. Brutus handed Hunter a plastic cup full of beer. "If you're gonna be here, you've got to drink something," he said. Brutus sipped his beer. Hunter slurped along the edges of his. Kait seemed to have disappeared.

Brutus's arms were marked with at least seven visible tattoos, all of which involved flames and/or skulls. Hunter was the only non-tattooed person in the room. At least three people had inked their throats. There were tattoos on knuckles and kneecaps and elbows, and even one person who was proud to show off that he'd recently marked the inside of his lips with the words BITE ME.

Everyone migrated to the basement, and Hunter soon found himself conscripted into a family darts tournament, partnered with Brutus. Kait was down there already, doing shots with her cousins; she introduced them and Hunter immediately forgot their names, felt them sizing him up from across the room for the remainder of the night. The other brothers were downstairs too, but they were still young then—Billy was sixteen, Max only ten—and they tailed uncles and cousins, aping their mannerisms and speech patterns.

Hunter and Brutus played the first game of the tournament, and even though he was the only sober one playing, Hunter missed the board entirely on his first two shots. Brutus punched the wall and shouted, "How do you get a name like Hunter when you can't aim for shit?" They were eliminated in the first round.

Hours later, still in the basement, the uncles and cousins having mostly dispersed, the younger brothers began furtively sipping on the dregs of abandoned beers. Kait was half-asleep, too drunk for conversation. When Brutus ran out of cigarettes, he asked Hunter if he smoked, and Hunter said, "Not cigarettes," thinking he could regain some credibility with the family by implying he at least did drugs, and Brutus said, "Jesus Christ, there's fucking kids down here."

Kait passed out around midnight, and nobody would help him carry her to the car. Uncle Somebody said a man ought to be able to carry his own woman. They had to sleep there, Kait in her old room, Hunter on the basement floor, a thin blanket between himself and the cold slap of the concrete. In the morning, he pretended to be asleep, even while the brothers stomped around upstairs, hiding behind closed eyelids until Kait found him. "Sorry about my brothers," she said, leaning over him, her breath tickling his ear. "You get fifty points for this one."

THE POINTS SYSTEM WAS a game they played, instituted early in the relationship, when she'd bought him tickets to see an indie band called Walrus Tuskers Trio, accompanied him to the show even though she hated the band, couldn't understand the appeal of anything classified as aggro-experimental rock; afterward, he told her she'd earned fifteen points for trying to tolerate the things he liked. She said, "I didn't know we were keeping score," and he said, "Oh yeah, definitely." He pretended to pull a scorecard from his back pocket, said: "And I'm winning." From that point forward, they kept a running tally of points earned. Some actions warranted a standard score—cooking dinner earned a minimum of three points, with bonuses for taste and degree of difficulty. Starting her car for her on frigid mornings was worth five points. Buying gifts on nontraditional occasions was worth twenty-five points. It wasn't possible to lose points, as that sort of punitive urge would undermine the spirit of the game. High scores were never the point; awarding points was like giving out gold stars, just a way to say thanks, to say *I've been paying attention and I appreciate your effort*. In the end, she was ahead, of course she was ahead, but he was close.

The only thing in his life he'd ever fully committed to was loving her, which he tried to demonstrate via the completion of what some people call *the little things*, things like washing the dishes and rubbing her feet without being asked and going dress shopping with her on weekends and making the bed even though he didn't care whether the bed was made or not and anticipating when she would come home stressed from work craving a glass of wine and a bowl of mint chocolate-chip ice cream. He often argued that romance isn't about Big Gestures, but rather about the accumulation of the so-called *little things*. Big Gestures are not repeatable and cannot solely be counted on to keep a marriage afloat. It's not the candlelight dinner on the waterfront, he said to her, but the guarantee of leftovers warming on the stove for you when you get home from work. It's not rose petals scattered across the bedroom floor, but the neatly made bed and the nights spent watching movies together while sharing popcorn. It's not about hot-air balloon rides and champagne, but the comfort of having someone holding your hand when you're stuck in traffic. She nodded and acknowledged that he did all the little things, agreed that the little things are the glue of a good relationship, but he could tell she was disappointed to hear that he was too cynical to even believe in romance, if only for her sake. So, during the Month of Being Romantic, he left a note in her lunch bag every morning, a reminder that he loved her, that he would miss her during the day. The first began with this line: "I can't see you right now, but you look beautiful." He bought a fresh bouquet of flowers every three days, so that there were always bright colors popping in the room to enliven a gray November. Cooked extravagant fish dinners (this month predated the vegetarian transition and also overlapped partly with the Month of Eating More Seafood) and served them with obscenely expensive wine. One Friday, he removed all the furniture from the living room by himself, rolled up the carpet and stowed everything in the basement, so that when she returned home from work he could serve her a glass of wine and invite her to join him on the Largest Residential Dance floor in Philadelphia. After dinner he cued a romance playlist and they swayed and rocked and gyrated for hours before desecrating the dancefloor and falling asleep in the flickering candlelight.

Sherry calls him in the morning. After a full night of web browsing on his phone, he's nursing an Internet hangover (symptoms: mildly blurred vision, headache behind the ears, stabbing guilt, a vague sense of impending doom). She says she needs to know where her daughter is, and Hunter says, "I sent you a picture. Should I have attached a GPS to the urn?" Sherry calls him a cocky little bastard, and he says he can't really talk right now, he has places to be. Before he hangs up, Sherry says, "If I was you, I'd stay gone. You ever come back, we'll be waiting."

Kait and Sherry were not close. The schism in their relationship was rooted in a longstanding dispute over Sherry's self-destructive attraction to abusive and controlling men, specifically an ex-boyfriend who, according to Kait, was ugly and petty and probably one of the ten worst people in the country besides her father (whom Hunter had never met and whose only contact with Kait was the occasional letter, mailed every few years from a different prison, saying this time was rock bottom for real, this time he'd cleaned up and made amends and gotten right with God). Sherry's ex-boyfriend, according to Kait, made everyone around him worse by association, and Sherry drank too much with him, became neglectful and too consumed by her own fear to care for her children, refused to listen to reason when confronted about him. They stayed together for six years, until Kait was in college, and only broke up because he had taken a swing at Max in front of the whole family on Thanksgiving. "No wonder I've dated so many assholes," Kait said once. "Not you. I mean—before. You know?" She rarely divulged information about her dating history, but he knew she'd strung together a solid half-decade of emotionally abusive and controlling boyfriends who had inflicted long-term damage on her, had taught her not to trust anyone, had convinced her to hate herself and to always feel a lingering sense of guilt and shame when she did something good for herself. One of those boyfriends, a deadbeat named Finn who still palled around with Brutus, was so jealous that he would sit outside the bathroom door with a timer because he was afraid that she would sneak out the window and run away from him, and even still sometimes drunkenly texted pictures of his penis to Kait, telling her to come back where she belongs.

After Sherry finally got rid of that boyfriend, she focused on mending her relationship with Kait via shopping trips and massages and pedicures and hour-long chats on the phone, but Kait was too old, had missed her opportunity to form the kind of unbreakable bond children are supposed to form with their parents. Still, she said sometimes, "It's nice to have a mom again."

And so, despite her lingering bitterness about her own unhappy childhood, she would disapprove of Hunter's callousness toward Sherry now, even though Sherry has never made any particular effort to make Hunter feel welcome, had obviously judged him as not enough of a man for Kait because he was such a departure from her past boyfriends. Kait would remind him now how hard she had worked to bond with Willow and Jack. Probably Kait would tell him *you are better than this*. In the myopia of his sadness, he's forgotten that her family is in mourning too. For all their tough-guy posturing, her brothers loved her more than they loved themselves; the morning of the funeral, Max kept repeating that he wished it had been him instead. They had all come to count on her as a surrogate mother when their own mother was incapable of helping them. Besides being sisterless, they are also essentially motherless, because Sherry isn't strong enough to cope with her daughter's death. She has led a sad, lonely life, and now she needs to self-medicate just to face her own empty home. She's groping for some piece of Kait to hold on to, to anchor herself back in the world. If Kait has any agency in the afterlife, then she would want to see her family too. Hunter does not get to hoard the memory of her, no matter how much he might want to. So when he hears Kait say *you're being selfish,* he knows she is right. And when he hears her ask why he would taunt a grieving mother, he knows it's a fair question, and the only answer he can produce is this: *because I'm angry and they're the only people I can hurt.*

A COUPLE MONTHS INTO their relationship, Kait spent a long weekend in Hartford, slept in the guest room at Jack and Willow's house. On her second night in town, the four of them went out to dinner at a steakhouse downtown. At dinner, Hunter saw her in full professional mode: the eye contact, the brief hesitation before speaking as she considered her words carefully, the firm but genial delivery, the prepared anecdotes designed to appeal to a man of Jack's sensibilities. It was cold in the restaurant, like a crypt, but she had come prepared with a spare cardigan for Willow to borrow. She got ribeye while Hunter got trout, and she impressed Jack by ordering a Knob Creek on the rocks. She listened patiently while Willow talked about the local government disturbing the area bird habitats. She asked Willow about her time as a volunteer at the shelter. Kait talked more easily with his parents than he ever had, and afterward, sitting on the living room couch, he asked her, "How the hell did you do that?"

"I'm exhausted," she said, her eyes closed already.

"I think they really liked you."

"Your dad's really not that bad," she said.

"People always say that. Just wait till you get to know him better." Soon after, she was asleep in the guest room, and she wouldn't wake until late the next morning, after everyone had already eaten breakfast. She was frantic then, embarrassed at having slept in, and here he saw the duality of Kait: she could carry herself with poise and confidence in any company, but it would sap all of her resources. People who only knew her casually or through work didn't understand how anxious she was, never realized that she woke up a half hour early on workdays just to do deep-breathing exercises and prepare herself for a full day of dealing with the world.

That morning, he told her she could relax, because he'd invented a game and all she had to do was follow his lead. He called it the Guided Life Tour, and it worked like this: he drove to significant landmarks from his past—say, the playground where he broke his first bone, or the hospital where he had his heart surgery—and narrated the story for her, complete with dialogue, scene constructions, fleshed-out supporting characters.

They stopped for a late lunch at Santucci's Pizzeria, and then he continued the tour, opening with a joke he'd been saving all day: "Be sure to tip your guide afterward." Led her to a rust-colored motel on the fringes of town. Noted the ninety-dollar weekly rates—"They've gone up," he said—and waited until she asked why he stopped at this seedy place hemmed in by liquor stores and strip clubs. "Because," he said, "this is where I lived when I ran away." He wanted her to see a dark side, a dangerous, brooding Mystery Man, wanted her to know he could be unpredictable and wild sometimes. Told her about the expulsion from high school because of the pot they found in his locker, the escalation of the fights with Jack, the guilt for resenting Willow for loving him as much as she did. The day he quit his first job, Jack threatened to kick him out of the house, and Hunter decided to call his bluff. Packed a bag and walked right past him, drove away and did not stop until reaching this motel. Jack wanted to do the tough-love bit, wanted Hunter to learn his lesson, so he let Hunter stay there for three weeks. He finally left when the hotel manager changed the lock due to outstanding debts.

When Hunter visited Kait in Philly a few weeks later—staying in a friend's apartment because Kait said there was nowhere for him to sleep at Sherry's house—he talked her into guiding him on a tour of her past. Although he'd been racing to tell her everything he could about his life, he realized one day that she'd barely told him *anything*. After a full day of prodding, she gave in, drove to a restaurant at the foot of the Tacony-Palmyra Bridge. Said, "I can't do this, I feel stupid." Hunter told her she would be fine, he wanted to know everything about Beef's Burger Barn, and so she started again: "Over here, that restaurant used to be a house. A very old house, where three people lived—No, forget it, this is dumb," she said, shifted the car into drive and sped away, said she didn't like the game anymore, and then she shut down on him the way she did sometimes, ignoring his questions, turning the radio up loud enough to discourage further talking, her jaw clenched as if wired shut.

When they parked outside his friend's apartment, Hunter told her, not for the first time, that she seemed depressed, and he wanted to help her. "I'd like to be alone tonight," she said, and she didn't call until the next morning, during which time he hadn't slept, showered, or eaten, and she said she was sorry, but maybe they should take a break from story time for a while. She wanted more secrets. For both of them. She said, "If we tell each other everything now, we'll run out of things to talk about later." She didn't want him to know too much about her too soon. "You're a good guy and I don't want to blow this," and besides, what would they talk about in ten years? In forty? "You have to ration your stories," she said, "because a relationship should gradually reveal itself over time," a stance on which she held firm until the day she died, and now Hunter is left with a host of untold stories, things he will never know about her.

WHEN HE BASHES THE car into a pothole, he doesn't stop to make sure everything is still in working order, and so he doesn't discover until another mile later that he's been riding on a flat tire. The flapping of the rubber, the imbalance of the car, and the grinding of rim on asphalt finally alert him, at which point he has no choice but to pull onto the shoulder and glower at his car as if he has been betrayed. He has no idea how to change a flat tire; Jack tried to teach him once, but he didn't pay attention, and anyway it looks even to his inexpert eye like he may have done permanent damage to the car by riding on a flat for so long. His effort to drive coast-to-coast has been derailed after a week due to his own incompetence, and Kait is in the car by herself, watching him while he stands outside sweating profusely, because dammit, it is *hot*, and why doesn't he know how to fix anything?

He picks up Kait, apologizes for ruining the trip already. Stuffs her into his duffel bag, slung over his shoulder. Uses his phone to take a picture of the broken-down car, and then retreats to the relative safety of the Internet, where he can control his own narrative. He loads the picture onto Facebook, the first photo in an untitled album. Caption: *Abandoned.* After a quarter mile walk down the road, he takes another picture—of the steaming line of asphalt cutting through farmland, dotted by white trucks and occasional state troopers. Caption: *Westward Bound.*

SEVEN

When you dream, you never see her. You only dream about being lost in a cavernous house and searching for her.

YOU HAD FANTASIZED SOMETIMES about her being dead; actually, *fantasized* is not the right word, because that makes it sound like you were thinking about killing her, which you decidedly were not, but you had envisioned her death from time to time, imagined what your life would turn into without her. You told her once that you worried that she wasn't born to be *a long-term person*, a feeling you couldn't explain except to say that when you looked at her you sometimes saw her fading away right in front of you. You worried, when she was late coming home from work, that she'd gotten in a car accident and someone was going to summon

you downtown to identify the body. You walked through the front
door expecting to find her twisted and broken-necked at the bottom of the stairs. Saw, when you closed your eyes, flashes of ca-
tastrophes occurring: lightning strikes, rabid dog attacks, tornados
touching down on top of her, abductions by Colombian drug lords.
Tried to imagine your emotions when she was gone, and beyond
the standard sorrow and mourning, here's the thing you couldn't
admit to her, were afraid to voice: sometimes when you thought
about these things, you zoomed past the sadness and loneliness
and focused instead on the positive changes her disappearance
would have on your life. All the sympathetic attention you would
receive. Not having to worry about impressing her every day with
surprises and gifts and declarations of love. The women with whom
you could conceivably engage in guilt-free sexual intercourse, the
varieties of inventive and acrobatic sexual acts they could teach
you. The movies you could now see without worrying that they
were too boring for her, the family gatherings you could skip, the
absence of pressure trying to shape you into a better man, and the
word you never considered but that summed all these things up
was this—freedom. And now the guilt is choking you, because
what you're feeling is nothing like freedom, and besides, what did
you need to be free from in the first place—her love? The best
things about you were tied up in her, so where did you even get the
idea that marriage was restrictive? How childish could you have
been to think life would somehow be better experienced alone, like
you're the High Plains Drifter?

You'd imagined so many different scenarios, and while it's
true that you never willed it to happen, it seems possible that you

generated enough negative energy around Kait that you caused this. And now you have nothing.

HERE ARE TOPICS YOU learn to avoid in conversations with strangers you meet on the road: marriage, children, where you're from, where you're going, reasons for traveling solo, the contents of your cube. And still, you want people to know. On buses and on trains and on ferries, you keep her by your side, display her, buy her tickets, because you want everyone to see that you're on a spiritual journey. You want them to sense the gravitas of your mission and to understand that their personal trifles don't mean anything in comparison.

You want them to know your wife is dead, and that any moment someone they love could be dead too. Sometimes kindly strangers ask what's in the box, and you want to tell them *it's my dead wife's ashes, wanna see?* but instead you turn away and pretend you can't hear them. You want them to figure it out on their own, so you turn the cube toward them at an angle so that they can read her name and the date of her death, and you slump and grimace and sigh to call your misery to the surface. There is an arrogance to your sadness, this idea that everyone should care about your circumstances even though they have their own losses to mourn, even though they don't know you or Kait, and you want them to understand that they *should have* known Kait. That they should be grieving too, because the world is missing someone important, someone valuable, necessary, like oxygen. There is no dignity in begging for attention, but you cannot stop displaying her, even when you know you should stop.

YOU DO NOT LIKE the word *widower*. You have written it, but cannot speak it without spitting afterward. You begin to worry that you might be contagious, that if you give breath to the words "my wife is dead," it will become an airborne virus, expelled and sprayed onto strangers, who will pass it on to their friends and acquaintances through handshakes, kisses, and hugs, and those un-hygienic friends and acquaintances will pass it on to their friends, and so on, until you've sparked an epidemic of widower-hood, and a worldwide search identifies you as Patient Zero.

EIGHT

A year into their marriage, Hunter decided he was done with Philadelphia and the whole East Coast. It was a place so unfriendly, so dysfunctional, so pathologically negative that he was convinced he'd been tainted by the atmosphere, a Regional Affective Disorder that had exacerbated all of his worst qualities and stunted his personal growth. He'd hoped to be many things by the time he was twenty-five, but he'd become none of those things. He'd hoped to be professionally accomplished, for one, to have a career rather than just a job. To be creatively engaged in something, even if it was writing music reviews for the community newspaper. To have a small circle of trusted friends with whom he had a monthly meeting for lunch or coffee. To volunteer every other weekend at a homeless shelter. To have the disposable income to buy rare gems for Kait and take her out to extravagant dinners. On the Internet, he saw photos of his acquaintances skydiving, attending black-tie events with the governor, getting record deals, going on safaris, winning fellowships for their research. It felt like he'd hit a ceiling at eighteen and everyone he knew had just kept rising. His two greatest achievements were his marriage and owning a home, but Kait deserved more credit than him for both of those accomplishments.

Without Kait, he was a failure, so he began researching new places to live, places where he could reinvent himself. Criteria: vibrant arts scene, large and diverse population, a wide variety of career opportunities, some historical importance, good restaurants, generally liberal, generally young. He narrowed it down to six finalists before telling Kait about his desire to move. The top choice was Chicago (runners-up: Seattle; Victoria, British Columbia; San Francisco; St. Louis; and Austin). In addition to meeting the other requirements, Chicago was a good hub for domestic travel, and Kait was familiar with the area from her time as a student at DePaul. She'd told him once the only reason she moved back after college was because she was too young to live on her own so far away from home, but now, he reasoned, she was older and more mature and they would have each other. He presented the case to her in as much detail as possible, including a three-page handout detailing demographics, average home prices, school ratings, and other data. "You really put a lot of work into this," Kait said.

"I wanted you to see I'm serious."

She crinkled the edges of the handout. "But we can't actually move."

"We can do anything we want. Literally anything. It's not like we're chained up here."

"But we kind of are. I have a job, and we have this house. And I like it here, and also how are we even going to find a good place?"

He produced another printout. "I've been looking. These ones all look pretty good, and if we fly out for a long weekend—"

"This is crazy. We can't just move halfway across the country on a whim."

"It's a two-hour flight. We can come back here any time we want."

"But if we stay in this house, it's a zero-hour flight to get back here." She skimmed through the home listings. "Anyway, you can't try on new cities like sweaters. That's not how things work."

"You're always talking about adventure," he said.

"Yeah, I want to go on *vacations* to other places, I don't want to live in them."

"Did you at least look? How great is that second house?"

"What's the rush to get out of here anyway?" she said. "You didn't kill someone, did you?"

"My parents have lived in the same town their whole lives. Did you know that? Jack grew up on the *same street* they live on now."

"You're nothing like your dad."

"This is just a place, you know? It's never been the right fit for us."

"Since when does everything have to be perfect? What if some things just have to be good enough?"

He shuffled his papers. Clicked on a few links. "What if also I killed a guy?" he said.

"Will you still love me if I testify against you? I think I'd be really good at being a witness," she said.

HE COULD HAVE THE car repaired, wait a few days in rural Illinois, and then continue, but he is afraid of losing his momentum. He takes a cab to the nearest bus station, buys a ticket to Chicago, and while waiting for the bus to depart, he decides to map out the rest of his trip. Without the car, he needs to have more of a plan, because he's now at the mercy of bus schedules and mass transit. Kait was the superior planner. Her intense level of organization was often a defense she'd erected against her insecurities, the dogmatic belief that if she spent enough time planning, then she could overcome all of her perceived deficiencies. She was the one who'd wanted to begin learning French and Italian, and who had bought atlases and European guidebooks. She was the one who insisted they spend at least two hours per week watching travel documentaries, just so they would know what to expect. She was the one who would have mapped out the itinerary down to the hour and who would be telling him right now that you can't just get on a bus and expect a trip to materialize spontaneously. *You need to act upon the world*, she would have said. He reminds her now that it's part of his charm (or at least he thought it was), one of the things she always loved about him (or at least he thought it was), the breezy nonchalance with which he's able to approach a major project, the way he provided balance for her Type-A anxiety. And yet, the nonchalance has led to a trip that is now two weeks and over a thousand miles long, with no discernible progress to show for the time and effort.

After looking over maps and bus routes, he thinks the only plan that makes sense is to start with Chicago, then work his way through the other finalists on his list of potential new homes. Now he has no reason at all to remain tied to that old place—Kait is here with him, and the thought of returning to the shell of his old life is terrible enough without even considering the possibility that Sherry, Brutus, and the rest will be waiting there to break him in half. So he will look at homes in Chicago. He'll go to open houses. He'll move from there to St. Louis and do the same. He will learn everything he can about each city, and maybe if one of them is as perfect a fit as he'd hoped, then he will stop there and begin a new life with Kait in a new home, with a new job and new friends and new family and a new self. Because this plan is coming together at the last minute and there are a few landmarks the Internet tells him he should see along the way, he devises a convoluted route that gets him to Austin, Texas, by way of Nebraska, then South Dakota, then Oklahoma. After that, he will head west.

THE GENERAL ATMOSPHERE OF an interstate bus ride is best described as oppressively sad, but at least Hunter doesn't have to drive anymore. As a passenger, he's not worried about crashing because he trusts the professional driver, and also how often are bus disasters reported on the news? Sometimes it happens, sure, but Hunter suspects those events are pretty rare and that their relative rarity actually leads to them being over-reported. Perhaps just as important as the safety, though, is the fact that this bus knows exactly how to get to Chicago and drives with a purpose.

In a college creative writing class, he once wrote a short story about a young man on a Greyhound bus, running away from home and going "anywhere the road will take me." The story ran twenty-seven pages (despite a fifteen-page limit), and was full of Big Revelations about Human Nature and The Way We Live Today. There was a Down-on-Her-Luck Single Mom. There was a Noble Stripper Chasing Her Dreams. There was a Gritty Blue-collar Worker. There was a Creepy Old Man, heaved off the bus by the group, which had cohered into a family halfway through the trip. A pivotal scene featured the narrator talking to a Wise Hobo who was tired of riding the rails and spoke entirely in homespun aphorisms. The narrator said to the Hobo, "At least you've lived; I'm a nonentity," a comment Hunter himself had once uttered to a beggar on campus, because the only problems Hunter had ever faced were the most generic suburban white-kid problems anyone could imagine, and it made him miserable to think how sad that was. In real life, the homeless man flicked the bridge of Hunter's nose and told him to go get fucked by a rhino. In the story, the Wise Hobo sympathized and told the narrator he understood, said it's better to live life in the muck than watch from the sidelines. Said if ennui and ironic detachment could bring someone down so hard, then the Narrator ought to challenge himself and face real drama in his life, see what he's made of. The last line of the story read: "Maybe we all have something to learn from one another after all." His classmates called it mature and funny and engaging, even though he could tell some of them hadn't really read it, and they'd just assumed it was good because it was long. He was also pretty confident that, yes, it was good, and, yes, he was witty and smart and talented, and so even when the teacher critiqued it, picking at all the loose threads and describing it as overwrought, Hunter decided that he was going to start telling people he was a writer, because he liked hearing people praise his work, and he liked the notion of being a Man of Letters, a person whose job it is to sit in his home and think about Important Things, then issue proclamations about those Important Things, living what appears to lay people to be a sedentary life, but which actually requires intense mental gymnastics. He knows now that it was a wrongheaded and juvenile dream, that very few people actually get to live the life of a public intellectual, and that anyway his great attraction to it was that it seemed important without actually involving a lot of labor, like a shortcut to being someone people cared about. He knows he's incapable of being that person he pretended to be, but the problem was he never found a new goal; by the time of Kait's death he still hadn't determined the person he was supposed to be. Envisioning a life of rubbing his temples and telling people *I've just been buried in my work all day long*, he changed his major to English, took a few more creative writing classes, read most of the books he was assigned, skimmed enough of the other books to be able to fake it (surely his professors had done the same; how could anyone have encyclopedic knowledge of hundreds of novels?), and graduated with a BA in English and a 3.1 GPA that he now admits could have been higher, but, as he contended to Jack and Willow every semester when his grades came in, aren't grades, after all, simply an arbitrary system of measurement designed to appease state accreditation boards and status-driven nerds, and isn't the true measure of intelligence how much knowledge has been gained rather than whether one received a B or a B+ on a reading quiz on *Beowulf*? When, a year into their relationship, he recounted these arguments to Kait, she cringed at his description of the grading process, boasted her 3.8 GPA in finance, and said,

"So what if grades are arbitrary? If everyone else cares about them, you have to care about them too," and to a certain extent she was right; it was the GPA (and the ancillary honors) that enabled her to get a good job out of college and maintain a strong credit score and would ultimately lead them to their house, which was not exactly an estate, but was the kind of place that people often called *adorable* and *charming*. Hunter admitted she was right; it had made him feel better at the time, he said, but rationalizations don't get you far on job interviews; recruiters want numbers and they want results. If he were back in school now, he said, he would put in a little more effort, spent more time actually trying to figure out what he was supposed to do with his life instead of deferring the issue.

At that time, he was still ostensibly pursuing the writing life, so she asked to see what he'd been working on, and all he could show her was the old Greyhound story, on which she made notes and copyedits and offered him feedback. She told him "This is really good, you should keep working on this." She prompted him, in front of her family, to tell them about his work, which only served to reinforce their perception of him as an effete intellectual, and later when he asked her not to do that again, she apologized, said she was just proud of him, said she *liked* that he was different from them, that his creativity and curiosity distinguished him from her friends' husbands and boyfriends. She sent him text messages in the mornings wishing him a good day of writing, saying, "I know you'll come up with something great." At first, he tried. Because it was good to feel like he was doing something worthwhile, to consider himself a writer again as opposed to considering himself nothing at all, and because he wanted to reward her faith in him, but within a week he realized he didn't actually like writing. He just liked the lingering cultural significance of having written. Still, he pretended for three months, holing himself up in his bedroom and skimming the Internet for hours, always deferring Kait's requests to read his work-in-progress. "You can't read it until it's done," he said. One evening over dinner, he told her he probably wasn't cut out for writing, and she said nothing at all, after which point he never pretended to write again.

AN UNABRIDGED LIST OF jobs held by Hunter Cady between ages 16 and 29 (plus: reason for leaving):

- Cashier at Santucci's Pizzeria in Hartford, CT (fired over philosophical debate with manager re: the practice of charging a quarter for extra napkins)
- Summer intern at Cady Manufacturing (terrible working relationship with Jack)
- Sandwich designer at Gaetano's Grinders in Hartford (fired for repeated lateness)
- Landscaper with Celtic lawns, Hartford (summer job only)
- Clerk at Underground Records, Hartford (shop closed)
- Barista at Whole Latte Love in Philadelphia (quit when he got a better job)
- Library assistant at Temple University (graduated, position limited to current students only)
- Intern at *Philadelphia Daily News* (quit, didn't want to work in a dead medium)
- Technical editor at Farrelly Information Services in Hartford

(job too soul-draining, left after ten days when he went to the
supply closet to hide from the tedium and his manager was
already in there *doing the same thing*)
- Substitute teacher in Hartford Public School District (a terrible idea from the start)
- Tour guide, Philadelphia Zoo (seasonal work only)
- Marketing and Development for Building Blocks, a nonprofit
organization supporting children in low-income areas of Philadelphia (failed to reach fundraising goals)
- Writer of fictions that will open minds and change lives (harder
than it looked)
- Contact Center Professional at Dependable Rentals (wife died)

There were times over the past half-decade when Hunter wondered
whether he should have skipped college entirely and gone into a
trade, learned to fix elevators—*an industry on the rise*, he would
have said every day—or building bomb shelters or just about anything besides having spent four-point-five years in pursuit of an
English degree with a minor in Philosophy that was long on in-
trinsic value and short on practical applications. Because understanding Petrarch doesn't pay the gas bill. Being able to quote Kant
doesn't help you upsell a customer from a compact car to an SUV.
But he'd been convinced, like so many of his classmates, that going
to college was some sort of guarantee of future happiness, and also
it delayed his entry into the real world and granted him what Jack
calls *the luxury of aimlessness*, a phrase he surely read in some book
filled with tips on how to become a tycoon. Jack enjoyed reiterating
the Legend of Jack Cady, self-made man, who never had the luxury

of aimlessness, and who made the mistake of granting that luxury to his son, who didn't have to pay for school and whose mother kept him on an allowance until he turned twenty-four.

In the months leading up to Kait's death, Hunter had applied to ten colleges to pursue graduate studies in a variety of business-adjacent fields. He wasn't enthralled by the subject matter, but at least this way he could make better money and follow through on some of his lofty promises to Kait. She didn't like the idea of losing his income while he was at school, but still it was her idea for him to apply. "You can't keep living like this," she'd said. "You're too smart to be renting out cars and sitting around the house." She helped him fill out the applications, copyedited his personal statements, tracked the deadlines. He'd wanted to keep the applications a secret as long as possible, but Kait had mentioned them to Jack, and Jack started e-mailing him grad school application tips and offering to look things over for him, to make calls to old friends with connections in admissions departments. By the time of Kait's death, Hunter had only heard from one school, a rejection from Wharton, which was to be expected, but he'd treated that application like a lottery ticket, just in case. The responses from other schools are probably piling up in his mailbox now, reminders of a time when he thought planning for the future was a sensible and responsible thing to do.

THE FUNDAMENTAL DISAPPOINTMENT OF the bus ride is that the relative safety and the direction are there, but what's lacking is what has been lacking from the start: nothing seems to be chang-ing. He is viewing the country at a remove, as if watching a docu-mentary about someone else's more interesting cross-country trip, which is not at all the point of travel, is it? The point is to engage with the world, to meet new people and experience adventures and accumulate stories to tell, and to return home a transformed man. What he should be doing is making footprints and taking soil samples and learning the names of the local flora and fauna. He should be hacking a new path into the wilderness rather than watching the roadside through a rain-streaked window. There's something too utilitarian about riding isolated across the country, flumping in the backseat of a Greyhound and silently gazing off into the distance; this is the sort of approach one takes when trying to complete a job, a courier delivering important documents to a client, and although Hunter has very important cargo in his care, there is no specific endpoint, there is no one waiting to collect Kait from him.

He decides the first step to improving his journey is to talk to the man seated across the aisle from him. The man is rumpled and musty, like he's been stowed and neglected in a trunk beneath someone's bed for the past ten years. His mouth is hidden behind an unfortunate mustache, and his nose is barely a stub, as though it's been punched deep within his face. Like everyone else on the bus, including Hunter, his ears are plugged with earbuds, and he is staring down at a cell phone, jabbing at the screen occasionally. He looks away from the screen every fifteen or so minutes, but then only to glance out the window or stare up at the ceiling as if engaged in prayer. He waits for the man to look up from his phone, and waves at him like a diner calling for his waiter, but the man pretends not to see. Fifteen minutes later, he tries again, and this time the man sizes him up, then points to his ears as if the buds in there have been inflicted upon him and he'd like to talk if only these damn things weren't here. Hunter gives up and fiddles with his own phone.

He snaps a photo of himself and Kait, adds it to his fledgling Facebook album, which he has since titled *Postcards*. Caption: *Kait, checking out the scenery*. Within five minutes, he has received a half dozen comments, people clicking on the little thumbs-up icon beneath the photo, *liking* it in the vaguest possible way (Do they like that he's on the road? Do they like having a distraction from work? Do they just like acknowledging the existence of digital photography?), and one comment, from a guy he knew in high school: *Dude, WTF LOL!*, a response that is admittedly not entirely comprehensible, but which is at least an acknowledgment.

Over the next hour, he will refresh the website twenty times, never fully clear what type of reactions he is hoping to receive, but he is certain that what he wants is reactions. And the responses do trickle in—more Likes and more comments, most of which express something along the lines of *still can't believe she's gone . . . RIP*, or else they're saying *that's not right, you shouldn't joke about this*, or they're offering help, as in *let me know if I can do anything for you*, and he devours the responses, finds them wholly unsatisfying but also needs to get more, wants more people to respond and validate his sadness, his right to feel broken, is deeply frustrated when he refreshes and nothing has changed, shaking the phone as if it is the phone's fault that not enough people care about his photo album.

The woman in front of him turns and says, "Something wrong back there?" She's missing a front tooth and her skin is so damaged it looks like she has spent her adulthood lying on the surface of the sun.

"No," Hunter says, "it's just that I posted this thing on Facebook—"

"Didn't ask for a story," she says.

"Actually, you kind of did—"

"I just asked you to shut the hell up and quiet the hell down and let the hell go of my seat," she says, turning away from him. He realizes he's been leaning forward against her seat, gripping it with his free hand as if dangling from a cliff's edge.

"Sorry," he says, "it's just that I'm on this road trip—"

"Don't care," she says, balling up a sweater against the window and burying her face in it.

When the bus pulls into a gas station, the driver announces that passengers have exactly ten minutes to smoke and buy refreshments and mill aimlessly about the parking lot. Most of the passengers are deflated-looking men wearing unironic trucker hats and dusty jeans; now they look away from their phones and they light one another's cigarettes and in conversation they become increasingly loud and animated, gesturing as if hoping to injure the air. The women are too thin to be healthy, cigarettes clamped between their lips, eyes like storm clouds. The men have bad beards and red faces the color of uncooked beef.

He sees, standing in a circle of older men, a woman around his age, in a tank top and cotton shorts with the word DIVA written across the butt, a trash bag full of clothing resting at her feet. When she bends to retie the flaps on her bag, he steals a glance at her cleavage, senses the eyes of every other man checking her out, the instinctive group eye groping that men do in crowds. Kait never wore clothing like that, didn't even wear lingerie on special occasions because she had some weird, lingering Catholic guilt thing regarding sex, which isn't to say she avoided sex with Hunter—that was never a problem for them, they still engaged in regular, satisfying sex, especially on weekends when she wasn't exhausted from work—but she was very traditional and reserved and would apologize to him when she screamed too loudly, believed that feeling pleasure was somehow sinful, so he knows she would frown upon him ogling this girl right now, and she would disapprove of the girl herself for choosing to present herself in such a way (Kait's preferred term in these cases was *skank*). The girl does not seem to notice him.

What people do in these circumstances is they cluster together into alliances of convenience, and they all scan the area trying to determine which passenger is the crazy one, because everyone knows there is at least one crazy person on the bus, and so Hunter knows that right now they're studying him and the handful of other loners, assessing his level of insanity in comparison to theirs.

Before reboarding, Hunter places Kait next to one of the gas pumps and takes a photo of her, uploads it to his album. He spends the next two hours bent forward in his seat, gazing into the window of his phone.

HIS FIRST STOP UPON arrival in Chicago is the DePaul campus, which he wanders for an hour and learns nothing about Kait or who she used to be before they met. It was a dumb plan, he now realizes. What did he expect would happen? That they would have her dorm room preserved like Salinger's at Ursinus? That they would be waiting to give him a tour? That he could have somehow driven into the past and met twenty-two-year-old Kait, warned her about her future, and saved her?

After leaving the DePaul campus, he wanders along the Magnificent Mile and stops to eat a quick lunch while overlooking the Chicago River. Watching the joggers and cyclists zipping by, he thinks, yes, I could have lived here. We could have lived here. He feels the back of his neck burning in the sun, but he waits a while longer before moving on, closes his eyes and allows the river to rush past, the bustle and the city thrumming behind him like a racing pulse, and for that moment, the length of an extended eyeblink, he feels okay.

THE REALTOR IS A stout woman with arms like clubs. She takes short, hurried strides like a handler at a dog show. Hunter follows her up the stairs to see the master suite. His next bus, headed to St. Louis, leaves tomorrow afternoon, but in the meantime, he's decided to visit a few open houses, just to see. Just in case.

Before they bought their house in Philly, they saw sixty-three other homes—Kait had a specific vision in mind, refused to settle for anything less—and so Hunter feels like an expert at this, notices the slight discoloration in the ceiling where there was once a leak, sees the hastily patched holes in the bathroom drywall, can tell from the obviously DIY nature of most of the repairs that there are some surprises and code violations hidden inside these walls.

The front door creaks open, and the Realtor scurries down to meet the new visitors, leaving Hunter alone. He tours the upstairs by himself. The second bedroom is decorated in an ocean theme, pictures of whales hanging on the walls, an awful seafoam green carpet, sheets covered with cartoony tropical fish.

A married couple passes him in the hallway. Hunter hears them debating the merits of the master. "It's too big," the woman says. "I feel like I'm in a cave."

"You wouldn't last one day in a cave," the man says.

"Like you'd be so great in a cave. Like you're the cave expert all of a sudden."

The man stops in the hallway, stares at Hunter. "Hey," he says. "I know you."

"Oh, Stan, you think you know everyone," the woman says. She's shorter than Stan, and dressed in all white—sandals, capris, tanktop, cardigan. His face is creased and discolored from years of outdoor labor.

"Look at him. We know this guy. How do we know you?"

"I really don't think you know me," Hunter says.

"I think I would know who I know better than you know who I know." Stan tugs on his goatee, steps into the ocean room. "Look, Edna. You recognize him too."

"You know what? You're actually right," Edna says. "We saw you on TV."

"I doubt that," Hunter says. The last thing he wants is for them to ask where Kait is.

"Just the other day you were on. You and your wife looking at houses. The hell are you doing here?" To Stan, she says, "I can't believe they broke up already."

"I can," Stan says.

Edna and Stan tell him *Happy Homecomings?* is one of their favorite shows. It went on hiatus for a while, but it's back and the reruns air in marathon blocks every few weeks. Edna watches because she likes seeing the houses and Stan enjoys predicting exactly when and how the couples will break up. They have their DVR set to record every episode, and so when Hunter confesses that he's never seen his own episode, they invite him back to their house. They live only a block away, had attended the open house just to snoop on the neighbors.

AND SUDDENLY, KAIT IS there in front of him, in HD, stretched across a fifty-two-inch screen. He is aware of being watched by Edna and Stan, even as he watches a younger version of himself and his wife walking through a south Jersey bungalow. Hunter turns up the volume, places the urn next to the TV just in case some mystical rift in the universe can pull her soul out of the set and revive her. He kneels on the floor only inches away, like a child enthralled by a Disney film.

Kait's first words are, "Sure, it's scary making a big move. But we wouldn't do it if we had any doubts." She squeezes Hunter's hand when she says it. He deadpans, "Well, I've got *some* doubts, anyway." She rolls her eyes and looks away—is it playful or is she annoyed? Had he spent his whole life with her interpreting that eyeroll as one thing when in fact it was another thing? Next, she is alone in Sherry's home, speaking to the camera: "No, I'm not worried about him not having a job," she says. "He's just trying to find the right fit for him." The camera lingers on her while she chews on her bottom lip, looks down at the floor, flips her hair out of her face. "But," she adds, "it would probably be good if he gets a job." Headed into a commercial, there is a shot of Hunter fumbling with a spackle knife while Kait watches. The narrator says, "Will straitlaced Kaitlyn have to put her slacker husband in his place?" After the commercial they walk through two homes before seeing the house they will eventually purchase; Kait carries a checklist of questions she pulled from a home-buying magazine, and she grills the Realtor about the condition of the plumbing, the pitch of the backyard, the age of the water heater. Hunter operates independent of the conversation, rifling through the bookshelf and smirking about the owners' paperbacks. Cut to Kait signing the mortgage documents; Hunter is in the room but signs nothing because Kait's credit is superior to his. The production assistant asks Hunter if he feels badly for not contributing to the house, and he says, "It's not like I do *nothing*." A week after they move in, the producers surprise them with cameras rolling at dawn on a Saturday; Hunter opens the door, rubbing the sleep from his eyes. An incongruous shot of a midday sun follows, and the narrator says, "Still recovering from a late night, the young couple struggles to stay organized." Boxes are half unpacked and Hunter steps over debris as he leads the camera on a tour of the first floor. It looks like they live in an opium den. Kait does not appear on camera until they are on the second floor, at which point she is visibly agitated, hastily dressed, no makeup, her long hair piled on top of her head like cold spaghetti. She avoids eye contact with the camera, shuffles behind Hunter while he describes the changes they're planning in the house: the paint colors, the new hardware in the bathroom, the furniture that still hasn't arrived. "It's been pretty stressful," Kait says. Sweat beads on her upper lip. The camera lingers on her, knows it can stare at her and make her keep talking. "Is there something else I'm supposed to say?" She laughs nervously, covering her mouth as if it's impolite to show one's teeth on camera. "I don't know. We're excited, though. We are." She looks over her shoulder at Hunter, who is straightening a photo on the wall. Hunter pauses the shot in that exact moment when the two of them lock eyes, and although it is impossible to quantify, he knows and everyone who has ever seen that shot knows: there is love there, real, actual love. There has to be. "It's going to be fun, even when it's not fun," she says. There is tinkling music with bells and harps like the sounds uninteresting people expect to hear in heaven. The host pontificates on the nature of relationships while the show alternates B-roll of the two couples unpacking their homes, the other couple putting finishing touches on a formal dining room while Kait digs, exasperated, through a pile of knickknacks. The credits roll over a black screen and then she is gone and Hunter is gone.

There are three Kaits, maybe more than that. There is the Kait of his memory and the Kait everyone else remembers and the Kait from TV, and it's impossible to say which one is the real one. One is filtered through his thoughts and perceptions, another is filtered through the perceptions of her friends and co-workers, and this third Kait is filtered through the lens of a reality television program intent on creating and exploiting conflict. Beyond the three he knows, there are infinite Kaits. The show was never going to accurately represent the two of them because the show wasn't interested in accurately representing them; they just needed a young couple to present as the nervous, troubled couple. On one occasion, the production assistant said to Kait, "It would make things a lot easier if you could just say you're worried about Hunter here," and so she complied, gave them the footage they wanted. The PA liked to talk about the importance of *playing ball*, in the sense that Hunter played ball and Kait did not play ball. On the morning of the first day of filming, she was so nervous she nearly vomited, but by the time they got on camera she'd pulled herself together. When the cameras surprised them at dawn, she first refused to leave the bedroom, yelled through a closed door at the PA who reminded her they'd signed a contract and agreed to play ball. "I told you I need time to prepare," she said. She stayed in the room for an hour while Hunter occupied the crew, and she only gave in because it was clear that nobody would leave the house until they got their shots.

"You want some soup?" Edna says. "You look like you need some soup."

"Soup's only going to make him worse," Stan says.

"Everybody needs soup sometimes."

He has soup. Spoon in his hand, steam rising up to his face. He is at the kitchen table, feels like he just awoke from a coma. There is a blank space in his memory between the viewing of the show and the serving of the soup. He does not remember telling them what happened with Kait, but their pity tells him he must have spilled the whole story. The linoleum at his feet is cracked like a pebble-sprayed windshield. The room is overwhelmed by the musty smell of domestic sadness, the vaguely moldy scent of nursing homes. It's the smell of old carpet that has absorbed too much. Duck-patterned wallpaper peels at the corners. There are absolutely no other decorations on any walls, no photographs anywhere. Edna lights a cigarette.

"Italian wedding soup," she says. "When my mother was sick, we ate this soup downstairs where we couldn't hear her. She was in pain and we couldn't do anything about it. My daddy told us stories about the war while she was upstairs dying, and the soup made me feel warm." She takes a drag on the cigarette. "You have to be warm to be happy. It's scientific fact."

Hunter blows on the soup, watches the pasta drift in the ripples. "I don't think I'm that hungry," he says.

Stan presses the end of his own cigarette against Edna's. There is a cat sleeping in the middle of the table while another struts across the kitchen counter. A bird squawks in another room.

"Elvis is hungry," Edna says, and rushes out of the room.

"You don't have to eat that soup. Here, gimme it." Stan takes the bowl and dumps it in the sink. "You know we're ninety-eight percent water already? We don't need more liquid in us. It's bad for you. Makes your organs soggy."

"That doesn't sound right," Hunter says.

"I used to not believe it either. My dad, he would say it to us, and he wouldn't let us eat soup, never. No stew, no chili, nothing in a bowl basically. But one day I had vegetable soup at a friend's house. Thought I was so smart. A week later, my insides are all torn up and I'm getting my appendix out." He stubs out his cigarette on the table, which is freckled with burn marks.

Edna returns to the room with a parrot on her shoulder and a parrot biscuit between her teeth. The feathers on the bird's head have been gelled into a mohawk. Edna leans toward the bird and lets it nibble the biscuit. "Elvis has entered the building," she says. "Say hi to our guest, Elvis." The bird lunges at the biscuit in her other hand. "Don't be nasty now. Be a pretty bird. Are you a pretty bird? Who's a pretty bird?" This performance goes on for a few minutes before the bird squawks "Hello Birdo!" Hunter waves to the bird. Edna crouches so that Elvis is eye-level with Hunter. "Do you want to feed him?" she says, handing him a biscuit.

"Christ, Edna, give him a break."

"Don't listen to Daddy. He loves you," she says, leaning in to kiss the bird on the mouth. "Dinner time," the bird says. It pecks at Hunter's outstretched hand, its beak piercing his palm.

"I don't love that bird and you know it," Stan says. He stands, circles the table to the opposite side of the room.

"But Elvis loves his daddy," Edna says, and she closes in on him, blocking his exit expertly, like a champion heavyweight cutting off the ring. Hunter pushes his chair away from the table, considers sneaking out before witnessing something ugly. The bird shrieks "Don't be cruel" and spreads his wings wide.

"Get your goddamn bird away from me," Stan says. He swats at it, then ducks beneath his wife's outstretched arm to escape, running like a soldier beneath helicopter blades.

"You do not hit Elvis!"

"It's not natural," Stan says. "You know birds come from dinosaurs? Look at his fucking feet!"

"Show me a dinosaur with blue feathers. Find me one goddamn dinosaur that looks like Elvis and I'll give you a dollar." She pulls a dollar from her pocket and slaps it on the kitchen table.

Stan lights another cigarette. "Cares more about that bird than she does about her husband," he says.

Elvis eats another biscuit out of Edna's mouth. "You're a good boy," she says. "You know mommy loves you." She kisses him on the head again, runs a finger down his chest. She coos at him and he spouts non sequiturs back at her, a mixture of Elvis lines and small talk and every now and then a name: "Dennis," the bird says, "Dennis Dennis Dennis."

"Who's Dennis?" Hunter asks.

"I told him to stop saying that," Edna says. "But nobody in this house listens to me." When she looks at Stan, there is a flash of hate in her eyes.

Dennis. Dennis. The bird stares across the room at Stan. *Stop it. Dennis.*

"Could you shut up the fucking bird?" Stan says. He flicks his cigarette at it.

"You're going to scare him!" The cigarette sits on the floor, smoldering. "He doesn't know what he's saying!"

Hunter crosses the room and bends to pick up the cigarette.

"Don't you pick that up for him," Edna says.

"Just leave it there, let the goddamn place burn down," Stan says. He kicks his kitchen chair over and storms out of the room, slams a screen door leading to the backyard.

Edna is still physically there, but she is no longer present, her eyes vacant, breathing silent. In the dim kitchen light, in profile, Edna looks like Sherry, and in the blink of an eye he knows the whole story, knows who Dennis was and that he died too young and they have never gotten over it and it has caused their lives to dissolve. He sees Sherry, as clearly as he's ever seen anyone, sitting in Kait's old bedroom and holding on to the phone in case Hunter calls to say he's bringing Kait back to her, Sherry talking to the dog to fill the void while people tell her she's losing it. He hears her saying, *So what if I'm losing it, don't I deserve to lose it?* She has her sons still, but she's lost her only daughter, the best of them, and Hunter now sees that in the best case scenario she is probably headed for a full-on crack-up, just like Stan and Edna, who have been estranged from the life they wanted—the one they used to have—so long that they're unstable and will never recover. Grief begins as a temporary condition, but left untreated it becomes a permanent sickness. Hunter knows that if he does not find a way to realign himself sooner rather than later, he is looking at his own fractured future. Some people face death and get over it and some do not; whatever the secret to saving oneself is, Hunter needs to figure it out before it's too late. He crosses the room to stand with Edna and says, "I'm sorry," and he hopes Sherry can hear him. "Dennis," the bird says, and spreads his wings as if taunting her.

NINE

A series of incomplete lists, lists you should complete sometime later, when you have the motivation and energy and fortitude to create and complete lists:

- Reasons to believe marrying you was the best choice your wife could have made rather than one of the great mistakes of her life;
- Means of making penance with your deceased wife who probably would not have died had she never met you, and whose likely willingness to forgive only makes you feel worse;
- Strategies for meeting strangers without seeming too lonely or too desperate or too weird, for presenting yourself as a

reasonable person worth knowing and maybe even loving or at least liking a lot;

- Arguments in favor of changing your name and hairstyle and growing unique facial hair and acquiring a new wardrobe and adopting a new identity in another time zone;
- Reasons to continue living even after your wife has died an untimely death and you find yourself suddenly cut adrift like a moon knocked off its orbit;
- Benefits of reconciling with your in-laws with whom you never would have interacted under any other circumstances but who also are understandably heartbroken by your wife's death, and who have legitimate reasons to be very angry with you right now;
- Rants and complaints you'd probably be better off keeping to yourself, especially when delivery of those rants interferes with other people's simple pleasures;
- Reasons your parents should still love you and believe in your ability to bounce back despite repeated failures throughout your life at bouncing back;
- Things to look forward to now that everything you had previously looked forward to is invalidated by the absence of your wife, whose presence was integral to those things being things you wanted to do, rather than things you felt like you had to do;
- Reasons to go home and get a job and rejoin the workforce and become a so-called *productive member of society* and contribute to the local economy and punch the clock every

morning at eight and every evening at four and take off every third Friday so you can go to the movies by yourself and then return to your empty home to heat up a frozen meal in a package labeled FAMILY SIZE because it's easier to have leftovers for a couple days than it is to heat something new every day;

- Reasons not to start drinking heavily—slowly corroding your insides first with plastic-bottle gin and becoming one of those faded men who walk into a liquor store at noon and count out a handful of nickels on the counter in exchange for one can of malt liquor and eventually don't even die but just disappear;

- Names of people who have worse lives than you and have faced more difficult situations and greater trauma without any safety net, people who you know are abundant, even if sometimes you want to feel like you are the only one;

- Reasons to trust other people, who you have never trusted in the first place and who now you suspect of all kinds of treachery, because the world has revealed itself to you to be truly sinister, has confirmed a lifetime of cynicism and convinced you there is no reason beyond unreason;

- Possible names for still-undiscovered planets and their respective moons, organized in order from most habitable by humans to least habitable;

- Pros and cons of leaping off a bridge, of throwing yourself in front of a moving train, of firing a gun into a crowd until a police sniper takes you out, of self-immolation, of overdosing on Tylenol, of cutting yourself and watching the blood swirl cloudy in the bathtub, of renting a boat and sailing into the heart of a mid-ocean storm, of leaping over the rail into the lion's den at the zoo, of hiring a hitman to take you out at an unspecified time so you don't know when it's coming or how it's coming, just that it is coming;

- Characteristics of the man you want to become, the man Kait knew you could be and you think you can be if you just figure some things out;
- Reasons to believe—in yourself, in a god, in redemption, in waking up in the morning and feeling better, in the possibility of getting back to normal;
- Things to look forward to in the future.

TEN

The next afternoon, he is on a bus headed south to St. Louis. Since leaving home, he and Kait have found nothing exciting to do, have made no friends or learned anything useful. The fantasy of traveling did not look like this. In the fantasy, it looked like luxury hotels with hot tubs and decadent feasts and romantic strolls in the countryside and rolling hills with castles looming in the distance. It did not include a rattling bus and morbid gray skies. It did not account for the possibility that tourism could be more limiting than staying at home, or that even after spending nearly three weeks on the road, after visiting famous landmarks, both natural and manmade, one can feel like they've still seen nothing worth seeing. Remarkable backdrops don't lend gravity to one's life, he thinks, don't magically transform the meanings of things; they're just backgrounds. Bad conversations are still bad conversations. Spinach is still spinach. West is west. Moving from place to place doesn't change that.

How many nights had he and Kait spent together planning, traveler's handbooks spread out on the coffee table, Kait listing tips on a legal pad while Hunter dog-eared important pages? How many weekends had been dedicated to swapping stories about things that *would* happen, someday? Together, they invented scenarios in which they met helpful Chilean strangers, spent the nights in their homes eating native food and conversing with the locals, immersing themselves fully in the culture and returning with a thousand pictures and a new appreciation for the depth and breadth of human experience. They imagined six-week trips through Australia, and she laughed at his dumb jokes about boomerangs and kangaroos and *Crocodile Dundee*. They developed emergency plans in case they encountered a tiger in India or a chupacabra in Mexico. Over countless hours and days of strategizing, they'd visualized themselves as travelers in almost every country they could name, and one night while she lay on the couch with her legs draped over his lap, she said, "I really don't care where we go, as long as you're with me."

"What do you think about North Korea?"

"I hear it's lovely in the fall," she said.

"Maybe Siberia after that?"

"If it was good enough for Genghis Khan, it's good enough for me."

"South Pole?"

"We could see penguins!" she said. She sat up, leaned in close to whisper like a coconspirator: "Maybe we could steal one and take it home with us."

"We'd have to buy so much fish then. The house would stink."

"Maybe we could train it to eat chicken fingers?"

That conversation led to the creation of one of Hunter's favorite running gags: any time he saw chicken fingers on a restaurant's menu, he would say something like, "This must be a big penguin hangout." Even on the hundredth repetition of the joke, she still laughed, sometimes smiled in anticipation of it when she scanned the menu.

Before arriving in St. Louis, he receives a terse e-mail from Jack: "Got a bill from Illinois State Police for hauling your car. Fun time's over. Tell me where you are and I'll come get you." Jack will eventually find him, will obsess over Hunter's whereabouts until he can track him down, which, briefly, makes Hunter feel like an international spy on the run. He is tempted by the opportunity to cut the trip short, to have an excuse to give up before he even reaches his destination. But—fun time? If that's what Jack thinks this is, if that's what Jack thinks Hunter is doing, then there is no reason to even talk to him.

Upon arrival in St. Louis, Hunter hails a cab, tells the driver to take him somewhere fun. If other people think he's out here goofing off, then he might as well have some actual fun.

They end up at a sports bar called ThrowDowns. He doesn't like bars, has never enjoyed drinking, and only had the occasional glass of wine for Kait's sake, because she worried about the implications of having a drink by herself, feared it was step one on the inevitable road to alcoholism, to turning into her father. Most of his nights at bars have consisted of nursing a soda while dodging stumbling coeds and waiting to drive his drunken friends home.

Inside the bar, there are forty-seven TVs lining the walls, half of them tuned to the Golf Channel, which strikes Hunter as the most boring network possible, but he's not particularly interested in sports. He played baseball growing up, was a pretty good second baseman through eighth grade, thanks in part to the evenings Willow spent with him in the backyard teaching him the nuances of the game. By high school, he'd lost interest and started skipping practices, got kicked off the team for insubordination. He isn't an antisports zealot, like some of his Chomskyan college professors were, has faked fandom before, has gotten caught up in the local teams' various playoff runs because it's almost impossible not to be swept up in the frenzy. He once tried explaining his disinterest in sports to Brutus and Max and Billy and Uncle Bobby when he and Kait were forced to host a Sunday football party. He and Kait had spent the morning scrambling to clean the house while cooking sloppy joes and slicing blocks of cheddar and otherwise devising ways to clog everyone's arteries, and once her family arrived, all wearing their Sunday uniforms, Brutus hurled a football at Hunter hard enough that Hunter caught it out of self-defense, and Brutus said, "Where the hell's your jersey at?" Hunter said he didn't have one and Brutus interrupted: "Don't worry, we brought a spare," and tossed a green Philadelphia Eagles jersey toward him. "Gotta wear one. House rules."

Once the game started, everyone hunkered into their positions and gathered their beer and chips and cheese and focused intently on the TV, conversing only sometimes during commercials, and

Hunter sat silently in the corner of his own living room. At half-time, Uncle Bobby invited Hunter into the backyard to have a catch, but Hunter said he wanted to stay inside and work on the fondue, a pronouncement that incited approximately fifteen minutes worth of limp-wristed mincing and gay jokes, the only remedies to which would have been Hunter chugging a beer or punching somebody.

Focused on melting gruyere and swiss over low heat, he missed the first five minutes of the second half. When he returned to the living room, Brutus's girlfriend occupied his seat. Because the Eagles had started playing well while he was absent, he learned that he was banned from the living room. "House rules," Billy said, apparently unaware of whose house he was in. Kait shrugged, said, "He's right," and so Hunter retreated to the kitchen, where he listened to their violent reactions to the game, tried to determine whether he even wanted to be invited back into the room.

After the game, Brutus cornered him in the kitchen and said, "You're not real big on football, huh?" and Hunter explained that Jack had never cared about football; Sundays growing up meant yard work and gutter cleaning and other chores that kept him from ever watching or investing in the games, and he came from a place that had no major pro or college football teams so he'd never formed an allegiance to anyone. Brutus shoved the football into Hunter's gut, knocking the wind out of him, and said, "You better learn to love football if you're going to be one of us."

That night, lying in bed next to Kait, he said, "Hopefully they won't make us do that again."

Her back turned to him, she said, "You know, sometimes I wish you could be more of a man."

"Oh, I'm all man, baby," he said, curling up against her from behind, cupping a hand over her breast.

"I mean, I know you're different. It's just, maybe it wouldn't kill you to meet them halfway now and then."

HE STEPS TO THE bar and orders two glasses of Chardonnay, sets one in front of Kait and takes a photo of the cube and the glass. Caption: *She's a cheap date!* Receives near-immediate feedback, more thumbs being upped, others saying, "Wish I was on vacation! LOL!" The people who write LOL most often are the ones least aware of what a joke actually is, who seem to think the acronym qualifies as punctuation, but at least it's positive feedback, as opposed to the growing number of folks who feel compelled to respond to his digital postcards with pitying comments such as "Please feel better. We all love you!" or, lately, with actual outrage, as in this just-posted comment from Billy Dixon: "This ain't funny, bro. A real man wud come home and deal with his problems!" He places the phone facedown on the bar, takes a sip of his chardonnay; it tastes like well-water two days old. He pushes it away, summons the bartender. Says, "Give me the manliest drink you've got," and so the bartender offers him a double Old Granddad, neat. Hunter drank straight liquor once, in college, tequila from a plastic gallon bottle, passing it around a crowded dorm room. The tequila was warm and nobody seemed to like it, so they all stared grimly down the barrel of the bottle, imbibing so that they could, at some point later in the night, feel drunk, because that's what they were supposed to do in college, get drunk and accumulate hundreds of nearly identical anecdotes of drunken escapades to share with one another when they became responsible adults. Hunter had joined the chase, and pretended not to be disgusted by the taste, barely suppressed his gagging, didn't tell anyone he was worried about drinking something that burned so much inside his chest, and at some point he probably did feel drunk, and probably danced and laughed and shouted with everyone else, but all he remembers is the aftermath, when he awoke facedown in his own vomit, bits of tequila-glazed chicken fingers encircling his mouth, and he felt sure that he had died overnight. In fact, he soon began *wishing* he'd died overnight, because then he wouldn't have to spend the rest of the day on the floor of a communal bathroom, vomiting and experiencing muscle pains in his shoulders and back and generally feeling like he'd been thrown from an airplane without a chute. He'd been smoking pot since he was fifteen, soon after discovering classic rock and Jim Morrison's poetry, and preferred everything about being high to being drunk, which was all around more painful and aggressive and sloppy and didn't even offer the possibility of profound thought or self-discovery. By the time he'd met Kait, he felt like he'd exhausted the possibilities of expanding his mind via marijuana, although they had smoked a few joints together over the years, usually at the end of particularly stressful work weeks when nothing else could help her relax. His college friends thought his first hangover was hysterically funny; there is no less empathetic audience in the world than a group of teenage boys. They told him he just had to get used to it, and the next time he'd feel better. Two nights later, they passed him a new bottle of tequila and he retched at the sight of it, pushed it away, tucked himself under the comforter on his bunk bed while they all talked about getting wasted and how awesome it would be to be wasted when they finally did get wasted and how wasted they'd been on previous nights in comparison to their current levels of wastedness, and eventually they *were* wasted, at which point he slipped out of the room and spent the remainder of the night watching TV in a student lounge, passing time until he could hear tomorrow's stories about the new frontiers of wastedness his friends had explored.

He swirls his Old Granddad, occasionally lifting it to his lips and pretending to sip, splashing it back down when the odor becomes too aggressive.

The place is fairly crowded for a Thursday evening; the patrons are wearing business clothes and they're charging through the doors as if the only thing that helped them survive the day was the knowledge that eventually they could drink alcohol. Many of them enter solo. They all stare beyond the bar, at the TVs, or into the mirror behind the liquor, watching themselves drink, pressing their glasses to their lips forcefully, and they sometimes check their watches or tap messages into their phones. They swallow hard and their glasses are refilled and they slide more money forward without speaking a word.

There is a band called the Hungry Hippos setting up in the corner. This is the kind of inoffensive live band Kait liked to see. She would clap and ask him if he wanted to dance, and he would try to hide his anxiety about dancing in public by ironically doing hokey dance moves like the robot or Vanilla Ice's high-stepping.

Six months ago, Kait brought him to a bar for what was origi-
nally supposed to have been a ladies' night with some of her college
friends. She needed him to go because she couldn't stand half her
friends anymore, and she didn't want to waste a perfectly good Saturday not seeing him, even though he was the one husband among
a group of single ladies. Kait told her friends he had come along to
be the designated driver. The girls got drunk and danced on stage
while the band played Bon Jovi covers and people spilled beer on
Hunter, and Hunter shuffled on the dance floor and tried his best
to look like he belonged there. Kait spent the first half of the drive
home recapping the night. She said, "That band wasn't bad, right?
They were pretty good even."

"Yeah, I guess," he said.

"What, you don't think they were good?" she said. "They were
good. Just admit they were good." In the backseat, her friend Abby
agreed and said the band was really, really good. Like, really good.

"I guess they were fine," he said. "It's just—every time I see one
of these bands, I keep thinking about what they really wanted to
do. Like, how did they end up here instead of playing in big arenas
and going on tour? And are they okay with it now, or do they still
wish they could be doing something better?"

"That's really deep," Abby said.

"No it's not—he's just being miserable again," Kait said. "They're
getting paid to do what they love to do. What's wrong with that?"

"Do you think their wives and girlfriends like it? Late nights,
constant practice, always acting like their big break is on the way."

"Well, at least they're *trying*," Kait said. She stopped talking then,
rode in silence for the remainder of the ride.

A TRIO OF GIRLS bustles toward the bar, crushing into him, barely aware of his presence. They're wearing identical pink T-shirts that say BACHELORETTE across the chest, and BAD BITCHES BAR CRAWL on the back. Each girl is adorned with a variety of penis-shaped accessories: earrings, flashing necklaces, bracelets, hats. They're drinking from penis-shaped straws, and every time one takes a sip, they make a sultry face, and the others take a picture. By the end of the night, there will be in existence, and surely uploaded to the Internet, hundreds of photos of these girls with plastic penises in their mouths. They stumble and slur and smell like they've all bathed in strawberry daiquiris. One of the girls sits in Kait's seat and shouts for the bartender's attention.

"I was saving that," Hunter says, and the girl ignores him. "Hey, seat's saved," he repeats.

She says, "I'll just be a minute, okay."

"No, that's not okay," he says, "It's not okay at all. I'm saving that seat for my wife."

"We've been here a half hour," she says, waving the penis straw in his face like a dagger, "and this seat's been empty the whole time." The bartender arrives, and the girl orders another round of something called Watermelon Throwdowns, which glow like isotopes and arrive in glasses roughly the diameter of salad plates.

"You don't believe I'm married?" he says, displaying his wedding ring. The other girls slurp on their drinks, strike sultry poses, cackle.

"Why should I care?"

He shoves Kait's cube toward the girl. Tells her his wife is in there, because she's dead and he's carrying her across the country to give her a proper goodbye and maybe spread her ashes in the

Pacific Ocean. The line about the ocean, he didn't expect to say that, but it sounds good enough. It seems like the sort of thing one is supposed to do. The girl eyes the urn, checks his face to see if he's serious, and then she says, "Oh. My. God. That is the *cutest* thing ever!" Grabbing his arm, she pulls him off the stool and leads him into the thicket of the Bad Bitches Bar Crawl.

None of the self-proclaimed Bad Bitches is married. They're all a year past college, mostly in long-term relationships, and mostly enamored with the idea of having a wedding, and they're all deeply, openly resentful of the bride-to-be, a girl named Jessa, who laughs every time someone in her group calls her a slut, and who will probably eventually realize that they mean it to be hurtful, but they know they can get away with saying anything to her while she's this drunk. The first thing Jessa says to Hunter, leaning in close and whispering, is, "Everyone thinks I'm drunk just because I fell off the bar stool." She holds on to his arm to stabilize herself. Her cheeks are puffy, nose red, hair disheveled and mascara streaked, but still she looks like she is probably pretty when she's not pumped full of enough toxins to require hospitalization. The rest of the girls keep feeding her drinks, and Hunter takes a few sips of her Watermelon Throwdown, ostensibly to protect her, at which point he learns that WTs are delicious. Kait did not drink what she called girly drinks, said daiquiris and piña coladas were nothing but sugar, too many calories, so Hunter has never tasted anything like this, did not real-ize alcohol could taste so much like not-alcohol, that something so sweet and fruity could even be in the same genus as beer. Within an hour of meeting the bachelorettes he has consumed three cocktails, and he finds himself following the girls to another bar, which they say has even better drinks than ThrowDowns does. They all think it's very sweet that he still loves his wife even after she's dead. "It's like something from a movie," according to the girl who stole Kait's seat. Her name is almost certainly Lindsay. It's possible they're all named Lindsay.

"I hope when I'm dead, my husband carries me around forever," another Lindsay says. "And if he doesn't, I'll haunt his ass." They have all been raised on Hollywood romantic comedies and seem to think the ideal representation of love is something like obsession or stalking. They think love means sex, still, and they are much more interested in weddings than they are in marriage, much more interested in naming babies than in raising them. They embrace every aspect of the mass commoditization of marriage, even the fact that the wedding day has now grown, through one-upmanship and clever marketing, from a single evening event to a full weekend affair. They want destination weddings and expensive brunches and white horses and the most expensive flowers in the world. They are only six years younger than he is, but they make him feel ancient. He surely had primitive views on love and sex when he was in college too, but he cannot remember himself then, and every effort he makes to do so feels like trying to access the memory of a stranger.

Another round of drinks. These places are all too loud for holding conversations, too loud sometimes for Hunter to hear himself speak, but the girls laugh at everything he says anyway. Probably they would be doing this for any guy who chose to follow them around for the night, but he has always wanted to be the Funny Guy in a group of people, often envisioned himself at the center of a circle spouting witticisms and eliciting rounds of head-tossing laughter, and for the first time in his life he thinks he gets the appeal of this lifestyle. The drinks keep coming. Hunter poses for his own set of penis-straw pictures. They'll end up online, captioned *Some guy we met . . . So random!* He takes pictures too, of the girls holding Kait, Jessa's lips firmly pressed against the cube. Uploads them. More drinks. The girls embark on a bachelorette scavenger hunt, which is how Hunter finds himself crafting a veil out of toilet paper, and also how he becomes the official Bad Bitches liaison to the other men, because the hunt entails the collection of items like condoms, men's business cards, and a man's boxers, in addition to the performance of a specific set of actions by Jessa. He recruits men to sample liquor off her neck, to remove her bra without removing her shirt, carry her on their shoulders while she shouts "I'm Getting Married!" The drinking continues. The scavenger hunt checklist tells Jessa to gives Hunter a lap dance. She sits him in a chair in the corner of the room beneath a strobe light. Her movements jerky and only semihuman. Grinding against his crotch as if she wants to hurt him. Hunter gripping her hips to keep her from falling off. Placing a shot glass between his legs and picking it up with her mouth. Then they're outside, strangled by still summer air. A dozen pairs of stylish heels clacking on the sidewalk. Charging toward another bar. More drinks. Hunter paying. The girls toasting him and Kait. Feeling like a mascot, entertaining but disposable. Onslaught of dumb questions about his dead wife. Do you miss her? Do you think about her a lot? Are you still sad? Was the funeral hard? Was she pretty?—the question they all repeat. He shows them her Facebook page and the girls are relieved to see that she was, in fact, pretty. So many Lindsays rubbing his back, telling him how pretty she was. Michael Jackson music, rhythm familiar like a heartbeat, the girls shrieking and rushing to the dance floor, Hunter drunk enough to join them. The girls encircling him beneath flashing lights, the floor disappears and re-appears at random. Group hugs and group photos. Jessa falling twice. Hunter's ill-advised Jesus joke when she falls a third time, the looks of drunken disgust from the good Catholic girls. Ordering a pitcher of water. A round of energy drinks spiked with alcohol, the taste of purple. The room rocking, floor lifting up and then gently floating back down like a ship in temperate seas. Memories of the African cruise he and Kait never took. Constriction in his chest, a nearly immobilizing fullness. The girls are chewing gum, mouths flapping open so he can see all the way down their throats, down past their souls and into their overfull stomachs. He tells Jessa if he looks hard enough he can see into her soul. No response, no movement, eyelids sagging. It is entirely possible that she is already dead. Hunter's touch, cursed. But then the James Brown songs, the speakers oozing sex and the voice demanding that they get up offa their things, Jessa resurrected by the funk, dragging him back to the dance floor, her ass against his groin, sweat against his sweat, her teeth scraping across his skin, telling her, "I want to kiss you on the mouth." Telling her, "I bet you look better naked than I look naked." Following her, or leading her, into the men's room. Pressed against the stall door, fumbling with Jessa's skirt. The air in the room sticky. Her pulling away. Him standing behind her as she vomits, she still grasping at his crotch as if reaching for a lever. Kissing her again, the taste like rotten apples, her tongue, rough. Hands crawling over him like spiders. Eyes closed, the room stands still. The sound of his belt unbuckling. Bouncers arriving. Disappearing into an alleyway.

IN THE MORNING, HE's by himself in a hotel room, and the ashes are gone.

He will spend the remainder of his life canvassing the country in search of his wife's remains. A mission of penance, of vengeance. He'll be a drifter, just another nameless creep lurking on the edges of towns, insisting that someone has stolen his wife from him. A phantom, driven by a singular, maniacal focus on retrieving the ashes, harboring dreams of someday hunting down the person who stole them. Like something from a campfire horror story—The Forlorn Widower.

The pen at his bedside tells him he's at the Days Inn in East St. Louis, but he has no idea what that means, or where he could be in relation to anything else in the world. Still half-drunk, his stomach upside-down, his vision backward, he tries to re-create the events of the previous evening, remembers noise and flashing lights and penis hats and Jessa. Sees no evidence of her in the room, assumes she left him here and then stumbled home to her fiancé to make a tearful confession of infidelity. The fiancée may be on the hunt for him now, seeking his own vengeance. If it comes to that, Hunter will not run.

The exhaustion of weeks on the road catching up with him; his joints ache and he feels a listlessness like he's oxygen-deprived.

Somehow his duffel bag made it here with him. He tears it open and dumps the contents on the floor, finds only soiled clothes. He remembers bringing the ashes to ThrowDowns and is pretty sure he left there with Kait, but maybe not? Maybe he dropped her when he ran off with Jessa. Maybe he forgot about her the moment another woman called him cute.

His knees ache from dancing, head throbbing and swollen, mouth dry like British humor. Somewhere in St. Louis, someone else is holding on to Kait. He flips the mattress, just in case, searches the drawers and finds only the Bible. Kait's mother was right not to trust him. Her brothers might actually murder him now, and who could blame them? He killed their sister then tossed the ashes aside for a drunken one-night stand. Kait insisted they were only hard on him because they were protecting her, and although that seemed a convenient excuse, he doubted it was true. A pair of chirping birds on the windowsill mocks him. The room smells like the inside of an old refrigerator, feels sealed shut. Jack would tell him this is why he shouldn't have left home in the first place, this is what happens when you never take responsibility. Willow would defend him, and Jack would rattle the ice in his rocks glass, shake his head, say he has work to do, and lock himself in his office until midnight, thundering away at his keyboard, rhythm steady as a freight train. Underneath the bed, Hunter's phone is buzzing and flashing, demanding attention. He has twenty e-mails to check, a dozen text messages, several missed phone calls. Out of the twenty, only a few will end up being worth checking. Ninety percent of all incoming communication is useless, but that doesn't stop it from coming. Kait enjoyed opening the mailbox at home even though it was almost exclusively junk mail and bills; she said you never know when you might find a surprise in there, and so every couple months Hunter mailed her a letter to remind her that he loved her and that she was beautiful and smart and better than him. The missed calls are from Sherry, who has left him three increasingly hysterical voice mails, the first of which says: "I been talking to the news stations. One of them wants to do a story on how you took Kait from us. See how funny you think it is when the whole city sees what a scumbag you are." The text messages are unintelligible, garbled messes sent by Jessa between four and five a.m. It's possible she's in some kind of trouble, but, taking inventory of his feelings, Hunter finds that he actually doesn't care at all what happens to her. If not for her and the Bad Bitches, he wouldn't have lost his wife. Her fiancée should kick her out of the house, cancel the wedding before he gets in too deep and she breaks his heart. Kait never cheated on Hunter, there is no doubt; if she ever had, she would have been so consumed by guilt that she would have told him immediately. He slipped once when they were dating, got high with hometown friends and found his high school crush sitting on his lap, his hand lifting up her shirt and kneading her bare breasts; their sloppy make-out ended abruptly when he felt his phone buzz in his pocket and knew it was Kait, took it as a sign from the universe, slid out from beneath the woman and then left the party without telling anyone. Later, he told Kait he didn't know how it had happened and didn't know how to stop it, but the truth is, he knew exactly how it had happened be-cause as soon as he'd seen the crush he'd remembered how much he'd lusted after her, and found the ounce of pot to be the perfect excuse to fulfill a teenage fantasy. Did last night count as cheating on Kait? Did he actually stoop to using his dead wife as a pickup line? For all his condescension to Jessa's attitudes toward love and marriage, wasn't his own view just as simplistic and unsophisticated? In so many ways, his life has been a fantasy too; it's all just a matter of degree. His e-mail delivers him comments on the latest additions to his photo album—photos whose existence he'd forgotten but which now offer the hope of solving the mystery of the missing wife. When he told Kait about the incident with the high school crush, Kait did not cry or shout. She said she appreciated his honesty, and said, "It's okay this time, as long as it never, ever happens again." Her forgiveness actually made him feel more guilty because he knew he deserved to be yelled at, to be banished to the couch for a week, to be periodically reminded that he was the one who had cheated and she wasn't. He took five photos last night. In the first one, Lindsay is on her knees in front of Hunter, grasping his unbuckled belt, a faux-naughty expression on her face, the other girls laughing. Kait is on the table beside them. In another, he and Kait are onstage, performing karaoke. According to the caption, the song is "Let's Stay Together" by Al Green. Photo number three shows them all posing with a homeless man, smiling gap-toothed as he grabs on to Jessa's hip with one hand and holds the ashes in another. Caption: *Making new friends.* Photo number four shows the group inside another bar, a pair of phosphorescent drinks resting on top of Kait midtable. She used to desert him at parties, have a few drinks and wander off—he called her the Mingler, a comic book character with the superpower of making small talk with any stranger. Hunter told her he'd rather do *big talk*, if only people would engage him, but she wanted to know how people were supposed to engage with him if he sat scowling in the corner with arms crossed. Where had she gone last night? Had someone stolen her? Only Hunter, Jessa, and one Lindsay remained in the last picture. They were slumped against the bar, eyes bloodshot and skin greenish in the light. After the Christmas party at her boss's house, Kait said, "I wish you were a real artist so I could at least call you eccentric." The name of the bar is visible on the glass Jessa is holding. He looks up their phone number, calls them, but no one answers. It is only eight a.m. He takes a cab there and waits, leaning with his back against the door.

The manager arrives at ten. A middle-aged woman, red hair pulled up in a ponytail, skin freckled and pale, a large coffee suggesting she worked late last night. Hunter intercepts her before she enters and tries to tell her the story. At first, she seems afraid, but then she takes his hand and tells him to stop crying, everything is okay. He didn't even realize he was crying, but now he feels the heat in his cheeks, the streams of tears that have rolled down the creases beside his mouth and dripped onto his shirt. She sits him down and hands him a glass of water, offers a shot of whiskey on the house. The thought of more alcohol makes him want to die a violent death. He finishes the water before saying anything. The manager busies herself rearranging glasses behind the bar.

He begins telling the story, and the manager cuts him off. Plops the Lost and Found box in front of him. Kait is in there, alongside a mixture of cardigans and umbrellas and earrings. The cube is undamaged, mostly. A few more nicks and scratches. The manager says it was found on the floor of the bathroom. The staff spent the night searching obituaries online; they were going to call home the next day, return her to her family.

He lifts Kait and cradles her against his body. Climbs over the bar and hugs the manager, who holds on to him longer than could be reasonably expected from a stranger. She inhales deeply. "My husband died last year," she says, and he feels a sudden perverse attraction to her, a surge through his poisoned blood telling him fate has arranged this moment and these two ought to be together. He pulls away, says he has to go right now, and exits before she can call him back, before he does something regrettable. He does not have enough breath to apologize to Kait in the way she deserves. But he tries, for the next two days, hiding in a hotel room and never looking away from her.

ELEVEN

E veryone has secrets," she told you again and again. "It adds to the fun," she said. You were talking too much and she was not talking enough, and you couldn't tell whether she was being cagey or if she was trying to politely tell you to shut up. You yourself are often mentally saying *shut up, Hunter*, sometimes in mid-monologue you're rebuking yourself for blathering on even though you can tell other people aren't listening anymore, but you have so many remarkable facts to share and funny jokes to make, and it's so hard to sit quietly listening, and the more you like certain people, the more you talk to them, because you're afraid the silence will encourage them to reassess their association with you, and once they start reassessing they'll find there is no particular reason to be near you besides convenience or a lack of options. Which is why you did about 80 percent of the talking in your relationship, and you would get annoyed when she didn't remember everything you told her, because you remember every word she ever said to you, at least you think you do.

COUPLES ARE SUPPOSED TO have Cute Stories to Tell at Parties, and they're supposed to have access to each other's internal lives in ways that no one else does, and you had that, but you also didn't have it, which made double dates frustrating, because one of the functions of a double date is to measure yourself against the other couple, to compare their cute stories to your cute stories, and to evaluate their shared experiences versus your shared experiences, so that later when you're alone in your home, you can assess the quality of their relationship and rank them as less in love than you, saying things like *They're kind of weird, right?* or *I don't understand why she stays with him* or *Did you see the way he couldn't stop playing with his ring? They'll be divorced within a year.* Or sometimes on good nights, *I really like those two, why don't we hang out with them more often?* You're sure other couples met you and then left thinking you talked too much and she too little, and they said things like *one day she's going to get sick of him*, and they started applying expiration dates to your marriage, not that they could have known it would have ended this way. The problem was they didn't see what you were like in private, the way she laughed at your jokes and trusted you and was happiest with simple things like spending an entire day at home with you, eating leftover Chinese and laughing at bad Lifetime movies.

• • •

A PARTIAL LIST OF things you will never know about your deceased wife:

- What she did—besides "taking a break"—during the year between high school and college
- How she could have gotten into the habit of opening a can of soda, taking three sips, then putting the can in the freezer and forgetting about it until several days later
- What she actually did at work, besides Boring Bank Stuff
- Why sometimes she seemed so lonely, even when you were with her
- What she thought about as she was dying

The Guided Tours never disappeared completely, but at some point you progressed from the urgent and performative early-relationship conversations and shifted into the comfortable chatter that is crucial to the maintenance of a long-term relationship. The ability to talk about nothing for hours. To accurately predict the other's reactions. The casual banter of sparrows chattering away on a tree branch.

THERE ARE STILL THINGS you've never told her, either because she wouldn't let you tell her or because you were embarrassed and afraid to scare her off. Which is why she will never know, for example, that, for reasons you cannot explain, you hated watching her tweeze her eyebrows. You try revealing your secrets to the urn, hoping the information can be conveyed through the ashes to her spirit, if such a thing exists, and so you want her to know that when

you'd only been dating for a few weeks, you got busted for posses-
sion and had to perform two hundred hours of community service
back in Hartford. At the time, you said you were stuck at home for
a few weeks because Jack was swamped at work and needed your
help around the office. You tell her about the mandatory coun-
seling sessions in high school because you'd written on a mental
health questionnaire that you sometimes had suicidal thoughts,
even though that wasn't strictly true, you were exaggerating to seem
deeper and more profound. She never knew, but maybe knows now,
that you sometimes resented her for not playing Trivial Pursuit with
you just because it made her feel stupid when she didn't know the
answers. You confess that last night you lost her and possibly had
sex with some girl who was on the verge of getting married. You tell
her the one thing you're sure she never knew, although you've said
it before: that she was infinitely more beautiful and charming and
intelligent than she thought she was, and that no matter how many
times you said it—not enough times, you owe her another hundred
years' worth of adoration—it never became routine or perfunctory
for you, you always meant it as deeply as one can mean something,
you just wanted her to believe.

TWELVE

Between the emotionally fraught night at Stan and Edna's in Chicago and nearly losing Kait in St. Louis, the last two stops have been too stressful, and so after recovering his wife, Hunter leaves town earlier than anticipated. He changes his tickets and ends up in Seward, Nebraska, with an afternoon to kill before he can get to Lincoln. His phone tells him that the most unique site in town is the world's largest time capsule. The capsule is marked by a white pyramid large enough to contain a car. It was planted here on the front lawn of a furniture store in Seward, because the owner of the store wanted his grandchildren to learn his life story by having physical access to his artifacts. A couple circles the pyramid, peering at the walls as if trying to see through them. Hunter and Kait do the same. The other man knocks on the walls, says,

"These are nice walls." His companion does not listen, is busy taking photos of the pyramid from every angle, photos of the store's exterior, of the plaque commemorating the capsule, of the winged bomb inexplicably placed on the lawn. Buried beneath them is an oversized crypt filled with thousands of relics from the life of a man who died a decade ago. A lifetime of carefully chosen possessions buried for future reference. Kait left everything behind, but she left nothing. It's all there in the house, her dresses and pants, her shoes and makeup, her movies and board games, her low-fat yogurt and skim milk, her loose hairs and skin cells. They weren't chosen, but rather were left haphazardly, scattered throughout his life, as if she couldn't wait to escape, and it's not her fault, but also how is it fair that Hunter now has to pick through all of her relics and curate them in some meaningful way? Does a house automatically become a time capsule the moment it is abandoned, or does it need to be consecrated first? The woman asks Hunter to take a picture of her and her husband. They pose in front of the pyramid, smiling. She asks him to take another, just in case.

Kait took thousands of pictures with her digital camera, printed and organized them into albums, stacked the albums chronologically on shelves in their living room in case visitors wanted to page through every moment of their lives. He'd always felt too self-conscious about how and when he was supposed to smile when posing for pictures, so too often he looked like a fool with curled lips and bared teeth, and anyway he worried that taking too many pictures made people forget to appreciate their lives in the moment. "You'll be glad we have these albums when we're old," she said.

Once the other couple is gone, on the run toward the next tourist attraction, Hunter places Kait on the ground next to the capsule, kneels, and snaps a picture of his wife in front of the pyramid. Uploads it. Caption: *Two boxes full of memories.*

LATER, WANDERING THROUGH THE center of Lincoln, Nebraska, he spots a TrustUs Bank, hulking on the corner of Ninth & H. The familiar sign—green and white palette, a font that can only be described as leafy—swings in the breeze as if waving him in. He enters, shielding his eyes against the sun glinting off the windows. Kait told him once why banks are so insistent upon huge windows, although he doesn't quite remember now; something about transparency and community. There's some kind of science behind the leafy font too, something about associations with security and tradition. The inside of the Lincoln TrustUs smells identical to the inside of the Center City Philadelphia TrustUs—like a dying pine tree, like Christmas five days later. The carpet in both places is exactly the same, a placid, foamy green that looks like it belongs in the Seward time capsule. The layout, T-shaped, is identical to Kait's branch. The employees here wear the same uniform Kait wore, speak with the same inflection Kait had. The women walk the same way Kait did, that hurried but controlled power strut. These are not Nebraska people, Hunter thinks. They're Bank People, a totally different species whose primary instinct is to look you in the eyes and smile as a greeting, to exchange money for money, to wear dark suits, to leave work at three o'clock and go to happy hour at the tapas bar before heading home.

Four tellers await customers along the horizontal line of the T.

A row of chairs is arranged along the vertical. Hunter sits in the chair farthest from the tellers and places Kait on the seat next to him, closes his eyes, and inhales deeply. When she came home from work, she smelled like this, the same way a cook at a pizza joint comes home smelling like heat and garlic and onions. What she smelled like, he used to tell her, was *expensive*. He inhales again, wishes he could pack the odor in his cheeks like a chipmunk and save it for winter. It's afternoon, lunch hour, and a steady line of customers processes from door to teller and back out into the world, where they will fade from Hunter's life forever. Most of them don't look at him, and when they do, they don't really see him, have no idea of his history, probably are assuming that container in the chair next to him is headed for a safe deposit box. Nobody else sits, because these seats are largely ornamental; why would anyone just sit down inside a bank? There's scientific research, probably, that says seeing chairs makes people feel comfortable or something, as in *well, as long as these people have six symmetrically arranged chairs, then I can surely trust them with my life savings.* Kait rarely sat at work, ordered the most uncomfortable chair possible for her office, so she wouldn't be tempted to get lazy. Took the stairs instead of the elevator wherever she went, always found a reason to be on the run. When she came home, she would flop on the couch, lay her feet on his lap, and he would remove her shoes, gently rub her heels while she complained about her boss's terrible communication skills. Sometimes he sneaked a hand above the knee, and sometimes she let him creep higher until his hand was up her skirt and she was grinding against him, but more often, she fell asleep, forearm crossed over her eyes because she was battling another migraine. He would slip out from beneath her legs and set a glass of water and a bottle of Excedrin by her side, then cook dinner for her while she napped.

A security guard lays a hand on his shoulder and says, "You can't stay here."

"I've been walking all day," Hunter says.

"We've all got problems," the guard says. "This isn't a halfway house."

"I've only been here a few minutes." Hunter looks up at the clock on the wall, realizes that, no, he's actually been here for over an hour—since Kait's death time seems to move both too fast and too slow.

"If you don't have business here, you've got to go."

"I'm a customer. Have a lot of money in here," he says, digging through the scraps in his pocket for a deposit slip. "My wife used to work here," Hunter says, tapping the cube. "Well, not here. But, like, here. For this bank." He doesn't know what he wants from this conversation, except that he'd like this guard to know Kait existed, to know she was important to someone, and so was he, once.

The guard hooks his hand around Hunter's elbow, lifts him to his feet. "Fine, but she's not here now."

"Do you know her? Her name's Kaitlyn." He and the guard are walking toward the door. "But everyone calls her Kait. And my last name is Cady, so she's Kait Cady." The guard pushes open the door, guides Hunter out with a hand on his lower back. "See? It's funny, is why I'm telling you."

"Funny."

"Like a double name."

"A double name." People used to think the double name thing was funny. They thought it was cute. The guard stands between him and the door. Crosses his arms.

"Where the hell am I supposed to go now?" The creak of the sign overhead sounds like laughter.

IN THE FACE OF another bus-schedule-imposed delay, Hunter decides to spend a day at a southeastern Nebraska nature preserve, because he's been told it is remarkable and also because the pamphlet promises "endless serenity." Standing at the foot of a hiking trail, he recites a passage from the Internet to Kait about the history of the preserve, when Lewis and Clark walked through here, when it became officially protected land, how many visitors per year it welcomes. He tells her how many species of birds thrive here. Reads the safety warnings about uneven trails and the unpredictability of wildlife, and details their different hiking options. On their honeymoon, he collected all of the tourism pamphlets from the front desk and sat next to her on the bed reading them aloud. She was tired from the drive and lay down with her arm draped over her eyes, giving perfunctory responses, nonverbal grunts and nods. By the fourth pamphlet, he paused. "I'm sorry, do you want me to stop? I should stop."

"No," she said, eyes still covered. "I'm just tired."

"I didn't mean to be annoying. It's just . . . I'm excited. You know?"

With her free hand, she reached out blindly groping for his. "I think it's cute."

"You should take a nap. I'll read you more later," he said. And almost as soon as he finished his sentence she had fallen asleep.

When she woke up a half hour later, she sat up and handed him the pamphlets. "Okay, lay it on me, Mr. Tour Guide," she said.

"I don't want to bore you," he said.

But she insisted. She told him about a friend whose husband brought an Xbox with him on their Hawaiian honeymoon. He'd spent most of the week playing video games and barely talking to his new wife. Kait's friend went to the beach by herself in the morning and had lunch alone and when she got back to the room, her husband was half-drunk on room-service daiquiris and still playing games. "So, what, I'm going to complain that my husband wants to talk to me? That he's excited to be with me?"

Squirrels skitter through the treetops. Groups of hikers pass him, cameras dangling around their necks. The website freezes; he shakes the phone, but nothing changes. He restarts, waits until he can access the site again and begin reciting more facts. The forest chitters and squawks and woodpecks and digs and scrambles. He takes a few steps into the woods, clouds of bugs hovering in front of him, waiting to devour him. He tells Kait there may be bears in the woods somewhere; wouldn't it be cool to get a picture of a bear peeking its head out of a cave?

Some mornings, he told her he was going to get up early to make minor repairs around the house, or read a book, and he tried to do those things until he had to look online for something like tips on how to use a power drill or the definition of an obscure word, and soon enough he would be sucked for five hours into an Internet black hole. When she would ask later about his progress with the repairs, he would tell her the job was harder than he'd expected, it would have to wait.

There are four paths to choose from. Most of the hikers are following the one to his left. He allows a small group a few minutes to establish a comfortable distance and then he follows them onto the left path, passes more signs offering dire safety warnings, telling him to act as much like a human as possible in the unlikely event that he does encounter a black bear. Stumbling on an exposed tree root, he fumbles Kait but manages to regain control before she slams into the dirt. The hikers ahead of him have already been swallowed by dense foliage. The forest is filled with eyes watching him. He tries to be as human as possible.

Willow and Jack took him camping once, back when Jack was still trying to reconnect with Hunter. Jack was always working and his intermittent and fumbling attempts at showing affection belied his own discomfort with raising a child. Willow and Jack weren't planning on children, and as Willow said during her Catholic phase, Hunter was "an unexpected blessing." Still, he and Jack had gotten along well enough until Hunter went to high school and discovered sarcasm and classic rock and recreational drugs all at roughly the same time, and Jack was utterly incapable of dealing with Hunter's transition into a surly and self-righteous teenager. But Jack Cady is not a quitter, Jack Cady gets results, and he worked to salvage the relationship. A few weekends per year, then, he would get away from work and try to cram all of his father-son bonding into the space of two to three days, as in the weekend of Hunter's fifteenth birthday, when, instead of seeing his friends and going to a pool party that would have been populated by bikini-clad girls who were susceptible to peer pressure, Hunter had to go fishing, golfing, and bowling with Jack. He was in college by the time of the camping excursion, wanted to join his friends on a Spring Break trip to some island, but never got a job to raise the money, and when he asked Jack for a loan, Jack told him he had a better idea—they could spend the a long weekend together in the woods. Jack tried to teach Hunter how to start a fire, but Hunter couldn't get the stupid flint to work, and Jack eventually took it from him, started the fire himself. He tried to teach Hunter how to raise a tent, but gave up after Hunter nearly snapped one of the poles in half. Jack caught some trout in a nearby creek, and began teaching Hunter how to clean a fish, but Hunter intentionally pierced his hand with the knife, made it look like an accident, so that Jack would send him back to the tent. Jack never had the patience to be a mentor, so by the next day he had relinquished any hopes of turning his son into an outdoorsman and instead spent the day working on the camp, improving their shelters, and foraging. Hunter stayed inside the tent, where there were no bugs and he could play video games on the portable system he'd sneaked along in his bag.

Nature is objectively nice, Hunter knows, and important and all of that. But it's also dirty and smelly and unpleasant to be in. He prefers his nature in postcard form, shot through a wide-angle lens and broadcast on PBS. Pictures of mountains and woodland creatures are dramatically more comforting than being near actual chattering woodland creatures that carry all sorts of strange diseases and it's impossible to tell when you've offended one of them. The scent of wildflowers like a funeral. The dirt an accumulation of hundreds of years of decomposing organisms. He came here because it seemed like a good place to visit, a tourist attraction with substance. It was a chance to get some fresh air after weeks of breathing recycled oxygen, an opportunity to plunge into the real world. A creature shrieks above him, but he cannot locate the source. According to his map, he ought to be approaching something called Beacon Bluffs, but all he sees is a stream at the bottom of a craggy downhill slope; close to the edge, he has a vivid vision of himself tripping on a tree root and dropping Kait, watching her tumble the whole way down and get swept away by the current. Stepping back from the precipice, he retreats into the woods behind him. He does not stop until the trail is just a vision in the distance. Over the groundswell of woodsy noise, he hears an anguished moan, muffled but persistent, like the sound of a woman trapped beneath a collapsed building. He follows the moaning, pausing every few seconds to recalibrate his direction. When he steps into a clearing, he finds the source.

There is a boy alone.

The boy sits on a log and kicks at the dirt. Above him, a tangle of tree branches hangs like a net. His knee is scraped, shirt muddy, cheeks red with tears. When he sees Hunter approaching, he looks too afraid to run.

"Do you need help?" Hunter says.

"Hell no," the boy says. He looks about ten or eleven, old enough that he's just learning how to curse. Old enough to want to act tough, but young enough to still be terrified. He hides his face, trying to swallow his tears.

"How long have you been out here?"

"I got lost this morning and my dad said if I get lost just to stay where I am and he'll come find me, but it's been a long time."

"How did you get out here in the first place?"

"I thought I saw a beaver and I love beavers so I chased it out here but then I looked up and there wasn't a beaver and I was here by myself and everyone left without me." He grinds his foot into the dirt.

The boy's arms are sunburned, his hair tousled. "Here," Hunter says, extending his hand to the boy. "Let's go find your family."

The boy takes his hand immediately. "I'm Zack," he says. His hand is sweaty, and although he has stopped crying, he seems like the slightest noise could set him off again. He sniffles and uses his free hand to dry his eyes with his shirt.

Hunter does not know exactly where he is going, but he moves with a sense of purpose, hoping his confidence rubs off on Zack. "Do you think there's bears out here?" Zack asks.

"I don't think so," Hunter says.

"But what if there's bears?"

"Did you know bears can't run downhill? Their legs are too short so they fall." Hunter knows this is a myth, but it's important to reassure the boy, and anyway if a bear shows up the truth is that they will be mauled and there's nothing either of them could do about it.

"How do you know that?" Zack asks.

"I'm a pretty smart guy."

"Say something else smart then."

Hunter repeats some of the facts about the park that he was

reading to Kait. Zack seems to accept this recitation as proof of Hunter's intelligence.

"Are you here with your family?" Zack asks.

"I'm by myself." Zack skips over a fallen branch, does not release Hunter's hand. "Aren't you scared to be alone?"

"Sometimes." A gust of wind causes tree limbs to creak overhead. They're so deep in the woods now that Hunter feels like he's living the opening scenes of one of Grimm's fairy tales. It's still midday but the sun will be setting soon and he does not want to imagine the terror of being lost in the dark here.

"What's that thing you're carrying?" Zack asks.

"It's kind of a long story," Hunter says. Zack stops and looks at him, his eyes blank and wanting. He has already placed all of his trust in Hunter and his face seems to say *okay, then tell me a story.* "I can tell you all about it when we get back."

"Can I hold it?"

Zack's hand is clammy and his cheeks are red and although he's doing his best to be stoic, Hunter can see a squall of tears about to be unleashed. "Sure, but you have to hold it with both hands and promise not to drop it. It's very, very important." Zack nods solemnly and then squeezes it against his body with the intensity of a secret agent carrying the nuclear launch codes. They walk slowly as Zack maintains a laser focus on protecting the cargo.

"What's in here that's so important?"

Hunter considers making a game of it by pretending it's a treasure he found in the woods, but why should he lie? Zack may not have a firm grasp on the mechanics of death and grief, but he's probably seen a thousand deaths by now in movies and video games. He may have dead grandparents and cousins and—who knows?—parents. It seems like a violation of his trust not to tell him the truth, and maintaining Zack's trust is essential to making a calm, composed return to civilization. "That's my wife."

Zack laughs. "You can't marry a box."

"Right. Smart kid. You cannot marry a box." Zack shakes it a little, as if trying to guess the true contents. "What I mean is, I was married. To a person. But she died. Do you know what cremation is?"

"*Everybody* knows what cremation is," Zack says, rolling his eyes. "When my friend Robbie's dog died they cremated it and they put the ashes out in the park."

"Same thing here. Except I didn't spread the ashes yet."

"You have to," Zack says. "Or she doesn't get into heaven. That's what Robbie's mom said. But she said dogs have a different heaven, but it's the same rules basically."

"Doesn't it seem like heaven has too many rules?"

Zack stops. "Was she nice?" He looks down at the cube as if hoping to see her in there. Hunter tries to wave him along, but Zack remains still. The answer to this question seems particularly important to him. Hunter tells him that, yes, she was nice.

"Is that why you look so sad?"

"I guess that's why, yeah."

Zack continues to look at the box and Hunter places a hand on his back. The boy's breathing is shallow and he looks like this news is too much for him to handle right now. If he's allowed to dwell in Hunter's grief any longer, he may sink into a panic. Hunter presses gently on his back and they begin walking again. "What about you? Who are you here with?"

Zack nods. "Me and my dad and my stepmom go here every year. I think it's boring but my dad and my stepmom like it a lot, and my brother likes it too."

"How old is your brother?"

This question prompts Zack to launch into a monologue in which he details his family's convoluted web of relations, the parents who divorced and remarried and divorced again a year later before marrying new people, the joint custody and visitation schedules, the brother and stepbrothers and half-sisters, the hyphenated names, the alimony and child support, the bartering over holidays, and with his expert knowledge of the intricacies of divorce law he sounds for a moment like the world's littlest lawyer. By the time he finishes speaking, the trail is in sight, and Zack begins walking faster. As soon as they emerge from the woods, Zack returns Kait to Hunter and is running a few steps ahead of him.

Following the park map now, they walk to the nearest ranger's station. The ranger uses his walkie-talkie to report that the missing boy has been found, and asks that the family come pick him up. The voice on the other end, presumably another ranger, says, "Oh thank god." It is clear from the ranger's demeanor that he thought they were possibly searching for a body instead of a boy. Within ten minutes, the family is at the door—father, stepmother, brother, stepsister, and half-sister—and Zack rushes to hug his father, the tears now relentless. The father holds on to him and kisses his head and he cries and laughs at the same time. He looks like a man who just found out his tumor was benign.

The father shakes Hunter's hand vigorously. "Listen," he says, his body seeming to double in size as he regains his composure. "We owe you. Big time."

"Anybody would have done the same thing," Hunter says.

"Nonsense," the father says. "They didn't do it. You did."

Standing next to his father, Zack tells him about the cube, about Kait. Then he says, "Can Hunter come eat with us? He doesn't have anybody to eat with." The father digests this information, tries to avoid looking at the ashes, smiles apologetically at Hunter. He turns to his children and says, "Kids, do you think he should join us for our pic-a-nic?"

The kids cheer and the brother high-fives Hunter, and they all seem to take joy in the simple act of hearing their father speak. Zack is the oldest of the children, and all four kids are still young enough that they love their parents unconditionally and would rather be here than any other place. The father is rugged and has a meticulous beard and his wife stands there taunting Hunter with her still-beating heart while the children watch both of them with idolatrous looks in their eyes. They seem very happy and healthy, and there is nothing Hunter wants less than to spend an afternoon with them.

"No, sorry, no, I can't," Hunter says. "I have to get home soon."

"We've got wine," the father says. "And sandwiches and all kinds of good stuff. Who doesn't like wine and sandwiches?"

"You don't owe me anything."

"You saved my boy's life," the father says. He pulls a twenty-dollar bill out of his wallet and adds, "At least take this." Even as he's doing it, he seems to realize it's a ridiculous gesture.

Given the choices, Hunter thinks the most dignified option is to just join them for their picnic. He stuffs his hands in his pockets and waits for the father to withdraw the twenty. On a hilly clearing behind the station, the father unfolds a large picnic blanket while the mother assigns a variety of small tasks to the children. The family works together efficiently, but not in a militaristic way; they're like a picnicking pit crew, everyone focused on their jobs and humming through them without even having to communicate. Within minutes, there are seven plates set out with sandwiches, grapes, an apple, and a granola bar. The adults have small plastic cups of wine. Everyone has a bottle of water. The whole family is smiling and talking and listening to one another. Hunter has never seen a family so bizarrely functional.

A breeze billows through the father's plaid hiking shirt while he sips his wine, and he looks like the cover model on a catalog for perfect fathers. He is comfortable being exactly who he is in this moment, surrounded by his loving family, and he has the confidence to sit quietly rather than imposing himself on the conversation. Hunter gulps down his sandwich in a few huge bites, and he finishes his wine before the stepmother has even taken a sip.

When the kids finish eating, they run off the blanket and roll in the dirt. They dig with their hands, looking for dinosaur bones, or at least interesting rocks. The stepmother slides closer to her husband, and he wraps an arm around her shoulders while she leans into him. Hunter feels a bitter lump forming in his throat. "So," he says, "You guys are like the perfect family, huh?" He means it as a compliment, but he's afraid it sounds aggressive.

The father laughs and says, "You just caught us on a good day."

The stepmother adds, "It takes a lot of work to try to look normal." She glances over her shoulder at the children. "They sure didn't make it easy on us at first."

"Things were ugly for a while," the father adds. "Between the divorce and their mom's issues, my job stuff, Zack's problems at school. I didn't know sometimes how we were going to get by."

It is comforting to hear him talk about his unhappy past, to be reminded that these people were not always like this. There have been crises. There has been doubt. People don't just spring fully formed like this into the world; they have to grind through an endless process of construction and collapse until they develop into a person they can like.

Hunter says, "Aren't you ever afraid sometimes that things are too good now? Like something bad has to happen to kind of balance things out?"

The father leans forward and refills Hunter's wine. Hunter can't tell whether he's ignoring the question or thinking about it. He realizes this is inappropriate picnic conversation, and his role here is to talk about how nice it is outside, to say something about the birds. But he so rarely sees people who seem uncomplicatedly happy, and he wants to know how they maintain. He needs assurance that there's a path from his current crisis state to some future in which he has developed into a man he can like and respect.

"I don't know," the father finally says. "Sometimes I think I've already hit my quota for bad news. But then today, we almost lose Zack, and, man . . ."

Both parents go quiet, unwilling to give voice to that alternate reality in which Zack really did disappear.

"He's a good kid," Hunter says.

They both nod, then glance down the hill to make sure all their kids are accounted for. The father says, "You have any kids?"

Hunter should have seen this turn in the conversation coming, but he'd let his guard down. Now the only direction it can take is a spiral downward into his depressing story and he doesn't want to ruin their day. He wants them to be able to enjoy their marriage and their children without the burden of his unhappiness weighing them down. He clutches at his pocket, pretends his phone is buzzing. He pulls it out and checks the display. "Oh, wow, I have to take this call," he says, and before he even finishes the sentence he is on his feet. "Sorry, I have to run," he says. He thanks them and then is hustling down the hill with Kait in his arms and the phone pressed to his ear, holding a fake conversation with someone very important. The parents try to call him back to the picnic, but he is too fast and they can't leave their kids to chase after him.

Kait loved children, smiled at them in supermarkets and was always the first in line to hold a cousin's baby and coo at it; Hunter was indifferent toward kids, but he knew Kait would be a great mother, selfless and generous and well-organized, and she had recently gotten in the habit of saying things like "you would be a good dad" and enumerating his dadlike traits (reliability, loyalty, intelligence), often in contrast to her own miserable father, so he knew that one day, sooner rather than later, they would probably have children, and these children would be universally beloved by Dixons and Cadys alike, and Jack and Willow could recoup their losses on Hunter, invest their hopes and dreams into these new little beings. As a couple, though, they chose to wait, wanted to travel first, and they waited too long—the catastrophic accident of the ectopic pregnancy notwithstanding—so now there will never be a child in the world like the one Hunter and Kait could have made together. If they'd had a daughter a year ago, he could be holding a miniature version of Kait in his arms right now, could feel like there was a purpose to his life. Or he could be looking resentfully down at the face of a little burden, a daily reminder that Kait abandoned them, saddled him with the responsibility of having to follow the child everywhere she went because he would be too afraid to lose her, because children are set at birth to self-destruct and most of their energy is spent seeking out new ways to get hurt, and a parent's job is to scramble behind them with outstretched arms in case they fall. Even when the daughter was forty years old, Hunter would feel compelled to follow her, to save her from the world itself. The daughter would complain about his intrusiveness, but that wouldn't change anything because he would need to be there and experience every second of her life vicariously because he'd already had his chance to live and wasted it.

Back near the start of the trail, he is again himself with nature. There is too much space here. That's one of the ostensible appeals of the park, he knows, of nature walks in general—the solitude. When he read the blurbs online, he considered stowing away here, uniting with nature, becoming a woodsman and living off the land. Self-reliant. At some point, he would scatter her ashes and free her, allow her to return to the earth. The soil enriched by her ashes would blossom into an Edenic oasis, which he would visit every day to pay homage. But about a mile into the forest, he looks around and sees nothing but menacing nature: rows of trees rising out of the earth like teeth, millions of bugs all aiming to drink his blood, whooshing winds that moan like rheumatic joints. If he were to die right now, nobody would find him for days, at least, and it's possible the only person who would care is now in his arms, voiceless and bodiless, confined to a steel cube. He thought he wanted to be alone, but the loneliness is the most painful thing he has ever felt in his life.

THIRTEEN

Some days you simply cannot forget and you cannot remember at the same time. The past is alternately suffocating and liberating. When you go too long without thinking about her, when you realize you've spent a whole morning without a single thought of Kait, the guilt threatens to strangle you. It's your job to remember her, but it's impossible for anyone to live inside his own memories. You want to move forward with your life, but if you move too quickly, you may lose everything you have left of her.

Some days, you simply cannot muster the energy to act like a human: to shower, and shake hands with strangers, and have thoughts about the weather, and order an omelet at the diner, and thank the waitress, and leave her a tip, and make small talk with the desk clerk at the hotel. And yet you still find yourself doing these things because some biological impulse drives you to persist. Your white blood cells are slowly manufacturing antibodies to fight back the viral strain of grief that's been draining you, and some small, hidden part of you perhaps even *wants* to do all these things, to feel normal again.

FOURTEEN

Since arriving in Tulsa, Oklahoma, two days ago, Hunter has seen only the highway from his hotel window and the sliver of carpeted hallway visible when he cracks the door open to accept room service. There are things to do in Tulsa, obviously. There are things to do everywhere. Hunter's problem is that he doesn't want to do any of them. Due to a confluence of mechanical issues and a scheduling mix-up, the bus to Austin was delayed, and so he is stuck here for another two days. Until then, he and Kait are under self-imposed quarantine. They are watching TV and they are doing crossword puzzles—they used to do the Sunday crossword together, alternating turns on clues and leaving the newspaper on the kitchen table for each other throughout the week—and they are playing video games on the Internet. Every night, he struggles to sleep, twisting himself up in his blankets for hours, sweating through the sheets.

If Jack were here, he would repeat his refrain about how Hunter should appreciate having the luxury of aimlessness. But right now, the aimlessness feels less like luxury than burden. To move without direction is unnatural; even the least sophisticated mammals have instincts to tell them what to do, but his instincts have been eroded by a lifetime of abject safety. He knows that when on vacation Kait would never have considered sitting in a hotel for several days; they would only have used the room for sleep, showers, maybe good-morning sex, and otherwise they would vacation vigorously. At the start of this trip, he was confident the requisite adventures would emerge on their own, but instead he has proven to be woefully inadequate at every aspect of adventuring. Even now, in the throes of this delay, he is losing faith in his plan; what happens if he gets to Austin and finds it even more unlivable than the other places he's been? Why should he expect Seattle or Victoria or San Francisco to offer him anything he hasn't seen already? What makes those better destinations than, for example, a dinosaur quarry in Oklahoma or the Texas Prison Museum in Huntsville or the World's Largest Uncrucified Christ in Arkansas? When one's choices are limitless, how is it possible to know what is the right thing to do?

He awakes to a single sharp knock on his door. Blanket wrapped around his shoulders like a cape, he looks through the peephole and sees Jack checking his watch. Even though the temperature in Tulsa will creep up to three digits before noon, Jack is wearing what he always wears: khakis, blue dress shirt, black tie. He doesn't cuff his sleeves or loosen his tie. His hair is unmoved by the weather. A bead of sweat trickles past his right ear.

Jack knocks again, a single gunshot crack. He jangles his keys in his pocket, checks his watch again. He will not go away until Hunter opens the door. If Hunter does not open the door, Jack will purchase a sledgehammer and knock the door off its hinges, then bill Hunter for labor and materials. It shouldn't be a surprise that someone has found Hunter. He's been leaving a trail of digital breadcrumbs—the most recent a photo of him and Kait hiding inside a pillow fort in this hotel room—but did it have to be Jack who showed up?

As Jack winds up to knock again, Hunter swings the door open. Jack walks past him into the room, flicks on the overhead lights and opens the blinds, floods the room with sunlight. "Get dressed," he says. "We've got a busy day."

AN HOUR LATER, THEY'RE sitting on a park bench on the campus of Oral Roberts University. Jack has a meeting here today, says he arranged it since he'd be in town anyway; a chance to check in on some of his contacts (Jack has contacts and he has business partners; he does not have friends). Over Jack's shoulder, Hunter has a clear view of the world's largest pair of praying hands—a sixty-foot tall bronze sculpture at the entrance to the school.

"Did you need to bring that thing here?" Jack says, pointing at the urn.

"This is my wife."

Jack looks away from Kait, grinds his teeth in that theatrical way he has to ensure people know he is frustrated. "How long are you going to do this?"

"It must have taken them forever to make that," Hunter says, looking at the praying hands.

"Your mother is worried about you."

"I read that thing weighs thirty tons. Can you imagine?"

"She wanted to come but not everyone can afford to wander around the country on a whim."

"You flew two thousand miles just to lecture me?"

"I came here on business." Jack stands, motions for Hunter to follow him on a gravel path toward an administration building. "And I came to bring you home."

"Why shouldn't I do this?" Hunter says. "I've got the money."

"You know what this is like? This is like that month when you gave up on cheese. Or do you remember that time you were going to take boxing classes?"

"This is nothing like any of that. Someone is *dead*." Hunter thrusts Kait into Jack's chest, and then releases his grip on the urn, lets her drop, wants Jack to catch her and be forced to hold her, to feel the physical weight of her death in his hands, because he is much more adept with concrete ideas than he is with abstractions. Jack steps backward, arms at his sides, and Kait thuds into the gravel. The urn gouges a divot into the pathway, a fossil recording Kait's brief passage here. Down on his knees, investigating the cube, Hunter finds no new damage. "How can you just let her fall?" Hunter says.

"You're the one who chose to drop her." He turns, continues

walking toward his meeting, does not look over his shoulder to check on Hunter. Hunter and Kait rise from the ground and follow him.

"You know, you're not the first person to have someone die," Jack says when Hunter catches up. "My mother died when I was eight. My father was dead before you were born. I lost three cousins last year. This is what happens."

"So, what, I don't have the right to be sad just because other people die too?"

"You sound like your mother."

"You sound like an asshole." They pass under the hands, swallowed by their shadow. Jack checks his watch.

"You want to be mad at me because life is hard, fine, be mad at me," Jack says. "I'm not the one who did this to you." When they enter the administrative building, Jack tells Hunter to sit in the lobby and wait for him while he goes to his meeting. Hunter sits, eyeing the floor like a high school student stuck in detention.

KAIT WOULD HAVE BEEN fascinated by the giant hands. Hunter was never particularly religious, never raised that way, and in college loved to quote the Marx line about the opiate of the masses, but Kait was raised in a Catholic family and a Catholic neighborhood. She rarely attended Mass, and when Hunter launched into diatribes about the institutional corruption of organized religion, she nodded and agreed. But like every Catholic he knows, she also couldn't shake the feeling that she should be doing something spiritual anyway. She was the one who insisted on getting married in a church, for example. He didn't like the idea, not only because of the length of the service, but because it would require him to spend months trying to convince a priest that he deserved to get married. She asked him, "Don't you believe in any god?" He said he'd never seen a good reason to believe in one. When she said, "I'm not sure what I believe in," he repeated one of Jack's favorite mantras: you have to have conviction because there's no room in life for doing things halfway. Still, she insisted that if they had children, they would be baptized. *Just in case*, she said, as if God is a contingency plan. She seemed to want to have faith, even though she couldn't explain why, and so they kept religious artifacts in their home—a crucifix in the bedroom, a small statue of St. Joseph in the foyer, supposedly for good luck—and she still prayed at night, crossing herself and willing herself to believe.

While they lay in bed one night, he asked her who she prayed to, and she couldn't say exactly. "It just helps me sometimes," she said. "Why does it bother you so much?"

"What's the point in praying if you don't even know who you're speaking to, or why?" he asked. "It's the same as having an imaginary friend."

"Just because you can't see God doesn't mean he's not there." She rolled onto her side to face him, pressed a hand on his chest, roughly where she assumed the soul was contained. "There are some things you have to take on faith."

"You're only saying that because that's what they teach you to say."

She made the sign of the cross on him, smiling, and said, "Tonight, I'm going to pray for you to see the light." That was funny, Hunter had to admit.

THE TV IN THE building lobby is muted. Occasionally a pair of shoes clicks metronomically past him on the tile floor. A secretary taps out text messages furiously. Fluorescent lights buzz like angry wasps. Hunter unlocks the cube and invites Kait to escape, to reveal herself like a genie and grant him his three wishes, and then he snaps it shut and locks it again. While locking and unlocking, a motion effortless as clicking a pen, he wishes now he'd had her faith, thinks maybe religion isn't entirely bad after all. Most of his thoughts over the past few weeks have been essentially the equivalent of prayers. Even though he thinks he knows who he has been talking to, there is no guarantee that she can hear him or that her soul even exists, and he could just as easily be unloading his emotions on a box filled with dirt, besides which, how can he even be sure the funeral parlor delivered him the correct ashes, maybe this is a stranger in the box or not even human ashes at all, so there is a certain leap of faith occurring even on that most fundamental level. Besides that, there is something appealing about the size and scope of the enormous praying hands at Oral Roberts, or any of the other colossal monuments he and Kait have seen on this trip, like the sculpture of the Native American warrior Crazy Horse being carved and dynamited into the side of a South Dakota mountain, a work seventy years in the making with perhaps another seventy to go. Besides a great accumulation of wealth, memorials on the scale of the European cathedrals and Egyptian pyramids require bottomless reservoirs of love. He thinks now that he could use his remaining insurance money to commission a sculpture of Kait to be displayed on their lawn, maybe even a whole series of them, so he could praise her in all of her natural states, from sleeping to eating blueberry muffins for breakfast to planting flowers to trimming her bangs in front of the bathroom mirror to relaxing in front of the TV with a glass of wine.

Everyone wants to memorialize their loved ones, but nothing they do ever seems adequate.

Jack's meeting lasts three hours, during which time Hunter pokes around on the Internet until his phone battery dies, and then watches the silent TV screen, which is populated by hundreds of women who were allowed to live longer than Kait for reasons still undetermined. When Jack emerges from the elevator, Hunter is half asleep. Jack says, "Did you just sit here doing nothing the whole time?"

STANDING AT THE RENTAL car, Jack says, "Listen, your mother wants me to give you a hug." He leans into Hunter, Kait pressed between them, and he withdraws after a few firm pats on Hunter's back. He tells Hunter to get in the car, and doesn't speak until they're about a half mile down the road, the bronze hands receding in the rearview. "Here's the deal," Jack says. "I'm meeting those guys tonight at a steakhouse in town. We have some hurdles to clear, so I might be out late. There's a seven-thirty flight home tomorrow morning. Earliest I could get." He switches lanes without signaling, speeds past a minivan. "I got you a seat. Cost extra because it was last minute, but I'll cover it."

"I'm not done yet," Hunter says.

"Oh no?" Jack laughs. "What's next on your big agenda?"

"I don't really know where I'm going," Hunter says.

"That's always the problem, isn't it?" Another lane change, stomping on the gas pedal.

They pass a sprawling RV park, filled to capacity, each RV with a happy family. It is only in Hunter's sightline for only a few seconds, and then it is gone, but he sees every detail. He sees the retired couple inside the bright blue camper near the roadside, the husband arranging turkey and swiss on crustless bread for his wife, and Hunter knows they are in the middle of a trip for which they've been preparing their whole lives. He sees the jumbo camper in the back of the park, teeming with six children and a golden retriever, the harried parents sending them to run around somewhere so they can be together in silence for a few moments and try to remind themselves why they thought this was a good idea in the first place. He sees brothers and sisters fighting with one another, and he sees teenagers twiddling with their phones to contact distant boyfriends and girlfriends. He sees thousands of camera flashes, everyone wanting to record this moment, envisioning future scrapbooks and online albums. He sees patriarchs double-checking itineraries and unfurling maps onto the hoods of RVs, circling destinations with their pens in order to convey a sense of authority. These are all people traveling with other people, which makes them tourists; he is a person traveling without other people, which means he long ago crossed the line separating tourist and drifter.

Jack jerks the wheel to zoom past another slow-moving vehicle, mutters something about Midwestern drivers. Says, "Tell me something—how are you going to survive without a job?"

"I've got plenty of money."

"Right now you do. What happens in five years?" At a red light, Jack drums his fingers on the steering wheel, stares up at the light, so that he can charge through at the exact moment it turns green.

"No answer. Let's try this one—is the money invested? Do you expect it to just grow on its own?"

Holding his phone, Hunter says, "Do you have a car charger? Battery died."

"Kait's mother won't stop calling. You know that? She keeps talking about lawyers and police. I'd say it's a bluff but she probably doesn't know any better."

"She'll get over it."

"Do you understand you're being selfish? That you're hurting people?" They pull into the hotel parking lot, engine idling. Jack unlocks the doors.

Hunter says, "Can I go out to dinner with you?"

"Not when you're like this. When's the last time you washed your clothes?" It has been a while. He started reusing dirty shirts last week rather than wasting time in laundromats. "This is business here, not family fun time." Jack makes a show of rolling up his sleeve to check his watch.

"Do you cheat on Mom when you're on the road?"

"You want to think everything's simple, but it's not all simple."

"Why would you marry her if you didn't want to be with her?"

Jack squeezes the steering wheel, stares straight ahead as if he's still speeding down the highway. "I know you're angry. This is not what you wanted your life to be. It's not what I wanted for you either. But it's how things are."

Hunter steps out of the car. "You should go to your meeting," he says. Jack waits a moment before backing out of his parking spot, and then he is gone.

. . .

BEFORE HE LIES DOWN in bed, he receives an e-mail from Sherry: "Because we don't trust you anymore, we're going over your house. I and Brutus are going to take what's ours and what's Kait's. You want to keep her, fine. But you can't lock us out forever, it's easy to break in a place." He pictures them rifling through his possessions, dumping out his drawers and ransacking the house. Cutting holes in the drywall on the hunt for hidden treasures. Like a family KGB searching for evidence to prove that Hunter was a bad husband, for reasons to justify their contempt. He thinks about the things Kait would never want them to see—the mess in the spare bedroom, the purple vibrator in her underwear drawer given to her as a gift by a bridesmaid and as far as he knows never used, the antianxiety meds she'd begun taking about six months before her death. He thinks about the things they'll take with them. Her clothes, anything that fits Sherry. Her boxes of college memorabilia—scrapbooks, graduation gown, old notebooks, his only connection to that period of her life. He imagines them physically tearing these memories out of his mind, severing all ties he's ever had to her. If they could get away with it, they'd torch the place after clearing it out. They're grieving too, it's understandable that they're so upset, why shouldn't they be heartbroken by their loss, but why do they want to punish him? For being depressed by his wife's death? For not being enough like them, not being a drinker and a fighter and an expert at darts? For not being the kind of guy they wanted Kait to marry, but instead being the kind of guy *she* wanted to marry? They want her possessions, but they don't know who she really was. They love who they think she was, and right now they're in the house trying to unearth a person they lost long before she died.

He should call a neighbor or a friend to check on the house, but doesn't have phone numbers for any neighbors and only interacted with them out of social obligation. He can't think of anyone who is a close enough friend to defend his house against a band of marauding Dixons. Telling Jack is out of the question; he may be able to help, but Hunter would rather have his house burned to the ground than to be deeper in debt to his father, to endure more of his condescension, another of his lectures. After landing on the East Coast, he will have to rush back to his home and survey the damage, call the police and insurance companies, waste even more time trying to recover his losses.

He wakes at six o'clock, buckling under the pressure of a migraine, which makes it nearly impossible to do anything. He feels like he's recovering from a bout with the flu. Jack will be at the hotel soon. He will force Hunter onto that flight, and then they'll be home, and Hunter will have failed to cross the country, failed to give Kait the trip she deserved, and then what happens? He just goes back to work for another forty years until someone tells him it's time to retire?

Hunter rolls out of bed, still wearing last night's clothes, and carries Kait with him toward the pharmacy two blocks away. He buys a bottle of pills for the migraine and consumes three times the recommended dosage, then sits on the curb by the pharmacy door, his head feeling like a cracked egg.

Maybe a half hour later, still on the curb, Kait in his lap, he takes his first photo in days, the pill bottle next to Kait. Caption: *Searching for a cure.*

A car parks directly in front of him even though the parking lot is empty. He assumes Jack has found him. He will not put up a fight, because he knows he will lose. But the driver is a stranger, looks like he's in his early fifties, wide-chested and spry, springing from the car toward the pharmacy, while two younger passengers climb out from the backseat. They're closer to Hunter's age, one male and one female, and he has to resist the urge to thrust Kait in their faces, warn them that no matter what has led them here, this is the ultimate fate of every love story.

The young guy looks like a hand-rolled cigarette, lumpy and pale, with bright red hair that curls out over his ears. His mustache sits like a caterpillar on his lip, dramatically darker than his hair, probably grown as a joke. He fits into his clothes like biscuit dough bursting out of the tube. He's clearly a strong guy, much more so than Hunter, like a former rugby player who has let himself go. His cheeks are stippled with acne scars. He wears a T-shirt that says THIS SHIRT IS ONLY FUNNY IF YOU GET THE JOKE. The girl looks like Kait. Except for the brown eyes, and the slightly shorter legs, and the narrower hips. And her hands aren't right either—Kait's were delicate with spindly fingers, and this girl's are meaty and perfect for opening jars. Her breasts are larger than Kait's, and her hair is dyed blonde, unlike Kait's natural chestnut. But when he looks, he still sees Kait, still sees himself standing next to her.

The couple stretches and leans on the car, movements synchronized.

The guy sneaks a kiss while the older man shops inside the drugstore. The young guy wraps his arm around the girl's waist as they gaze off into the distance. They look like they've just reunited after a long absence, like he's returned from the war and she's afraid to let go.

The older man bounds outside and calls to Hunter. "Hey," he says, his voice rusty and sharp. "You from around here?" Hunter shakes his head. "We're looking for some place to eat."

"There's probably something down that way," Hunter says, waving down the road.

"Well, where the hell you been eating at?"

"I've been sticking to room service."

"Looks like you haven't been eating anything at all," the older man says. The young couple closes in and all three stand over him. "You okay?"

"It's been a long couple of days," Hunter says, looking up and shielding his eyes from the rising sun.

The girl says, "He looks like he needs help. Do you think he needs help? I think he needs help." Her lover nods and the older man makes a *humpf* sound to indicate agreement.

"I'm fine."

The girl eyes Hunter like he's a stray dog. She touches the old man on the elbow and gives him a look Hunter understands immediately: it's the same one Kait would have given him if they'd found a stray, the look that says *we need to save this poor guy.*

The older man takes a deep breath, then extends his hand toward Hunter. "Come on," he says. "Let's go find a diner. Get you something to eat." He pulls Hunter up to his feet. The migraine still pressing on him, Hunter blinks through the dizziness he feels upon standing.

Jack will arrive at the hotel within the hour, and if Hunter isn't ready to go, he will be irritated for the rest of the day, making the flight home unbearable. But these strangers are friendlier than Jack and he can't remember the last thing he ate, so suddenly his hunger seems urgent. Given the circumstances, he would prefer almost anything to sitting alone in his hotel room for an hour and waiting for his father to take him home. This trip needs to end on his terms, however it ends, not because his father is dragging him home like a child out past curfew. What if this drive to the diner is the key to the whole journey? What if Kait is waiting there for him at the door, and she takes his hand and they fly away to some other, better time and place? What if he's really hungry and just wants to shove some fried food in his mouth and forget it all for a minute? He conceals Kait in the bag with the pills and follows them to the car, riding in the front while the young couple piles into the back.

THE OLDER MAN SITS next to Hunter in a diner booth, Hunter trapped against the wall, the couple across from them. The man's name is Paul, and he is much older than Hunter had guessed. Beneath his baseball cap, he has only a horseshoe of silver hair to match his thick mustache. He is barefoot, his moccasins sitting vacant beneath the table. He's in his sixties, the grandfather of the girl, Amber, and they're in the midst of a road trip from North Carolina—a college graduation gift. Thirty years ago, Paul drove Route 66 with his wife, and for years Amber has wanted to replicate his trip. The lumpy guy, whose name is Austin, is here because he is the boyfriend, and Paul thinks he needs to get some living in before he starts working long hours in the insurance industry, which Paul sees as the exact opposite of living. It took no effort for Hunter to learn these things, because the three of them haven't stopped talking since he got in the car. The waitress delivers stacks of pancakes to each of them.

"These are the best damn pancakes I had all day," Paul says, smirking, and Hunter can tell by the others' blank reactions that this is a pretty standard Paul joke, a variation on something he's probably said every morning of the trip. He claps Hunter on the thigh like they're old buddies and asks, "So where you headed?"

"Trying to get out west," Hunter says. He shoves a forkful of pancakes into his mouth.

"You got work waiting for you?" Paul says.

Still chewing, Hunter says, "Kind of," and forces more food into his mouth. He focuses on his plate as if to make sure the pancakes won't run off. He's glad Paul isn't across from him, because it's easier to avoid eye contact this way. To derail the line of questioning, he asks: "Where are you guys going next?"

Paul heaves a sigh, then says, "Depends who you ask."

"He won't let us get off Route 66, so we can't see all the stuff we wanna see," Amber says.

"What they don't understand," Paul says, "is this is the way me and her grandmother went."

"We don't have to do everything *exactly* like you and grandma did," Amber says.

"I know it."

"If it's Amber's gift, shouldn't she get some say in it?" Austin says.

"The giver decides what the gift is," Paul says.

Hunter's phone buzzes in his pocket. Jack is calling. He has ten minutes to get back to the hotel.

"What if we just, like, take a couple detours and then come right back?" Austin says. "Make the trip longer, but don't skip anything."

"That's a great idea, babe," Amber says.

Paul digs in his pocket and rolls rosary beads between his index finger and thumb.

"Seems like it wouldn't be bad for you to see some other stuff," Hunter says. "Get on a different road awhile."

"Maybe you all should've done the planning instead of me." Paul stands and thrusts his foot into his moccasin as if trying to smash a spider. "Why even listen to the one who's been here before." He tosses his fork onto the table and stomps toward the bathroom.

Amber twists a strand of hair around her index finger, looks like she wants to yank it out. Hunter says, "Was that my fault?"

"He gets like that sometimes," Amber says. "The trip wasn't even his idea. Me and Austin were gonna do it alone, but then at the last minute he kind of forced his way in. Offered to pay for everything, so we figured why not? But then sometimes he seems annoyed we're even here."

"Weird."

"We get along and all, so it's not *that* weird. But, yeah, also it's a little bit weird."

"The problem," Austin says, "is we're looking for a little more, I don't know. Fun? Adventure? Something."

Hunter's phone buzzes again. He pictures Jack standing outside his hotel room, banging on the door. Going to the front desk to demand entry. He nearly answers, but then thinks he should at least finish his meal. Thinks he'd rather not have to run away from breakfast without an explanation. Thinks how much more pleasant it is to be with people who don't know anything about him. Amber asks him who's calling, and he shrugs. "Must be a wrong number," he says, switching the phone to silent.

Paul emerges from the bathroom shaking water from his hands, walks past them into the parking lot. But Paul is just getting something from the car. He returns to them a minute later, drops a map on the table along with a handful of tourism pamphlets, and says, "Listen, I know you're not having fun." Amber opens a pamphlet. "Look it all over and let me know what you want." He downs the rest of his coffee.

While Amber consults the pamphlets, making check marks on the ones she wants to visit, Austin unfurls the map and Hunter notices a small town about a thousand miles southwest of their current location: Peridot. Kait's birthstone, the peridot earrings he'd given her for her birthday and that she was wearing the day she died, fluorescent light glinting pale off her ears as she lay in a gurney, rolling away from him.

Paul orders another round of coffees. He and Hunter sip quietly while Austin and Amber spend the next twenty minutes scribbling all over the map, circling towns, writing notes in the margins, and running their index fingers alongside each other's in lines steady as railroad tracks.

• • •

THEY LEAVE THE DINER at seven o'clock, just about the time when his flight will be boarding. Hunter asks Paul to take him back to the hotel, because there is no other place to have Paul take him. There is no other explanation to offer. On the short ride, he prepares himself for a confrontation with Jack, during which Jack will revel in telling them that he's a fraud, that he's just some lost boy who needs his daddy to come and save him from the world.

When they pull into the lot, there is no sign of Jack. If he were here, he would be leaning on his car, arms crossed over his chest like a bouncer. He must already be at the airport, having decided the best punishment for Hunter is to give him exactly what he wanted, to leave him alone.

"Thanks for joining our little breakfast party," Paul says, engine idling outside the hotel entrance. He shakes Hunter's hand.

Amber smiles and says it was fun to meet someone new. Austin claps him on the back and says, "Good luck getting west, buddy."

If Hunter returns to that hotel room, he may never leave it again, at least not until the money runs out, and then he might start working there, cleaning rooms and checking businessmen into their junior suites for the night. He has only one opportunity to salvage this trip. It will mean sacrificing his itinerary, but there is no other reasonable option. He is still holding on to Paul's hand. "Son, you okay?" Paul says.

"How bad would it be if I asked to hitch a ride with you?"

"You trying to pull a game on me?"

"I'm stuck here. My car's broken down. And the rentals are all booked. And I need help." Paul eyes him warily, clearly trying to determine whether this scene will one day be part of a dramatiza-tion on *Unsolved Mysteries*. "And my wife is waiting for me."

He shows them his wedding band, tells them his wife got a job in California and had to move out ahead of him. He had to stay be-hind and tie up loose ends, was hoping to see some of the country on the way out to meet her.

Amber thinks this is a very cute story, and she makes the *awww* sound young girls make when they hear cute stories. "It's like the dude in that book," Austin says. "You know. The book from fresh-man year? The long one."

"And, what," Paul says, "you tie us up and rob us ten miles down the road?"

"I think I'm the one taking the bigger risk here," Hunter says. "How do I know you three aren't murderers?"

"Boy, if I was a murderer, you'd be dead by now," Paul says, which is not nearly as reassuring as he seems to think it is.

"I read somewhere that you should try to do one good deed ev-ery day," Amber says. "This would be perfect. And anyway, this is why you do road trips. This is what's supposed to happen."

"Think about his wife," Austin says. "I know Amber would be freaking if that was me."

A plane roars overhead, causes the car to shudder. Paul rubs his eyes and stares down at the floor as if the solution to this problem is written on his moccasins. Amber grabs Austin's hand, squeezes it while watching her grandfather hopefully. Paul says, "You got to pay tolls and gas."

Hunter thanks him and then runs upstairs to get his bag. Paul,

Amber, and Austin could turn out to be kidnappers or sadists or evangelicals, but they could also become friends, and so even though there is a zero percent chance Kait would have approved of this plan—there is adventure and then there is recklessness, there is opening yourself to new experiences and then there is risking your life just to avoid a confrontation with your father—he decides she's been outvoted and buries her in the duffel bag before stuffing her in the car trunk. A few minutes into the ride, Amber says, "So, Hunter, tell us about your wife."

FIFTEEN

Mornings are the worst. That moment before you open your eyes and your brain starts working again and you return to the conscious world. Remembering.

SOMETIMES THE WEIGHT OF the sadness presses down on you so hard you can't breathe.

CRAZY PEOPLE TALK TO inanimate objects. In a few months, you will stop being bereaved, and you will become eccentric, and then you will become disturbed. This is the progression. But what if that's the only way to grieve? What if it's the only way to be fair to her? It worked for people in the Middle Ages. Why shouldn't you be allowed to cling to this? Why shouldn't your misery be a monument to your love?

ONE OF THE JOYS of marriage is complaining to each other, huddling cynically against the outside world, viewing it together and deeming it undeserving of your presence. Sitting in a café and quietly judging other people and knowing intuitively that your wife agrees with your judgment. So who are you supposed to complain to now? Who is supposed to confirm your worldview and let you know you're right? If you don't have a partner for this activity, then it becomes antisocial behavior rather than the connective tissue of a relationship. The presence of that other person validates your continued membership in a society.

FOR THE REST OF your life you will be the man with the dead wife, and people you haven't seen in years will still dumbly ask, "How's Kait?" which will make you feel guilty for answering honestly, so sometimes you'll say, "She's fine," because they're not comfortable with the truth and because it's easier to pretend that's what she is. They will move on with their lives and continue assuming everything is fine with you because you said it is fine, and because it is impossible to allow oneself, no matter how charitable or empathetic, to be burdened by every neighbor's quiet struggles.

WHEN YOU SEE ANOTHER tourist losing his composure over a minor setback—like the man who hurled his phone out the bus window because he got bad reception on the highway to St. Louis, or the woman who suffered a complete meltdown at the

Arby's in Davenport, Iowa, when they ran out of roast beef and who berated the employees so ferociously that they had to call the police to remove her—you feel smug in your misery. They're everywhere, these people who cannot function in the face of inconveniences, like long lines or a broken pair of sunglasses, people who explode into rages because someone ruined their picture in front of a historic monument, and when you see them, you think, what would these people do if they faced real trauma? How could they possibly survive an actual loss? Would they just stop breathing on the spot? You, you're sad and you're on the run, but you also are maintaining a stoic façade, and seeing these unstable people makes you feel better about your own weakness.

You LIKE TO THINK your grief is individual and unique and objectively worse than the rest of the world's, but the brutal truth is, it is not, and this fact is not as comforting as some people seem to believe.

SIXTEEN

Here is what he tells his new companions when they ask about his life: he tells them he's moving to San Diego because Kait works for a major environmental advocacy firm and she was just promoted to Manager of West Coast Operations. She's really into the earth, he says, and she had to get out there right away to start organizing her staff. Yeah, he's proud of her, loves that she's pursuing her passions. They're in the midst of forest fire season, so she'll probably be busy for the next few months, but they'll have plenty of time together, and anyway you can't beat the climate in San Diego. The best part about Kait's position is that her income alone is double what they were making combined back home, so she told him to quit his job and start chasing his own dreams. He's a musician, he says. Bass and harmonica, a little keyboard. Playing helps him relax, it's a refuge. He's got auditions with a few bands set up already. In the meantime, he'll be doing a lot of writing, because, oh, didn't he mention that? He's a writer too. It's lonely work, but he loves it. He does not mention that he hasn't written a single creative word in almost two years. Tells them there's this roof deck on the new house—he hasn't been there yet, but Kait has sent him pictures—where he can set up a few chairs and a table and write for hours, looking out over the cliffside toward the ocean. He's really looking forward to spending long days up there, absorbing the sun, because he finds nature very inspiring, he says, and Amber agrees, she likes nature too. The inside of the house is nice, has plenty of room to start a family, which Kait wants to do, although not right away, not until they see the world. He'll be a stay-at-home dad, because that's the tradeoff you have to make if you're willing to let your wife bring home the bacon. She knows he's running late, but she's fine with it. Trusts him. All that matters in the end is getting there and seeing each other again; they have the rest of their lives to spend together, so why not enjoy the sights along the way?

THEY'RE DRIVING A STEADY four mph below the speed limit, occasional thrill-seeking teens whizzing by while Austin and Amber watch them wistfully. Acres of desert lie on either side of them, a landscape that demands silence. Paul is listening to Arlo Guthrie, tapping fingers arhythmically on the steering wheel. Even in the air-conditioning, sweat beads on Hunter's face, rolls down his side, and funnels into the grooves above his hips. Feverish. Like the car is hauling victims of typhoid.

Paul has this way of talking—in bursts, loud and declarative.

Like thunder. You can't predict exactly when it will happen, but you know it's nearby, the storm clouds forming inside his head, sparks jumping from his mouth. "You all are bored," he says. He seems unaware of the existence of question marks. Does not ask how people are feeling, but rather tells them. Nobody responds, so he turns up the music.

THEY CROSSED THE ARIZONA border about two hours ago. Cities arise like mirages out of the desert. Not cities, but towns. Villages. Every one of them is a city in miniature, a one-street downtown, a weird landmark, curious tourists, and then nothing. People live here, probably, but it is hard to comprehend why. These towns barely exist—they are places sustained entirely by tourism, and whose residents on any given day are primarily tourists. These are not actual places so much as they are fabrications of places.

Many of the roadside attractions are quirky and bizarre and manmade with no particular history attached. They've seen a large wooden blue whale in someone's yard. They've seen the Cadillac Ranch, they've seen a famous gas station and a giant milk bottle and another famous gas station. And he has taken photos of everything, because that is all anyone can do at these places. Everyone lines up to take pictures of themselves alongside the World's Largest Pair of Concrete Legs, loads them onto the Internet for others to see, and then drives away. It does not seem to matter to anyone whether ten thousand other people have produced the exact same photos and the same memories. The function of travel, so far, has been not to experience things so much as to look at things, nod, and then move on down the road until it is time to look at another thing. Kait wasn't interested in quirky roadside attractions. She liked major stops, huge museums, memorials to soldiers. Places that attract a dozen tour buses a day during the summer. Had she been in charge, they never would have passed through Texas without first visiting the Alamo, Dealey Plaza, a real rodeo. Maybe her route would have been more fulfilling, or at least more informative. Or maybe it wouldn't have mattered, because the real problem isn't the itinerary so much as the company.

Between towns, Hunter tries to will himself into hallucination as he looks out into the undulating, endless desert. Maybe they could get stranded here, so that they would have to band together and become real adventurers, lopping off the tops of saguaro in search of water, sucking rattlesnake venom out of punctured thighs. They would discover their inner strength and carry one another (metaphorically, physically if necessary) toward salvation—an oasis, or the road, or an uninhabited cave. Inside the car, it is easy to lose that will to survive. The world blurs by in the window like an unpleasant dream.

On the morning of the second day, he receives a phone call from Jack. Amber is in the shower and the others are getting dressed. Hunter steps out into the hallway to answer.

"You checked out," Jack says.

"I told you I wasn't done."

"Yeah, okay, sure. But I'm done. You understand? Your mother and I, we are both done." A cleaning cart parks at the end of the hall, a tiny Latina assiduously avoiding eye contact.

"What, am I supposed to apologize? You still want *me* to feel bad?" Hunter says.

"I don't care what you do."

"What if I got kidnapped? Or killed? You would have just left me there."

"This is what you have to understand: I tried to help you and you didn't want my help. So you are on your own. Let the whole damn thing crumble to the ground. Just do not come back here looking for sympathy. I've instructed your mother not to help either."

Jacks hangs up before Hunter can respond.

SITTING NEXT TO PAUL in a diner in Ash Fork, Arizona, Hunter keeps an eye on the car—and Kait—through the window, prepares himself to spring into action if anyone attempts to steal her. Amber is wearing a tank top, her shoulders shaded with muscular definition, like she used to work out three times a week but recently took a break. Her skin looks sticky in the heat, she breathes through slightly parted lips, her nose irritated by the dry air. She is not Kait. She is young and alive. Unscarred, undamaged. Pulsing and energetic. Under normal circumstances, he wouldn't ogle her, would have more tact than that, but she is the first woman with whom he has spent any time since Jessa, and Jessa does not count because Hunter is trying to believe that the Jessa incident never happened. Amber does not look at him, which makes the ogling more discrete but also more discouraging. She rarely looks at anyone besides Austin. When Austin excuses himself to go to the restroom, she watches the swinging door in the rear of the restaurant, doesn't say a word until he returns.

The diner sounds like every other diner in the history of the world; silverware scraping against cheap dishes, a squealing kitchen door flapping open, unnecessarily loud conversations, a hodge-podge of oldies and Motown on the jukebox. The vinyl seat sticks to the backs of Hunter's legs; he peels them up, the sucking sound audible to everyone in the booth.

Paul, drinking the first of his four daily coffees, says, "Good trip so far," his throat rumbling. Hunter nods. Amber nods. She does not look away from Austin. Her fingernails are brittle and unevenly gnawed. Eyes brown like loafers. She looks much more attractive when she's not smiling than she does when she's smiling.

Paul twists a coffee stirrer between his teeth. "Your grandmother and I were on a lot of drugs back when we passed through here," he says. "I ever tell you about when we were in Nevada? In the desert, it was a hundred and ten. And we were all doped up on quaaludes, so we stripped down. Naked as a pair of shaved cats. Ran as far into the desert as we could until it hurt our feet too much to touch the sand." Austin pokes Amber in the ribs, gives her a look like he's picturing her naked now, and she presses her shoulder into his. "Only, once we got out there, we couldn't figure out how to get back. Burned my feet up real good that day," he says, arms crossed over his chest, a hollow laugh rattling out of him.

"I guess that's not on the agenda either," Hunter says.

"Naw, my partying days are over." He digs a poker chip out of his pocket, shows it to Hunter. "Sober six years," he says. That explains why no one has even suggested going to a bar on this trip. It explains the rosary that dangles out of Paul's pocket while driving, his fingers rolling over the beads during long silences. "Cold turkey.

Ask her," he says, gesturing toward Amber with his knife. "I used to be crazy."

"We weren't allowed to see him much," she says. "Me and my brother."

Austin swirls pancake bits in a pool of syrup. Hunter has already finished his meal. He hears Kait criticizing him for eating too fast. "Why'd you quit?" Hunter says, partly curious, but partly because he knows Paul wants him to ask.

Over the rim of his mug, Paul says, "Quit the day my wife disappeared."

"She left because of the drugs?"

"Vanished. Like one day she was there and the next day she wasn't."

"Where'd she go?" A dumb question, he realizes after he asks it.

"They say she's dead, but I never seen no body."

Amber squeezes Austin's hand, and he shakes loose so that he can keep chopping at his short stack. Paul watches the steam rising out of his mug. Hunter keeps an eye on the car, Kait's ashes pulling on him like a full moon on the sea.

BACK ON THE ROAD, Amber sleeps with her head on Austin's shoulder, Hunter remembering the exact feel and chamomile smell of Kait on his shoulder, the nights he sat perfectly still, his leg going numb beneath her while she slept on the couch and he struggled not to disturb her, remembering the times he shrugged her away or intentionally dropped something to wake her up. He turns the radio down, apologizes to Paul for prying about his wife.

"You didn't make her disappear." Paul turns the radio back up—John Prine now, singing about the hole in daddy's arm where all the money goes. The engine's drone sounds like someone snoring. Paul plows through a pothole and Amber's head jostles like a puppet's, but she does not wake up ("That girl could fall asleep on a picket fence," Paul says). She is sprawled across the seat, her shirt pulling up, and Hunter watches the strip of exposed skin above her waistband in the rearview, pictures his lips pressed against it, swallowing her whole. "Her name was Annalisa. Everyone called her Anna, except me, I used the full name." Paul fingers the rosary. "I left the house to buy some more gin and when I come back ten minutes later, she was gone. No note, no struggle, nothing. Like she never existed."

"Police?"

"Tried to pin it on me, but no matter how crazy I ever got, I never would have hurt her."

"They didn't look for her?"

"Said they did, but what the hell are they doing now? Who ever heard of just giving up on finding a person?" He stomps on the brake, skids to a stop behind a slowing eighteen-wheeler. Amber jolts forward, but Austin catches her before she slams into the back of Paul's seat. Hunter slaps his hands on the dashboard, his breath rushing out of him. This is exactly the problem with driving—even on an empty road, you can die mangled in an accident. "Didn't see that one coming," Paul says.

. . .

THE ROAD CARRIES THEM through the Petrified Forest National Park, a place that defines desolation, too barren to even look like Earth. Hunter sees tumbleweeds for the first time in his life. Then the second, third, fourth, and fifth times, until he stops noticing them. The wind here is stronger than he would have expected, sandblasting them. The land itself seems to reject life. There are creatures, naturally; there are creatures everywhere in the world, even in the worst possible places. Some turn up dead on the roadside—armadillos and snakes, victims of drivers like Paul; even though he looks like he is focusing, quietly staring down the center of the road, he doesn't seem to actually see anything. In the distance, something that looks like a jackrabbit skitters away from the road. Then there is nothing besides rocks, ranging in hue from dark gray to lavender to fiery red, so that the world appears radioactive. Rust colors set against a brilliant blue backdrop so striking it looks fake, like real life digitally enhanced and then posted online. Conical hills loom behind piled stones, the landscape looking simultaneously haphazard and meticulously planned.

They pull over because Amber wants to take a few pictures. Paul snaps a shot of Amber and Austin, arms wrapped around each other's waists. Behind them, the world looks necrotic.

Hunter wants to take a picture of Kait here, but he cannot risk revealing his lie; if the others feel betrayed by his deception, they might leave him here, exile him to the desert for the rest of his life. He mouths an apology to her through the rear windshield, wishes for the others to disappear too so he can dig her out and hold her again, if only for a moment.

The sun feels like it is drilling into Hunter's skull, his head throbbing already, battalions of sweat marching down his face and his back. He squats behind the car, sheltering in the only shade he can find but afraid to touch down on the asphalt. Amber lays a T-shirt on the ground and sits a few feet away from him, legs folded up against her chest, shorts cutting into the tops of her thighs, sweat pooling up on the back of her neck, on her knees. He wants to taste it. Austin settles between them. Paul strolls down the road while they gaze out into the distance as if willing something to appear.

"Your wife really isn't worried about you?" Austin says.

She would be in abject panic at this point, would tell him this is the dumbest thing he's ever done. Would deduct a hundred points from him, even though deductions are a violation of the rules. "She's okay with it," Hunter says. "Kind of a free spirit. Did I tell you she paints in her spare time?"

"If you ever do something like this, I'll kill you," Amber says to Austin. "That's how people end up getting chopped up and stuffed into trunks." Her hand rests on Austin's knee, his legs stretched straight out in front of him. She caresses his bare skin lightly, twists a leg hair between her fingers.

Amber sees Hunter craning his neck to look for Paul, and she says, "Don't worry about him. He wanders sometimes." He's looking for his wife. He knows Paul is afraid that if he doesn't keep checking, he'll drive right past her.

"Hey, let's race," Austin says. Hunter wants to say something about his heart condition, but then Austin adds: "Like your grampa and gramma did." By the end of the sentence, he has already removed his shirt and flung it to the ground. Amber shrugs and pulls her tank top over her head.

"Won't we get burnt?" Hunter says. "I mean, wasn't that the point of the story?"

Austin has stripped down to his socks and boxers. "We'll bring our shoes with us," he says. Amber wriggles out of her shorts, hips like a pendulum. Her underwear is white with a yellow smiley face on the crotch. Above the face are the words HI THERE!

"What if Paul comes back?"

Amber shrugs, unhooks her bra and her breasts droop slightly, nipples turned outward and pointing in opposite directions; bikini tan lines make the breasts look alien on her. She throws her bra in Hunter's face and says, "You're gonna lose if you don't stop talking." She and Austin finish stripping, their bodies fully exposed. Austin chases her out into the desert. Hunter yanks off his pants, tosses his shirt aside as he begins running, and soon he's streaking fully nude through the sand, like running on a skillet. Austin actually looks better nude than he does in his ill-fitting clothes, like he used to be in great shape before he discovered beer and late-night takeout, like he'll be able to work out for a couple months before his inevitable wedding with Amber and suddenly he'll have his old body back. Powerful calves drive Austin past Amber, and he slaps her butt as he passes. Amber's body ripples on each step, ponytailed hair bouncing, breasts swaying and allowing Hunter to peek at them as they expose themselves at her side. He doesn't feel the burning, at least not as a pressing concern. It's there, but there in a way he can live with, like a squeaky front door, like an ingrown hair on his arm. Wind tearing at his chest and his genitals, he chases until he's alongside Amber. He grabs her arm, pulls her with him. Just ahead, Austin is hopping on one foot, slowing down so quickly that they plow into him, tumbling into the sand, which at first feels like being submerged in a vat of boiling oil, but then feels something like normal. The three of them tangled, they're all laughing despite the pain, because of the pain. Delirious. The heat, the feel of skin on skin. Amber's bare leg draped across his shin, each exhalation of her breath tickling his cheek. She doesn't think twice about this level of intimacy because he's not even on her radar; a married man, physically the opposite of her boyfriend, not much older but older enough that he seems old.

They push back up to their feet, Hunter twisting to hide his erection, Austin not noticing, and Hunter realizes he forgot his shoes. Austin lends him one of his, and together, they hop back toward the car, Amber walking between them to keep them balanced.

Paul is standing at the car when they return, twirling the keys on his index finger. He has folded their clothes. Eyeballing them, he says, "My fault for telling the story."

PAUL SAYS THE TRIP has been running over budget, so they all share a single hotel room at night. Although Hunter could pay for them to have separate rooms, he would rather deal with the snoring and sleeptalking and clutter of a crowded room than ever spend another night alone in a hotel room. While they all get ready for bed, he steps into the hallway to catch up on his missed correspondence; poor reception in the desert had prevented him from checking in on his phone during the day. Willow has left several messages, via voice, e-mail, and text. She is concerned that he hasn't contacted anyone or updated Facebook in days. In her e-mail, she writes, "You think I haven't thought about it? But you can never run fast enough." She ends the note by saying, "He's not good at showing it, but your father is worried too."

An acquaintance from high school has left a comment on his Facebook wall saying, "Hey, bro, where u been? No pics for a week . . . u didn't kill urself did you?" An e-mail from Sherry arrives with no text, but a subject line that says "i told you" and three attached photos: they've pillaged his house, doors kicked off hinges, food smeared on the walls, windows left open with rain puddling on the carpets. It's hard to tell from the images the extent of the damage or exactly what they've taken, if anything, but the thing that is clear is that they have murdered his home. For what? Spite? His legs crumble beneath him and he feels himself being turned inside out, suddenly he is weightless and looking down at his useless body on the hallway floor and thinking, What is this person supposed to do now? Where is this inside-out person going to go when his trip is over, why did he ever buy into the dumb dream of owning land and having the perfect life with the perfect wife, and why didn't he ever consider how easily it can all be stripped away without his permission, without the signing of forms in triplicate, without setting up a contingency plan, without reason, without time to establish a so-called *support system*, without that support system there to *support* him now, without some sign of a benevolent god, without any fucking reason, without a single warning that no matter what he did there was the distinct possibility that his entire life could be ruined in seconds, without him ever realizing that his desires and his will have *no bearing* on the way the world turns out because the universe does what it wants when it wants and his only so-called option is to brace himself for the worst and then when the worst happens to deal with it by saying something not-comforting like *well, that could have been worse.*

It's impossible to calculate how long he lies there waiting to be pieced back together, but at some point he reinhabits his body and he manages to sit upright and he sends Sherry a text message to tell her he's going to call the police. Because that seems like the thing he should do here—call the police. Sherry responds instantly: "Ha!" she says. "Lol!" she says. "Go head call them," she says. "They're looking for u." She sends a half-dozen more messages to gloat about her victory, to tell him she has called the police herself, they have a friend on the force who's going to fix this situation, and although Hunter hasn't committed any identifiable crimes, he still tenses at the thought of being pursued, wishes he could change his story in the hotel room, telling his companions that he really is a fugitive on the lam, and he needs to know he can trust them. He can weave an elaborate backstory, a criminal enterprise begun for noble pur- poses, trying to feed his family, then a failed partnership, a betrayal. He could be mysterious and dangerous. He could make veiled ref- erences to violence and deals gone wrong. He could duck in his seat when they pass police cruisers and always sit with his back to a wall in restaurants to prevent sneak attacks.

He returns to the room, lies on a cot positioned between the two beds, unzips his bag and presses a hand against Kait, the cube cold and unyielding.

Hunter awakes at five-thirty, the sun framing his face on the pillow. Paul is already gone on his walk. Amber and Austin are asleep, her arm snug around his waist. Hunter drags his bag into the bathroom with him. He sets Kait on the counter while he brushes his teeth and whispers to her that these people might be a little strange, but isn't everybody, and anyway they're nice. Tells her she might like them. Tells her there's nothing going on with Amber, he's not going to do anything, she's just friendly, and that's how girls that age are. Tells her he's sorry he's been ignoring her, but it just seems easier this way.

He puts her back in the bag before he showers. Post-shower, he hears heavy breathing on the other side of the door, a headboard rocking, Amber telling Austin to be quiet. If this were a porno film, he could walk into the room and join them, no questions asked. He thinks about peeking but worries he'll get caught and ruin their fun. He listens on the other side of the door, imagines the look on Amber's face during orgasm, the feel of her tongue in his mouth. After a few minutes, the noise settles. When he emerges from the bathroom, they're both fully clothed and pretending to be asleep.

SEVENTEEN

I f you'd only known. A cliché among clichés, but also the sort
of thing you find yourself thinking constantly.

If you'd known she wouldn't make it to thirty, you would
have crammed a lifetime of loving into the brief window when you
knew her. When you're young, it's easy to be arrogant and assume
you have unlimited time, but it only takes one day to feel like you've
aged sixty years. You wouldn't have allowed her to waste so much
energy dusting bookcases or searching for the right brand of high-
fiber cereal or stressing about properly folding her work slacks,
because that sort of stuff was unimportant *even then*, but now it
seems tragic that she spent so much of her existence worried about
things that had no bearing on the outcome of her life.

And you wouldn't have wasted so much time staring blankly

at the TV. You wouldn't have sneaked in a half hour of playing video games while she showered; instead, you would have sat on a stool beside the shower chatting with her, followed her to the bedroom, helped her pick an outfit, or even told her *forget the outfit, we're staying in tonight*, the sort of take-charge thing Paul Newman would have said to Joanne Woodward.

IF YOU'D ONLY KNOWN, you would never have allowed the Month of Being Romantic to expire, but one day you ran out of ideas and were tired and just wanted things to be easy again, so it was over. If you'd known, you would have continued giving her what she needed, which was an occasional Big Gesture, rather than relying on steady adequacy to keep you afloat.

If you'd known she would be dead by thirty, you wouldn't have envied her successful life while yours was a ragged mess. You watched her getting ready for work and you were proud of her, knew you were lucky to have a wife who had figured things out and was making money and doing something useful, but also you had to admit there was a little kernel of bitterness in your reaction, because you wanted that self-assurance and accomplishment, but never knew how to find it.

You wouldn't have burned any energy being angry about stupid things, like her tendency to pick at her teeth in public, or the way she sometimes talked over your favorite TV shows. You wouldn't have compared her to other women you saw on the beach, or spent any time thinking that even though she was beautiful, she could look *even better* if only she lost three, four, five pounds, if she stopped with the white chocolate and the sweetened iced tea.

You wouldn't have watched the women on TV and thought, *why can't her arms be just a little more toned* or *why can't her eyes be iridescent like the ones on that woman in the cell-phone commercials?*

Instead of trying to improve her, you would have perfected yourself, would have devoted yourself to loving her better, giving her the life she deserved but never got, organized yourself and pursued an actual career so you could afford all the things she dreamed of owning and doing. Got into shape and paid for a trendy haircut and bought stylish new clothes. Tried a little harder to get along with her family instead of grimly enduring the gatherings and then insulting them on the drive home. Taken some personal agency and made an effort to be a better, more likable, friendlier person instead of who you are. Would have convinced her to work less overtime and instead go on spontaneous trips to romantic weekend resorts in Cape May and Virginia Beach. And you would have saved enough cash to help her see the whole world before she died, because the narrative of her life at this point is not a love story, but rather a tale of unfulfilled dreams.

The future is nothing but the steady unraveling of the order we try to impose on the present. If you had known this sooner, you would have stopped waiting for life to happen to you and taken control of it instead, would have made important decisions rather than avoiding them. When strangers asked you about children, because strangers universally seemed to believe that the status of your wife's womb was their business, you danced around the answer, said you didn't know about kids. Maybe eventually, someday. But kids! Yes, of course kids! Kids with freckles and braces. Kids with asthma and pointy elbows like their mother's, kids with frequent ear infections and allergies to peanuts, kids whose noses curved upward at the tip, kids whose fat little fingers would charm you to no end even though you've never had a moment of interest in the fat little fingers of other people's offspring. Kids with precocious ideas about religion, rebellious kids with bizarre piercings, loving kids, beautiful kids, homely kids, kids who broke the state record in 200-meter hurdles, kids who couldn't walk, kids with bad hearts and kids with powerful lungs, kids with superpowers, kids who could read minds and could communicate telepathically with animals, kids who composed symphonies when they were five, kids who represented the entire world of possibilities, all the permutations of yourselves, from 99 percent of you to 99 percent of her, kids you would love regardless of what they looked like or how efficiently their bodies processed lactose or what talents they had, because in their postures and their expressions you would see her, and in their voices you would hear her, and in every movement there would be a century of her genetic history mapped onto them. Hundreds of kids, just to see what they'd look like. Just to hold them and smell them and dry their tears on your sleeve. To repopulate the earth with facsimiles of Kait.

EIGHTEEN

Austin and Hunter take five minutes to dress themselves in the morning, and Amber is ready soon after, wearing jeans and a T-shirt, her hair pulled into a ponytail. On days when Kait's self-esteem was particularly low, it could take over an hour before she felt ready to leave the house, trying on a dozen different outfits in front of a full-length mirror and engaging in a complex series of tugs and wipes and corrective smoothing of hair and clothes and makeup such that she looked like a baseball manager signaling for a runner to steal second, a process which sometimes ended with half of her clothes balled up in a heap in the corner of the bedroom. Hunter had gotten in the habit of helping her dress, sitting in the bedroom and talking to her while she applied mascara, and laying potential outfits on the bed for her while she dried her hair.

When she dressed and posed in front of the mirror he would stand behind her, arms wrapped around her waist, and before she had the chance to start thinking negative thoughts and insulting her body, he would say, "You look amazing in that," which was true, but which didn't always convince her, especially because his proclivity toward sarcasm made even his most sincere comments seem like they could be insults. But sometimes it did convince her, and on those occasions she would turn, kiss him on the lips and say, "You just scored yourself twenty points, Meatball."

SINCE PAUL HAD CEDED control of the trip to Amber, the group has been visiting more traditional tourist venues—what Hunter keeps calling *tourist traps*, which comment doesn't faze Amber, who says, "Well, we *are* tourists." It was inevitable, then, that they would end up at a place like Wild Bill's Wild West Outpost, about ten miles south of Flagstaff, Arizona. It is one of dozens of such places in this area of the country, theme parks designed to re-create the Old West experience, built on the graves of actual ghost towns. The whole park is centered on one dusty main street that runs through what is supposed to be the heart of a bustling western town. There are actors dressed in period costume— prostitutes, drunks, prospectors, sinister looking men in black, gallant and friendly deputies—moseying among the tourists. Unlike at the Renaissance Faire, most of the visitors here are not in costume, aside from little boys with plastic sheriff's badges clipped to their shirts, but this place still reminds him of the Faire, in that it's trying to help people relive a time that was probably actually not all that great a time to live in, especially if, like many of the patrons, one is

not a white, land-owning Christian male. Everything is scrubbed a
little too clean, everything is a little too nice.

Amber and Austin picked this place because they said they were
tired of looking at random things, and they wanted to go somewhere they could *do something*. Paul grumbled that the only thing
they would do here is pay attendance to look at different random
things, but he obliged anyway, and so now he's sitting in the saloon gulping from a mason jar full of root beer while the others
investigate the town. Amber and Austin race from one building to
the next, poking their heads into the doorway of the bank before
turning away, taking one step into the sheriff's office but refus-
ing to progress any further, as if allergic to whatever lies inside.
They want to be here, but they also want to fast-forward through
it; they're impatient and eager and youthful and they still have faith
that something better is waiting for them down the road. Hunter
is holding them back, because he walks into each building, reads
the plaques and the descriptions of the exhibits, examines the guns,
nodding knowingly at nearby men who look like gun aficionados.
During the Month of Being a Man he went to the shooting range
once, fired a Desert Eagle, handled a variety of other firearms,
dipped his arms into a stockpile of ammo. He liked it, actually, felt
the lightning strike of machismo when he fired, relished the tearing of the paper target's shoulder, imagined himself keeping a gun
under his pillow and defending his home from thieves, becoming a
cable news hero for administering vigilante justice on home invad-
ers, hauling a shotgun out into the woods, and dropping a moose
big enough to feed him and Kait for months. Imagined sitting in
his backyard cleaning his gun, telling Brutus about the mechanics

of it, taking the brothers to the range with him to demonstrate his pulsing virility. Wanted to be able to say things like *the Glock is a good piece and has cheaper mags, but I prefer the combat accuracy of a Walther*. But Kait was never angrier than the day he told her he'd fired a gun. There was no fight or simmering rage, but a firm declaration: "If you buy a gun, you are moving out," which marked the end of the Month of Being a Man.

Amber enters the sheriff's office, tugs on Hunter's sleeve, says, "Don't tell me you're one of those people who read everything."

"Someone spent a lot of time writing this." People glance at paintings and valuable artifacts and race ahead, unconcerned about establishing anything like meaning or context, propelled by a desire to be done before they accidentally learned something.

"Me and Austin get souvenirs from every state we see," she says in response to a question Hunter did not ask.

"I'm not holding you hostage here," Hunter says, still eyeing the gun. Finally, she says, "Come find us when you're done," and then he's alone again.

Probably the most authentic feature of the town is the dustiness, the swirling dirt, the choking particles in every breath. The boarded sidewalk groans beneath Hunter's feet. The sun looks distant today, but it is boring into him as if pursuing a vendetta.

One of the actors—a miner type—shouts for help. A thief has shoved him to the ground and is running off with a sack of gold nuggets. The sheriff cuts him off on his horse, and the outlaw turns back the other way, but he's hemmed in by a deputy. A crowd gathers along the perimeter, children in the front row cat-calling the evildoer. The sheriff, his mustache perfectly trimmed, his outfit sinlessly clean, tells the thief to give it up. The outlaw reaches toward his hip and both sheriff and deputy fire their guns. The outlaw drops to his death. When the miner retrieves his sack, the crowd applauds. The sheriff jumps down from his horse and struts around the perimeter, shaking hands with the patrons. Having just witnessed a faux murder, most people disperse, returning to their picnics and stepping over the dead man as if he is a fallen branch.

Hunter visits a building called the Vault, and inside he finds five rows of wooden folding chairs aligned in front of a projection screen. Only one other person is in here, a wheelchair-bound grandfather who has fallen asleep in the front row. The movie mixes historical reenactments with staid shots of academics talking in front of bookshelves and continually cuts to stock footage of cupped hands sifting through a pile of gold nuggets. The voice-over is too high-pitched, the voice of an old man who probably works for the local historical society and can trace his lineage in this town back two hundred years. The narration deifies those who founded the settlement, calls them courageous and heroic, spending ten minutes on the owner of the park, a guy named Frank Frankmann (a direct descendant of an outlaw named Frankmann, famous for having survived a scuffle with Wild Bill Hickok), declaring him a visionary and a leader for our times and detailing the genius innovations he has pioneered in the historical recreation industry. Hunter remembers how awful these filmstrips at historic sites invariably are, how they are a poor substitute for actually interacting with a place, how bizarrely hagiographic they are concerning the owners, as if the visitors care that Frank Frankmann graduated cum laude from Arizona State. The video is dull like church, dull like watching football with the in-laws.

After the film, he finds Paul in the saloon watching a G-rated burlesque show, which mainly involves women in ankle-length skirts making terribly labored double entendres (i.e., "Whaddya call a cowboy that's got no legs? An easy lay!"). But the old folks are laughing and the kids get French fries (aka *fried taters*) so they're happy. The unfortunate thing about this show's obvious low budget is that the women would all look much more attractive if they were just dressed in their regular clothes and makeup instead of the costumes. Hunter and Paul sit at the bar with their backs turned to the stage.

Paul offers Hunter a shot, throws one back himself. The shot is just corn syrup, which is about equally as disgusting as straight whiskey; Hunter holds it but does not drink it. "Can't drink much more root beer before I get sick," Paul says. Hunter orders a lemonade, which is served in a cup shaped like a barrel. "I know those two ain't having any fun," Paul says, pausing to do another shot.

"Why'd you come with them?"

"Just remembering is all. Out on the road again, like it was before." The burlesque show reaches intermission and a piano player plinks through a version of "She'll Be Coming 'Round the Mountain." Children square-dance beside the stage.

"This goddamn song. Fifth goddamn time I've heard it," he says, peering back over his shoulder. He grabs a handful of peanuts from a bowl on the bar and crunches into them.

"What would you say if you found your wife after so long?"

Paul inhales as if prepping for a deep-sea dive. "Look, I know I'm never gonna find her. It's been six years. But you got to look *everywhere*," he says. "And this is all I've got."

"But if you did find her. I think I would make a joke. Like—Sorry I've been gone so long!" Paul clinks his wedding ring against the bar rail. Hunter says, "You know, like you're the one who was missing. To lighten the mood."

"I got to piss like nobody's business," Paul says. "Go and find them others so we can get on the road."

IN THE CAR, TO fill a yawning chasm of silence—by mid-day they've run out of things to say to one another, and the two in the backseat are nodding off—Hunter announces he is going to call his wife. The silence is dangerous, an invitation to reflection and to questions. Silence is the greatest threat to the walls Hunter has been trying to erect around his sadness, a hungry wolf that will blow his defenses down in a single breath. He dials her cell phone and speaks to her voice mail. He has left her a half-dozen messages, and soon her mailbox will be full. He mimics a conversation. Says, "Hey, lover," and laughs. Says, "How's the dog?" because in this version of his life, he has a two-year-old Akita named Oliver. Says he can't wait to see the new furniture she's bought. Discusses the neighbors, Bob and Sandy, a nice couple even though they seem like gossips and Bob is a neat freak. Says he'll cook her a gourmet meal when he gets home, she deserves a break after taking care of the house by herself. Tells her about the various stops he's made and says he'll be home soon. Says, "I miss you too."

AUSTIN WANTS TO SEE the inside of a cave, so they're all standing in line for a guided tour of a cave. "I hope we see bats," he says. He is wearing a Batman T-shirt and plaid cargo shorts, both pockets stuffed with bags of peanuts that he's been shelling on their walk, a trail leading back to the car. It's hard to believe he is about to become an insurance agent. He grins constantly, not in a stupid way, but in a clever, quippy college-boy way. His laugh is hearty and strong, the laugh of a lumberjack, or the contractor at the neighborhood bar. Hunter does not remember if he ever looked or felt like that when he was twenty-two. Amber walks with them, her arm hooked around Austin's, but she won't enter the cave because she's claustrophobic.

A group of twenty people single-files behind a guide. Hunter is in the back of the line, so he can barely hear the guide, still does not understand the distinction between stalactites and stalagmites, does not know the origins of the water trickling in through the walls. Someone asks if there are bears in the cave, and the guide says, "No, they spend the day exploring people's homes while we're in here." Hunter is the only one who laughs.

The walkways are narrow and uneven, the walls jutting out at odd angles. Now and then, they pass piles of ceramic bones meant to replicate fossils that were discovered here decades ago. Austin walks with head upturned like a child catching snowflakes on his tongue. He points toward a particularly dank corner of the cave and says he's spotted a bat, but it is only a shadow. The walkways clank beneath their feet, metal girders that make it sound like a brigade of robots is on the march. Cameras flash like lightning. Some people are photographing every individual rock. A middle-aged man walks with a video camera extended in front of his face, and Hunter wonders under what circumstances this man will ever watch a video of motionless rock, wonders how many even duller videos the man probably keeps stored on his computer, wonders who is forced to watch these videos with him, or if he watches them alone.

The guide leads them down a small flight of stairs into a lower chamber of the cave, which he assures them is totally safe, an assurance that makes Hunter feel deeply unsafe. He says, "Down here, I'm going to let you experience something most people in the world never do—total darkness." Even though he warns them he's about to turn off the lights, someone still gasps when he flicks the switch.

A black curtain drops over their world.

Hunter listens to Paul's breathing, a slight rattle on his inhalations, as if his larynx has come loose and needs to be screwed back into place. Austin shuffles his feet and cracks his knuckles constantly. Someone tries to take a picture of nothingness, and the guide asks everyone to please stop taking pictures. Just exist in the tranquility for a moment, he says. The mucky ground seems to rise around them as if to suck them down into the earth. Hunter itches away the feeling of bugs on his arms, his neck. A clump of dirt shakes loose from the ceiling and lands on his shoulder. The subterranean chill is like being submerged in a grave. Kait's absence throbs in his head.

The lights flick back on, and the relief is palpable. Nearly everyone pulls cell phones out of their pockets to check for missed calls or to add a little more light to the cave. Hunter's phone tells him he has received four e-mails so far today. Tossing peanuts in his mouth as they leave, Austin says he thinks he heard a bat's sonar when they were in the dark. Paul, moving stiffly, says, "Well, I'm never doing that again."

IN THE PARK'S PICNIC area, they purchase sandwiches and sit at a bench to eat them, Amber and Austin across from the two widowers. Austin eats amiably, gesturing with his sandwich to make points while talking, offering his potato chips to everyone, seeming to find joy in the acts of chewing and swallowing. Loud smacking and chewing, one of Kait's pet peeves, admittedly unpleasant, but not ill-intentioned. Amber is a nibbler. This sandwich could last her all day if Austin weren't here. Her teeth are shockingly white, so white they look new, a stark contrast to her tanned face. She leans down over the table to bite into her sandwich, as if dipping into a trough, her hair falling down over her face, a blonde veil. Paul grinds his food, works methodically. Overhead there are exactly zero clouds. Birds of prey circle above, a prodigious sight, their massive wingspans unfurled, none of the frantic flapping of a sparrow, the talons that seem, even from afar, large enough to lift Hunter and carry him away.

Amber passes half her sandwich to Austin, who acts as the group's garbage disposal. She asks Hunter what he's reading, and he says it's an e-mail from Kait.

"When's the last time you saw her?" Amber asks.

"A while." Almost two months, almost three thousand miles.

"What about your families? Are they upset you're leaving?"

"Nah, we don't really get along with her side," he says. "Part of the reason for the move. And my parents have a summer house in LA, so they'll come visit."

"So at least you've got somebody out there."

"Yeah, my dad works a lot but we see him sometimes. And my mom and Kait, they're like best friends, basically." Paul finishes his sandwich, excuses himself for a short walk.

"Yeah, we're lucky too," Amber says, and launches into a story about how she and Austin both mesh well in each other's families, how lucky they are to get along with their future in-laws, and Hunter stops listening once he realizes she only asked about his life as a pretense to talk about hers.

"I don't think I could leave all my friends behind," Austin says, interrupting Amber.

"I'll have the band eventually. Most of my friends from home, I lost touch with them anyway." Hunter crumbles up his sandwich wrapper and tosses it toward a nearby trashcan, watches it rim out and land in the dirt. "It happens after college. Everyone gets distracted."

Austin says that's not going to happen to him and his friends, even though Hunter knows it has happened to every group of college friends that has ever existed. Hunter somewhat admires Austin's naïve optimism, even though he knows one day Austin is going to be tossed headfirst into the real world and find out that things end all the time without first asking permission. He tries to listen while refreshing his e-mail in hopes of an update on his house, which he knows is probably rotting now and needs to be saved soon if it's to be saved at all.

The next morning, in Prescott Valley, Arizona, Paul spreads the map out on the bed before taking a walk. While Austin and Amber attack the map with a marker, Hunter thinks again about the explorers who walked off the edge of the known world into new territories and mapped them. Everything on the planet, above the sea anyway, has been discovered, explored and analyzed, but what does that mean for him? Even though others have already seen everything before he has, he doesn't know anything about it. He's still charging through the curtains of his own limited experience into unfamiliar territory, filling in the blank spaces, because how can he know anything about anything until he's seen it for himself? And so he thinks maybe that what Kait wanted out of travel wasn't to broaden her mind or to find herself or any of that stuff; what she wanted was to be with Hunter, but in different places. She wanted to see the sights, but the real impetus was her love for him and her desire to share as wide a variety of experiences as possible. Or maybe what she wanted was for them to record the nuances of the earth together, because their map would be totally different from any other in existence, just like the unique map Austin and Amber are creating together. They could invent a universe that belonged exclusively to them. The world that is unveiling itself to Hunter on this trip, the world he is creating for himself, is desolate and pointless and not all that remarkable. But to explore together, to fill a globe with shared experiences and personal landmarks—not museums, but picnic tables where they had a romantic lunch, not goofy tourist attractions, but memories of the night they discovered a quaint neighborhood café in a European village—is to make meaning where there was no meaning before. What she wanted, he thinks, was for them to have that sense of discovery Amber and Austin have, to be oblivious to the reality that by virtue of the existence of maps and pamphlets and public restrooms and long lines, their vacations are not unique but are in fact mass manufactured. But then again, maybe not, because it's the first time these two specific people are experiencing this specific event. Kait obsessively documented firsts, from the big ones (first kiss, first date) to the idiosyncratic ones (first time they went to the zoo together, first time eating soup without an appendix), and every trip they took would have presented another series of firsts she could add to the list.

The map on the bed is nearly unrecognizable under the marker's hieroglyphics, a love letter written between Amber and Austin across the world.

Hunter lingers in the room when they all go to breakfast, says he's not feeling great, has lost his appetite. As soon as they're gone, he digs Kait out of his bag and places her on the desk, opens the blinds so she can feel the sunlight. It has been almost a week since he's been alone with her. He promises it won't be so long next time. Kneels behind her and takes a photo of them in the desktop mirror, posts it on Facebook. No caption—he doesn't want to give away his location.

Still on his knees, he rests a hand on top of her, tells her about the trip, everything she's missed. Some of the finish has been scraped off the cube from banging around the trunk, scratches and dings gouged out of the surface, scuffed like a used-up baseball. He tells her he's sorry their vacation is ruined, knows this isn't what she wanted—to wander around the southwestern US sealed inside his bag while Hunter sees a series of arbitrary landmarks. Nothing about this trip resembles their dreams aside from the fact that they are away from home. The regret tingles in his jaw like a heart attack.

Lost in his mourning, he does not realize until too late that his companions have returned from breakfast. Austin and Amber maintain a frightened, awkward distance, rooted in the doorway, but Paul stands over him, says, "Who's in the box?"

He tells them they're his grandmother's ashes, but that lie crumbles quickly. They keep pushing, and he initially demurs, says there's no story to tell. Pulling Kait down with him onto the floor, he makes them ask several times before filling them in on every detail: the ectopic pregnancy, the insurance money, the Facebook photos, the broken-down car, the buses, the scorned Dixons in his house, and the confrontation with Jack. He tells them Kait would have really liked the three of them, would have loved Amber's enthusiasm and Austin's sense of humor and Paul's devotion to his missing wife.

They interrogate him for another twenty minutes, and he answers their questions as honestly as he can, giving them a rough outline of the trip so far and telling them everything they want to know about Kait. When silence descends over the room again, he takes it as his cue to leave, putting Kait back in his bag and hoisting it on his shoulder. "I'm sorry," he says, the only explanation he can offer, inadequate as it is.

NINETEEN

You're a single man again. Some men think this is a dream come true, like to joke with other men about how they can't stand their wives, who are nagging and old and boring, and they dream of being back on the prowl, making up for lost time with nubile and enthusiastic young women, but you haven't been single in almost a decade, and being single when you're thirty is so vastly different from being single when you're twenty that they barely qualify as related experiences.

Some days, you cannot stop thinking about having to live another fifty years like this.

Now and then, you thought about the girls from your past. Fantasized about running into them on the street, striking up a conversation and going out to grab coffee. Finding out they're single and they've been missing you all this time. Showing them how much funnier and more mature you are than you used to be. Feeling what it's like to be flirted with again, because you couldn't remember the last time anyone, anywhere, had flirted with you. Kait didn't know how to flirt, felt uncomfortable trying to act sexy, and even though you knew she loved you and you thought she achieved sexiness without any effort, it wasn't quite the same as sitting down to lunch with a woman who wanted to seduce you. It would be gratifying to know that you still represented a viable option for at least some women somewhere. And, okay, the fantasizing wasn't always so innocent. You thought that if you were ever single again, you would enjoy it in a way you didn't in college, because you were awkward then and didn't go to parties, and so you missed out on a crucial element of the university experience. In the aftermath of Kait's death, Uncle Bobby tried to cheer you up, said something about how you're free to go out on the town again, and you played along, laughing, but then here's what you thought: *actually, maybe he's right.*

EVERY MAY, SHE HAD to use up her accumulated vacation days, burning them all off before they expired, and for two weeks you found yourself spending every free moment with her. She crammed the days full of outings and expectations—movie dates, day trips to Amish country, nights out at swanky restaurants, repainting various rooms in your house, an interminable series of chores so that sometimes it felt like your life was devoted to running errands. Your life became regimented and overwhelmingly active, and she kept saying, "This is so much fun," and you nodded, because it was fun at first and because you knew this time was important to her, knew she sometimes felt disconnected from the real world when she was working every day. But you found yourself sometimes wishing for extra space, thinking it would be nice to just have a couple hours alone to watch TV uninterrupted or to play around on the computer, both of which suddenly felt pressing when you couldn't do them at your whim. You suggested she go out with her friends, catch up with them while you stayed home, you didn't want to monopolize her. And you were relieved on the days when she finally went back to work, but in hindsight you can't identify exactly the source of the relief, besides that you were able to return to your hollow and perfunctory daily routine while blithely assuming she would always be there for you.

WHEN YOU SEE BEAUTIFUL women out in the world—and they're everywhere you look—you can't help comparing them to Kait. You search them for the curve of her hips, the jetstream curl in her hair, the constellations of freckles on her right forearm. Think of how much work is involved in getting to know these new women. Your life had been completely built around the idea of being a married man until the day you died, but now that plan is ruined and it's difficult to know how to begin again. You're not even sure exactly who you are anymore; your personality and hers molded themselves to each other over time, subtle alterations, gradual erosion of certain habits, accretion of new beliefs and mannerisms, the accumulation of inside jokes and a shared history. The expertise you both developed in reading the other's nonverbal cues, so that you could process an entire conversation with no words, and barely even any motion. You could look at her and know what she was thinking, and she could do the same with you, but what if that language isn't adaptable? What if you evolved into a person who is capable of only being loved by exactly one other person?

You have no concept of what adult dating entails. You were still living with your parents when you started dating your wife. How does one even begin to retrain oneself? It all seems so harrowing: the careful crafting of an Internet dating profile, checking e-mail every day until you find someone who wants to meet for coffee, the meeting and worrying about ordering the right kind of coffee and the small talking, the stressing every night about whether they like you and whether you really like them. The near inevitability of rejection. The cumulative agony of being dumped by your rebound relationship after your wife's death. The baggage you carry with you forever, the way your wife's death will infect all future relationships, and the lingering concern in the back of women's minds that you're a hex, that marrying you might doom them too. The fact that they might be right. The fact that right now you're not old, but soon you will be. Old. And undateable. And this persistent thought that if you're undateable, then what that means is you're unlovable.

Everyone you used to know is married and has kids now, and is too busy panicking about amortization schedules and changing diapers and watching cartoon shows about talking alligators to worry about your depression. They're at least ten years removed from regaining some measure of independence, and if you're still single by then, you will have become a weird guy to hang around with, because people do not trust single men at that age.

AFTER YOUR WEDDING, YOU stood in a receiving line so everyone could shake your hand and tell Kait she looked beautiful and tell you *you clean up nice!* as if they were surprised that you could look presentable in public. Family and friends insisted on saying things to her like *I don't know what you see in him* or *good luck with him, you'll need it,* and the path of least resistance was to chuckle along with their insulting jokes, but she defended you every time, saying things like *he treats me good, I'm the lucky one* or *I think I'll hold on to him a while.* You shook hands with limping uncles and hugged teary-eyed aunts. Every time a married man patted you on the back and said *welcome to the club,* you pretended they were the first to have come up with that one. They barraged you with advice about compromise and never going to bed angry. And they all kept saying things like *marriage is tough* and *you have to really work at it.* But that never seemed particularly true, not even on days when you lost patience with her or when she complained about your lack of ambition. Marriage was easy, the easiest, most uncomplicated thing you've ever done, the most unambiguously pleasant and satisfying and *right* thing you've ever engaged in. Maybe, you thought but didn't say, *if your marriage is so hard, then you married the wrong person.* Maybe, you thought but didn't say, *if you can't handle it, then you shouldn't be the one giving out advice.* But you were arrogant then, younger and sheltered and drunk on love. You both thought you were the only ones who had ever loved the way you did, and thought nobody could ever match or understand the depths of it.

TWENTY

Each of his companions has distinct reactions to Hunter's story: Paul, who seems to have gained respect for him now that he can see Hunter has also endured legitimate anguish, welcomes him to the club; Austin keeps saying, "Dude, that sucks," and now stands closer to Amber as if to prevent her from escaping; and Amber becomes deeply invested in the issue of the ashes themselves, suddenly very concerned about Hunter's need for *closure*. She is young and she still believes in simple solutions to complex problems. By now, Hunter has heard many promises of impending closure, this notion that at some point if one performs the right action, chants the right series of words at the right time, then suddenly everything will be better, the well of grief is stopped up and everyone can pretend the past never happened. And she is convinced that for him to progress from his current state, what he needs to do is let the ashes fly, send them out on the wings of the wind and watch as Kait wisps across the earth, destined to land, who knows where, maybe in an eagle's nest atop a craggy mountain somewhere, or to whistle into somebody's nose and be sneezed out into a handkerchief, or to tumble and settle back into the soil. Austin seems to have only a casual interest in the ash-spreading cause, but wants to support Amber, who keeps saying things like, "It's no big deal, I like to be helpful," even when nobody has thanked her for doing this or called her helpful, and so they are both grilling him for background information in order to develop a psychological profile of Kait and make an informed decision.

AMBER'S IMAGINATION IS LIMITED to things she has seen in movies and on TV, and so she chooses the Grand Canyon as the perfect setting for the release, envisioning a purely cinematic moment in which Hunter stands on the precipice of the canyon, delivers a heartfelt—not to mention long overdue—eulogy, and then frees Kait from her confinement, liberates himself from his heartache. She's more animated now than she has been for most of the trip: flinging her arms about like a visionary film director, she is preemptively teary-eyed as she describes the beauty of the scene. In the car, she does not sleep, asks to hold Kait, sometimes shakes the box beside her ear like a child investigating a Christmas gift, like she's expecting to hear Kait's voice whispering secrets of the afterlife to her. Hunter has made no promises to open the urn, only says they should see the canyon regardless, and along the way, he holds Kait up to the window so she can see the landscape, first flat as a dinner plate, then furrowed like a shar-pei's face, now jagged and imposing. The roads become more populated as they approach their destination, broken-down cars pulled over on the shoulder as men kick tires and pop hoods. The heat still incredible, the night sky red like a cooked crab, the sun rising early and angry like a colicky baby. Over time, it becomes easy to take for granted that those towering hills in the distance are actually eight-thousand-foot-high mountains, to become inured to being surrounded by postcard views of the world. Vacationing sometimes is nothing more than a hunt for the best views possible, but the current views are cheapened by the promise of the majestic sights that might be just down the road.

A pamphlet told Amber about a new structure called the Grand Canyon Skywalk, which at the moment can only be reached by driving for about fourteen miles on an ungraded, unpaved road. Paul turns onto the non-road, loose stones pinging off the wind-shield, the car rocking like a rowboat tossed in rough seas. Paul is grumbling about the car being dinged, about ruining his tires. He says, "Goddamn canyon is a thousand miles long and we have to go to the worst part." Amber assures him it will be worth it, because the majesty of the place will be such that they will be ren-dered speechless, and they'll be able to conduct a somber farewell ceremony to Kait, who Amber says is kind of like a sister to them all now, the way they've bonded. She says, "You owe her this. She would have wanted this," with such conviction that it is almost pos-sible to forget that Amber knows nothing appreciable about Kait or what Hunter owes her or what she would have wanted. Since the revelation of the ashes, Amber has spent an inordinate amount of time saying things about Kait like *she sounds great* and *she was an amazing woman* and *she was a beautiful person.* They all talk about her like she was an inspiration, putting her on a pedestal just because she's dead, probably because they think this is what he wants to hear, but it's not at all what he wants, because he already *knows* all the lovable and admirable things about her, and what he really wants is for someone to just tell him it's okay to feel broken and he's under no obligation to feel better. What they're doing is they're commandeering her memory and twisting her into the image of someone they can admire. They're allowing her to act as an avatar for their own deceased loved ones. They're stealing her from him, and he needs to reclaim her by making some kind of decisive action.

When they reach their destination, Paul parks behind a line of seven tour vans. Only three hundred feet away, a U-shaped walkway juts out over the canyon like a plexiglass tongue. There are about two hundred people on the skywalk, leaning over the rails on both sides and searching toward the bottom. What happens here is what happens at most tourist venues: tour groups arrive, stroll around aimlessly, take dozens of pictures to prove they were here, then they go away after a few minutes because they're hungry. Many of them have no particular interest in experiencing their experiences, as opposed to simply recording those experiences. If Kait were here, she would want to pose for a nice picture along the edge of the skywalk, and he would pose with her, despite his worries about both of them falling over the rail in a freak accident, and despite his longstanding objections to vacationing just for the pictures. Years ago, standing on the beach in Portland, Maine, watching all the other couples lining up for their photos of the sun sparkling on the water, he tried to explain why he hates how *a good vacation* is defined not as a time for growth and learning about other cultures but rather as going to a place where you get a lot of good pictures as evidence of worldliness or wealth or whatever. She listened quietly and said: "You would have a lot more fun if you let yourself have more fun." And here he is, still in line for the skywalk, and posing in a group photo with his companions and Kait. As much as he complained about the proliferation of amateur photography, he finds himself playing exactly the role he once rejected: a man in an interesting place, just hoping to capture *something*, even if he doesn't know what it is. He's wasted so much energy in his life raging against things without any particular reason besides that he didn't understand them; would it have been so hard to just take some more pictures with Kait? Would it have been so bad to smile for two seconds and wait for the flash and then move on without needing to editorialize? Amber uses Hunter's phone to snap a picture of him with Kait standing at a rail along the edge. But he decides not to upload it, hasn't uploaded a photo since revealing the truth about Kait to the others. He thinks about deleting the picture entirely but also has to admit, it is pretty amazing, the view.

Being surrounded by tourists is like being besieged by funhouse mirrors. There are old people, young people, fat people, thin people, slovenly people, well-dressed people, and they all look a little bit like everyone else at the same time that they look slightly different. Most of them move in pairs.

When Hunter's group gets their turn to test the skywalk, Paul

grips the interior rail and does not look down, shimmying rig-
idly along the frosted opaque edge of the walkway. Austin stomps
through the middle, stares down and jumps, causes the walkway
to vibrate and sends a few people into momentary panic. It is more
frightening up here than Hunter thought it would be; obviously
thousands of people have done this same thing before them, and
obviously the skywalk has passed countless safety tests conducted
by certified engineers, but still he holds on to the rail, shuffling as
if walking on ice, and steps gingerly into the middle of the walkway
as if dipping a toe in a freezing lake. He wants to stay away from the
rail because the thought of dropping Kait over the edge is night-
marish, and so he forces himself to stand in the middle and look
down—a vertiginous view into a seemingly endless scar gouged
into the earth, a wound dealt to the continent that eventually became part of its character. Standing here is like levitating; at any
moment he could plummet like Wile E. Coyote and disappear in
a cloud of dust. He loses himself in the search toward the bottom,
scans the layers of sediment in the walls, the changing colors like
the test pattern on a TV, a visible record of millions of years of evo-
lution. The reminder that nature is prehistoric, is infinite. When he
looks up, they're all gone.

He finds them outside the gift shop. Amber and Austin have
bought a Native American dream catcher, which she says they can
hang over their baby's crib, a comment that causes Austin to physically recoil. Amber turns to Hunter. "So when are we going to
do the ashes?" she says, clapping her hands in a school-marmish
chopchop way that makes him feel like he has somehow failed her.

"I don't know," he says. "It just seems a little bit arbitrary."

"But it's amazing up here," Amber says. "If I was . . . if I had passed on, I'd want to be spread out here. One last romantic gesture."

"She liked nature and everything, but this is just a place." Austin wanders off, kicking up mounds of dirt and then sifting through them as if searching for fossils. Paul jingles his keys in his pocket.

"You have to do it *somewhere*," she says. "Why not here?"

"What's the rush?"

"Are you kidding me?" she says. "That was the whole point of coming out here." She looks like she has to restrain herself from yanking the urn from his hands and disposing of Kait in front of him. Hunter grips Kait tighter, prepares himself for a fight.

"Who ever said I wanted to come here?"

"Oh, I'm sorry, did we inconvenience you?" she says. "When you invited yourself to join our vacation, should we have asked you for permission to do what we wanted? Was it rude for us to ask you to stop lying? No, no, don't say anything, I'm just trying to apologize, I feel so bad about going out of our way to do everything for you while we're on our vacation." She sucks in a harsh breath. "Maybe next time instead of telling us what's wrong with everything you can do something about it." She waves a dismissive hand at him and turns away, kicks a loose stone into the canyon. "I mean, what the hell do you *want*?"

Hunter listens for the sound of the rock hitting bottom, but it is a sound he will never hear. Austin has returned, and rubs a soothing hand on Amber's back. It took less than two weeks for him to alienate his new friends; the only people who have ever been able to tolerate long exposure to him were Kait and Willow.

Paul sidles up to him, says, "You're looking hungry." With an arm on Hunter's back, Paul guides him toward the car.

THE NEXT MORNING WHILE Paul is gone on his walk, Austin asks Hunter if he drinks. Hunter says no, not really, so Austin asks him what he does for fun. Hunter says, "I like to get high sometimes," and before he has finished speaking, Austin unfurls a plastic bag containing a half ounce of musty smelling marijuana. "Why didn't you say something sooner?" Austin says, but he doesn't wait for an answer, because he's already packing a glass bowl that Amber has extracted from her suitcase. In hindsight, Hunter realizes that Austin and Amber have both been getting high throughout this trip—the glassy eyes, the frequent use of Visine, the constant snacking, the inexplicable and sudden onset of fatigue every afternoon. It's hard to figure why they've included him now; maybe they had thought he was a narc. Maybe news of Kait's death humanized him. Maybe they're just feeling generous. Or maybe they're offering an olive branch after yesterday's blow-up.

They smoke in the bathroom with the exhaust whirring, towels stuffed under the doors, water running in the sink, and the pot hits Hunter harder than he expected because he hasn't smoked since that night months ago with Willow. The others, they're fresh out of college, so their tolerance is high as it will ever be. They shotgun hits into one another's mouths, Amber grabbing Hunter's cheeks, closing in on him intimately and blowing the smoke into his lungs as if delivering CPR. They alternate between giggling and hacking and listening at the door for Paul, and when they emerge from the bathroom, a thin line of smoke trails them like a pursuing wraith. After opening the windows, they run down to the hotel's vending machines and load up on snacks for the upcoming ride.

On the road, the world looks more vibrant, the colors on the mountainsides bleed into one another, blurs of light surrounding the car. Conversation progresses in stops and starts, bursts of noise that mean essentially nothing but seem incredibly important and also hilarious. The joy of meaningless language. The comfort of swaddling oneself in empty banter. The satisfying crunch of potato chips in desert-dry mouths. They're laughing at nearly everything, avoiding eye contact with Paul. Hunter smirks at them in the side mirror, and they smirk back, a shared secret. Paul was a drinker and an addict, maybe he knows, he probably knows, so what if he knows? But he might know. Enjoying inside jokes again. Feeling like a college student, harmlessly sneaky, losing oneself in the present, living without consequences. Feeling not at all old. Ravenous. The sensation of limitless possibility. The car still humming as they head west. Uterine warmth, heavy-headed fatigue.

THEY STOP AT THE California border so Amber and Austin can take a picture of themselves standing at the sign welcoming them to the state. Hunter stays in the car, which Paul keeps running, the air conditioner roaring. The effects of the pot have faded and they've had their naps and their food, and Amber is back on her quest for closure.

Kait once told Hunter she had the perfect place for his ashes. They were talking about death, having one of those hypothetical conversations couples have about the inevitable, but it was such an abstraction that it barely qualified as a real consideration. They agreed on the do-not-resuscitate issue, the cremation issue, the no-funeral issue, and then she said what she said. About the perfect place. She never told him where it was, said it should be a surprise for him after he was dead, and even now he can't think of where he would want his own ashes to be spread, so how could she have figured it out so quickly? He told her then that he had a place for her too, but actually he had no ideas at all, still doesn't, probably would hold on to her forever if nobody was pushing him.

They visit several more potential ash-spreading sites—an organic farm, an outer-space-themed bowling alley shaped like a UFO, a Methodist church, some sites chosen more carefully than others. Some places choose to remain stuck in time like Wild Bill's Wild West Outpost, while most others evolve naturally and become what they have to become because they have no choice. A building that once served as a general store for gold-rushing pioneers has been revamped as a boutique hotel. An elementary school is built adjacent to the site of a bloody battle waged between settlers and the Mohave Indians. Everywhere they go, the functions and meanings of locations have deviated from their original purpose. An old warship is now an aspirational dining restaurant. A governor's mansion burns to the ground and is rebuilt as a nightclub. Turn-of-the-century factories, long abandoned, become luxury condos. Even the Grand Canyon, with its ancient geology, is changing constantly.

When they arrive at a lake surrounded by rental cabins, Amber takes three steps onto the property and declares, "This one isn't right for us," and then they continue driving.

At a rest stop, Hunter tells Austin he doesn't really want to do this, says, "I feel bad taking over your trip," and Austin looks over his shoulder at Amber, who is scouting out new locations on the map, and he rolls his eyes. Says, "There's nothing you can do when she gets like this."

"If something needs to get done, I get it done," she says. She directs Paul to keep driving west. They are headed inexorably toward the sea.

While Amber crams another gift-shop knickknack into her bag—a coffee mug that says CALIFORNIA GIRLS HAVE ALL THE FUN—Paul says, "How about we stop screwing around and get you three some real souvenirs?" He pulls up his shirt and shows them the tattoo on his right pectoral, a pair of daisies crossed at the stem. He tells them he got it done when he and Annalisa took this trip three decades ago; he chose daisies because she had told him her name was Daisy when they started dating, and for the first six months of their relationship, he had known her only by that name.

Paul has no intention of getting a tattoo himself; he's saving space on his other pectoral for when his wife returns. Austin wants a tattoo because it's something to do and some of his friends have really cool ones on their biceps and on their backs. Amber says, "Tattoos are stupid, and anyway they look terrible on people when they get old."

"If I make it to seventy," Hunter says, "I'm probably not going to be too worried about people laughing at my tattoo."

"God, do you ever agree with anyone on anything?" Amber says. She smiles to make it seem like she's joking.

Austin attempts to sway her with romance logic: "We could get matching tattoos and have them forever."

"What, so then we both look stupid?" she says. "No deal. You're on your own, Hunter." The tattoo parlor is a small place, a storefront business on a main street in some town they can't find on the map. There is no room inside for the others to wait with him, no one to squeeze his hand at the first bite of the needle, no one to give him a pep talk and assure him he is doing the right thing. Amber is in the car, holding on to Kait.

Actually, Hunter has considered getting a tattoo since high school, thought it would make him seem edgy, like owning a pet python or wearing vintage Black Flag T-shirts to family functions.

The permanence of the tattoo makes it difficult to choose a design; the inking of tattoos is the most lasting commitment many people will ever make. Even marriage ends at death, but tattoos linger beyond. Based on the samples hanging around the room and the suggestion binder sitting on the table, Hunter gleans that this particular shop specializes in folkloric images—wizards, dragons, trolls. He flips through the book but knows he can't pick something from there; a tattoo is supposed to be a deeply personal accessory that will reflect one's values, beliefs, and sense of humor, so what does it reflect about him if he selects something from the back page of a binder full of generic choices? He briefly considers requesting a pair of family crests—Dixon and Cady—but he still hasn't figured out what his crest would be, and he doesn't want a reminder of that other family etched into his body forever.

In the back room, he tells the artist he wants something simple to commemorate his dead wife, and without much discussion, they begin. It hurts more than he thought it would. Like a swarm of yellow jackets. He wishes he were stronger, or fatter, or something. The needle feels so close to the bone. To cry now would weaken the gesture, would make him seem uncommitted. The buzzing ends as abruptly as it began.

Before he even leaves the chair, he regrets the unoriginality in his design. *R.I.P. Kait* on the inside of his right forearm, no ornamentation, no color, no flourishes on the font. Just seven letters and three periods, like a discount telegram. He's shamed by the limits of his own imagination, the consistent failure to do anything the way it ought to be done.

He could have made literary allusions, or gotten a true artist to create a portrait of her on his back. Could have covered his entire body in tributes to her, become the Twenty-first Century Illustrated Man. Could have turned his body into a work of art and been invited to stand naked against white museum walls while people trekked across the country to see him, studying him for hours while unraveling the history of Kait Cady. He could have used his otherwise useless body to promote the story of the most remarkable person he has ever known, inspired hundreds of thousands of people to talk about her in the same way they talk about Mona Lisa and Flaming June and the Girl with the Pearl Earring. A living memorial to her. Could have disappeared into Kait and let the world filter his existence through hers, worn her like a second skin and carried her with him forever.

. . .

EVEN THOUGH SHE'D NEVER shared his enthusiasm for moving, Kait had been convinced by Hunter's presentation that they should at least visit San Francisco, to see the barking sea lions piled on top of one another at the ends of the piers, to stand on a cliffside while the fog rolled over them and they disappeared momentarily from the world, to take a hot air balloon over the wineries in Napa. Hunter never thought they'd make it there, thought the European trips would supersede domestic tourism. And yet, with Kait in hand, he is standing on Fisherman's Wharf, the pungent air sour with yeast. They'd hit the end of Route 66 two days ahead of schedule, and so Hunter had convinced them to head north for this final stop. Three thousand miles from home, he and Kait are watching a line of street performers entertaining people in all directions. There are musicians and dancers and mannequin people and magicians and washed-up hippies with funny panhandling signs.

On the walk toward the cable cars, they pass a group clustered around a street magician. The magician guesses that the dupe's card is the ace of spades, but he is wrong—the dupe is actually holding the king of hearts. Still, the crowd expectantly leans in toward him as if this is all part of the setup, an intentional incorrect guess as prelude to an even greater trick. The magician shuffles his deck and announces, "My apologies, ladies and gentlemen. I have failed you all." Staring down into his top hat as if searching for answers, he walks away from the dumbfounded audience, never turns back to look at them.

Hunter and the others are here to ride the cable cars and to take photos of Lombard Street, carved into the hill like a regrettable tattoo. They've already been through the Haight, a necessary pilgrimage for any pot smoker or classic rock fan or white kid who went to a liberal arts college and at one point identified vaguely with the freewheeling countercultural spirit of the place. It was maybe the most depressing stop on a trip full of them, a dismal hippie haven overrun with people trying too hard to re-create a moment they barely remember.

After the cable cars take them up some hills and back down again—Austin leaning out the door and high-fiving pedestrians—they continue west. The drive to the coast is easy; the beach doesn't seem like big business here, especially not compared to the New Jersey beaches, which at this time of year would be congested and overwhelming. They park at the foot of the beach and walk on the sand, shoes in hand, jeans rolled up and cuffed. Wind whips Amber's hair into a cyclone above her head. The sun is visible through the fog, dull and distant, not so much setting as drifting away.

He and Kait never watched a sunrise together. Nor a sunset. She wanted to, of course she wanted to, because that's what lovers do: they watch the sun rise and fall together, symbolic, a validating moment for a relationship. He wanted to do it too, but always overslept, talked her out of it, distracted her. Found reasons to put it off. Said they should save it for later, for a special day, took too long to realize that special days cannot be predetermined but can only be remembered after they have occurred. Is finally realizing that *later* is a time that does not necessarily exist.

Austin and Amber stroll down the beach hand in hand, Austin sometimes bending to pick up loose shells and skim them across the water's surface. Hunter sinks down into a hump of sand, sets

Kait beside him, and pulls his knees up against his chest. The waves roll in steadily, one on top of the other. Paul approaches Hunter from behind, says, "Amber's a good kid, but she don't know anything." Paul twists a coffee stirrer between his teeth, sits to Kait's right. He digs his feet into the sand, buries himself up to his shins. "Closure." He makes a sound like a whale spurting from its blowhole. Tosses his coffee stirrer toward the water.

Hunter thinks right now is the exact time when it would be convenient to be a drinker, because they could fill the silences by passing a bottle back and forth, let the burning in their chests do all the talking. "How long did it take you to get back to normal?" Hunter says.

Paul stretches back, leans on his elbows. "No such thing as normal." Waves crash in harder, eating away at the shore. Out toward the horizon, the water looks nearly black. "After a while, you just keep on living. You don't have a choice."

Windblown sand piles up along Kait's left side, nearly obscuring her name. A boat edges out toward the line of the horizon, and Hunter contemplates the terrifying leap of faith people made centuries ago when they piloted themselves toward what appeared to be the planet's shelf. Completely ensconced in darkness, surrounded by sea monsters, they still pushed into the unforgiving night because they wanted to see what would happen when they reached the other side. They trusted that it would be worth the danger, and they took comfort in the rhythms of nature, knowing that the sun would absolutely rise in the morning at the right time and place and set in the evening at the right time and place, and the stars and the moon would absolutely be there to guide them. They knew better than anybody that the world would go on regardless and they had to learn to trust it or it would destroy them.

Austin and Amber reappear in the distance, headed back toward them, Amber tiptoeing between broken shells. Paul pushes himself back to his feet and says, "You got to do something with those ashes. Get her off your case." A trip that began as an attempt for Paul to relive the happiest days of his marriage has been hijacked by Hunter and Kait's ashes. The three of them have been preparing for this trip for months, if not years, but Hunter's status as recent widower overshadowed their carefully considered plans. He became a burden to them, even to smiling, persistent Amber, whose helpfulness manifests itself in pushiness and a pathological need to be acknowledged as helpful, which has made Hunter feel guilty for not having made himself available enough to have been helped. And, frankly, Hunter's trip has also been hijacked by this quest; even the way Amber has begun talking, like she and Kait are old friends and like she somehow relates to Kait, is a hijacking of Hunter's memory; it is Amber glomming onto his heartache because it seems romantic in some way. Both parties latched on to each other and used the other: they to add meaning and depth to their trip, and he to alleviate his loneliness, yes, but also to excuse himself from having to make choices.

As Paul walks toward the ocean to dip his toes in the water, Hunter turns away, digs his phone out of his pocket and extends his tattooed arm out in front of himself to take a picture—Hunter and Kait, sitting together with the Pacific at their backs. The other side of the world as he knows it. Thinks about uploading it so he can caption it *from sea to shining sea*, but decides not to share it with anyone. Paul wanders off in the other direction, and Hunter pivots to look again at the ocean. Lines of whitecaps roll toward them, endless and relentless. A wave rises and swells and claws at the shore, and the mist from the crash washes over him. He finds a seashell in the sand next to him and lifts it to his ear. Twenty-five years ago, when he and Jack were walking together along a New Jersey beach, Jack knelt down and pressed a shell first against his own ear and then against Hunter's. "I'll tell you something your grandfather taught me when I was your age," Jack said. "Not every shell is the same. If you find the right one, it doesn't sound like the ocean at all." He listened to another one, tossed it away. "Some shells have magic in them. If you listen really closely, you can hear voices from another world." He tried another. "They're hard to find, though. Unless you know what to look for," Jack said, winking at Hunter to let him know that this was to be their secret. They tried a couple dozen shells that day until Jack found one that he said was filled with his own father's voice, but when Hunter listened, he only heard the white noise of the ocean. Now, sitting alone with the ashes, Hunter knows that somewhere on this beach, there is a shell containing the message he's been looking for. The first shell does not work and neither does the second, but in the third one he hears a sound like a whisper. He closes his eyes and concentrates so he can hear it more clearly. The whisper he hears is Kait's voice. *The journey is over*, it says. When he opens his eyes he sees the waves still charging toward him, and in each wave's crest he sees Kait rising up out of the sea and then diving back down. In the mist he feels her touch covering him completely; in every cloud he sees the outline of her body; in each grain of sand he sees her face; in the oxygen and nitrogen of the atmosphere, he feels her physical presence with him in a way he hasn't since he drove away from home. Nobody in the world can see it, but she is sitting next to him and her arm is draped over his shoulder and she is saying in his ear: *I was real and you were real and that's all you can ask for.* And she is saying: *You kept your promise.* And she is saying: *It's over, it's over, it is over.*

The sound of the shell cuts out abruptly. He shakes it but it will never channel those sounds again. He stuffs it in his pocket, one of the few souvenirs he will take home with him. Then he snaps the cube open and turns it upside down to release her. He watches the ashes ride on the wind out across the beach and into the ocean and he knows they will travel across the globe on their own now. Austin and Amber, still by the water's edge, are closing in. As he walks away from the beach, he quietly says goodbye, because he is never coming back to this place and he is never going to see these people again.

TWENTY ONE

You see old couples everywhere you look, couples whose marriages have lasted longer than Kait's life, and who flaunt their good fortune by strolling hand-in-hand along sidewalks and in shopping centers and in airports. They don't have the decency to be considerate toward people like you, who can't help parsing their relationships, seeing what they've done to deserve a literal lifetime of happiness, why they're so worthy while you're not. You compare visions of your unlived future with these people you're seeing, wondering, would your love have lasted? It takes forty or fifty years for most people to finally become the person they want to be, and Kait never got that chance. Over time, would she still have laughed at your jokes, and would you still be able to see in her eyes the glistening girl you met on that rooftop? What happens when the joy of discovery gives way to comfortable complacency? Would you still share a bed and watch movies together and have things to discuss? How do people never run out of things to say to each other?

You worry you wouldn't have been as selfless as the old man you see pushing his wheelchair-bound wife through the airport, his back permanently humped from a decade of leaning down to serve her. At some point, many years ago, his presumably fulfilling life was wrested from him and replaced with this one. You would have panicked and put her in a nursing home. Would have found a way to rationalize it and told her *it's for the best, I don't know how to take care of people anyway*, and you would have had to find a way to ignore the look of betrayal in her eyes during your thrice weekly visits, and you would have had to explain to everyone that yes, you're still married but she's living in the nursing home now because she needs that kind of care, and they would treat you with a mixture of pity and admiration for at least sticking with your invalid wife, but the reality is you would be looking forward to your time away from her, free from the pressure and expectations, those quiet nights at home when you could get high and watch comedies on TV and forget all about her miserable fate. Because what she would be is an inconvenience. Some people get off on that suffering-servant routine, demanding that others see them tending to their disabled loved ones so that others can say *you're such a good person, I could never handle that,* and then the suffering servant can respond *if you really love someone, it's not a chore at all, it's a privilege*. Is it too cynical for you to say that's probably a façade, to suspect that some mornings those people must wake up resenting their disabled loved one for taking every-thing away but still hanging on, half wishing they will find their partner dead just for the relief? Roles reversed, Kait would have cared for you to her detriment, would have sacrificed everything to ensure you had something resembling a quality life, and while she changed your diapers and bathed you and spoon-fed you and wiped the mess from your face and smiled sweetly through your memory lapses, you would be consumed with guilt for ruining her life by having had a stroke, but you would be rendered unable to apologize because you would have lost your ability to speak. And she would not complain. She would take her responsibilities seri-ously and somehow find reasons to love you more. And so maybe, knowing how she would have sacrificed for you, you would have discovered depths of resolve and compassion that you didn't know you had, would have happily cared for her for another seventy years. What's not fair is that you never even got the opportunity to find out. You never got to prove yourself to her. You find yourself sometimes wishing for the withering old age, the mutual degrada-tion of your bodies and minds, the immobility and dementia. In a just world, couples would all have the opportunity to break down together.

HOW MANY THINGS ARE there that you've left undone? How many old to-do lists will you find in your pockets and in your house? How else to describe your life but as incomplete? Is life sup-posed to be about completing a long series of tasks, or is the whole point that no matter what you do, there will be things you've only partly finished?

When you collect someone's ashes, you're supposed to spread them somewhere. Ritual, the social contract. You're supposed to do something poetic and moving. You've never understood any of this, the expectation that you should be so willing to send her soaring away from you. Even eight hours after emptying the urn on the beach, now flying east toward Philadelphia, you feel piercing regret at having left her behind, terror at the thought that you let go too soon, a magnetic attraction that tugs you back toward her at an atomic level. But sitting on the beach with her, it occurred to you that it's selfish to keep holding on forever. It is detrimental to both of your spirits if you refuse to move on. You need to liberate yourself from the burden of her death and you need to allow her the freedom to go where she wants to go. If she wants to come back to you, she will. You can't force it on her. Her soul has to choose you.

There are no fairy tales. No looking over in your bed and seeing her lying there again. No magic potions to bring her back to life. No spells you can cast or prayers you can recite that will solve this problem. No dreams in which her spirit appears and comforts you. No speaking to the dead through psychics and Ouija boards. No meeting another woman whose body has been inhabited by Kait's soul. There is only a hole where a life used to be, and there is you sitting beside the hole, looking in and hoping to see something you cannot, will not ever, see.

Like most people, Kait believed in some version of heaven. Not necessarily the clouds and harps and wings and the reunion with her beloved pets, and maybe not even the promise of enlightenment, but some amalgam of various popular visions of the afterlife.

She believed she would still exist after death, believed that, wherever she would be, it would be a fine place, and she would still be able to interact with the material world on some level. You've never been able to conjure a vision of an afterlife that makes any sense, never been able to reconcile yourself to this idea that somehow everyone gets a life on earth, and then for some reason they're also rewarded for simply existing by getting to enjoy themselves for eternity. When you die, you do not expect to go anywhere. There will be no reunion where you and Kait get to clink champagne glasses and rekindle your love affair while observing Earth's dramas from afar. You will be dead and you will be ashes and someone will toss you somewhere too, and that's the end. But wouldn't it be nice if there *was* a reunion? Wouldn't it feel good to believe?

TWENTY-TWO

It took over two months for him to wend his way across the country via car and bus and car again, and it takes only six hours for his flight to carry him from San Francisco back to Philadelphia. There is no one to pick him up at the airport when he lands. He boards a shuttle along with a six-person family returning from vacation. Looking down at his phone, he studies the photo of him and Kait on the beach, tries to learn something new about that moment, tries to imagine Kait sitting there with his ashes in the urn.

His house looks relatively undamaged from the outside, with the exception of the waist-high grass waving in the late summer breeze, and bundles of mail spilling from the box, stacked on the porch, catalogues and magazines and sympathy cards and unpaid bills and second and third notices for unpaid bills. The inside of the house is ransacked, more damaged even than Sherry's photos had indicated. Dishes swept out of cabinets and shattered, couch cushions gashed open as if they had been concealing bricks of cocaine, mattress flipped, books and DVDs strewn across the floor. Refrigerator left open and running, the food inside fuzzy with decay. Kait's drawers picked clean, his drawers removed from the dresser and overturned. Toilet clogged, overflowing. Evidence of rodents everywhere, frayed wires and gnawed drywall, trails of mouse droppings lined across countertops and floors. The smell of moldy August rain. The house is a corpse, Kait's family the scavengers.

When fishing a pillow out from behind the couch, he finds the globe that started this whole trip, the last gift she ever gave to him. Impossible to tell how it ended up there, whether he had left it on the floor, or whether her family had tossed it aside like it was trash. He lies on the couch, the globe sitting on his chest, and he spins it, watching the colors swirl past him, a life in fast-forward.

Sleep should not come easy in the house, not with that belligerent odor, not with the chaotic mess, but lying on the torn cushions he still fades away for a few minutes. The exhaustion of months on the road, full days sitting in cars, nights curled on hotel floors, the fatigue hitting him organ-deep. When he wakes up, he calls Willow and tells her he's home. Tells her he needs help.

He thinks about calling the police to report a robbery, but if he presses charges, then he will have to see Kait's family again, be reminded of how much she looked like her brothers, the way they all had the same noses and the same teeth and the same posture, the fact that every time any of them spoke, he heard only Kait's voice.

Besides, whatever they wanted from him, they've taken it, and now they will leave him alone. They never actually hated him, Hunter thinks; it was the situation that made them so angry, imbued them with this need to lash out at everything that had survived Kait. Was it any different from the way he'd been sabotaging their efforts to overcome her death?

He can never be friends with them—that wasn't even possible when Kait was alive—but he at least wants to stop being an obstacle between them and being whole. He sits on his floor with a pad of paper—the computer keyboard is smashed and unusable—and writes a brief letter to Sherry:

You don't deserve this and I don't deserve it and nobody does, but it's what we've got to deal with now.

Kait's gone and I'm sorry, and I'm back and I'm sorry about that too.

I've been trying to figure it out. How to get by. And I have no idea.

But one thing I realized is, Kait didn't belong to me. I acted like she was mine but she wasn't. I want you to know I understand that now.

THE NEXT AFTERNOON, WILLOW arrives, a bag of groceries in hand.

The first thing she does is cook him a meal. French toast, his favorite as a child, drowned in syrup. She says, "You look like you've been starving yourself," and although that's the kind of thing mothers are supposed to say and he has always been thin anyway, he realizes she's probably right, because when she asks him what he's been eating on the road, he can barely remember; he knows he ate every day, but it was rote consumption, instinctively shoveling food into his mouth when it was placed before him, the unthinking way a dog eats. Probably there were a lot of rest-stop sandwiches and French fries. Probably there were gallons of soda, mounds of salt and sugar, saturated fats that have ruined his arteries, squeezing his heart and solidifying it into a rock. Probably there were no local delicacies and none of the kinds of restaurants Kait would have wanted to visit, their names circled and starred in the guidebook in her purse.

Willow makes him sit outside on the front porch to eat. Says the environment in his house is toxic and there needs to be a cleansing. Says he needs to see neighbors, reintegrate himself into his own life. The wild grass of the lawn raises up at him like the hair on a threatened cat.

Everywhere there is something broken.

The second thing Willow does is suggest he move back home with her and Jack. "It would be good for you," she says. "And I could use the company."

"I've got a house here," he says. "I have friends here," he says, which is not actually true.

The third thing Willow does is offer him a joint and retreat with him into the bedroom where they sit on the floor and get high and stare off into the distance and devour a bag of cheese-flavored snack foods. She tells him Jack has been accusing her of being unhappy, and she says, "I'm not an unhappy person am I?"

and he decides to treat this as a rhetorical question. She tells him Jack is talking about retiring soon, and says that might be the end of them when that happens. There is no way they can spend all day together; his temperament is not suited for a sedentary lifestyle.

Hunter asks, "Do you still love him?"

"He's a better man than you think," Willow says. "Raising you wasn't easy on him."

"How do you end up with a guy like him anyway?"

"It just always felt right. How does anybody explain it?"

They smoke until it is dark and the clock is still red-eyed and flashing *12:00* and strips of moonlight sneak between Venetian blinds and rest on his legs, like pale fingers holding him there.

THERE IS WORK TO do. There are rugs to vacuum, floors to sweep, pests to exterminate, walls to paint. There is grass to cut and trash to remove. Standing in the living room where his coffee table used to be (they had stolen it; how had he not noticed that immediately?), Hunter feels like a man who was dropped in the middle of the Pacific and told to drain the ocean. How does one even begin? Willow flits from room to room tilting pictures and swishing dirt off of surfaces arbitrarily, making cosmetic fixes where dramatic changes need to occur.

What Kait would have done is she would have sat down at the dining room table—now positioned next to the front door of the house, a sign that her brothers tried to remove it but couldn't fit it through the door without detaching the legs—and made a list. Divided into sections by room, comprehensive enough to include items like dusting the ceiling fans. And so: Hunter makes a list. On two sheets of paper. He then lists the necessary materials to complete the task, and drives Willow to the hardware store in a rental car, because his car is in an impound lot somewhere in Illinois.

THE CLEANUP ITSELF IS tedious and painful and more than occasionally nauseating. Halfway through the first day, Willow suggests he hire a service, but he says, "I feel like I ought to do this." He assigns Willow upstairs while he starts outside, where malicious creatures scurry from the lawn as he charges through first with a scythe and then with a weed whacker and then again with the mower. Sweat burns in his eyes, unidentified objects launch and sting his shins, sending a fine trickle of blood down each leg. Each swipe with the mower reveals a patch of land he hasn't seen in months, every moment leading to a new discovery as he labors under the stubborn September sun.

Taking a break, he goes inside to refill his ice water and finds Willow also on a break, fanning herself with a feather duster. She says, "These hands were not made for hard labor," displaying them as if modeling jewelry. "Neither were yours," she says, grabbing Hunter's hands and pointing out the calluses, the blood crusted beneath fingernails. She has taken several breaks already, but he does not criticize because he doesn't want to sound like Jack, and anyway this isn't her mess. Later, he takes more frequent breaks himself, lingering on his porch with a quart of lemonade, presiding over the conquered lawn for all his neighbors to see.

By the third morning, he knows they have made progress, but it's hard to gauge because there still is so much to do. At times, it feels like he is just shifting the mess from one room to another and then back again. Their morale sinking, he and Willow break for an early lunch.

Willow volunteers to pick up takeout while Hunter sits outside on his porch steps. At least here he can see the lawn, weedless and orderly. He hunches forward, leaning on his fist, and feels himself falling asleep.

A car engine hums down the street and stops in front of his house. He looks up and sees Jack, not wearing his standard khakis and dress shirt but jeans and a T-shirt. "Your mother told me there's a lot of work to do here," he says, walking past Hunter and into the house.

THE PROCESS TAKES FIVE full days of hard labor, inside and outside. It entails the hauling of dozens of heavy-duty trash bags to the curb. It requires the sorting of sentiment from waste. It demands that Hunter face the limits of his endurance. Willow renounces physical labor and assumes the role of supervisor, offering well-meaning but unhelpful tips like, "I'm not sure that's the best way to use a roller," and "I don't think you're supposed to do it like that," and "There has to be some easier way to get this done." Jack barely speaks. He consults the list and moves on to the next task and later crosses items off the list. He seems to have adopted an argument-avoidance strategy that is based largely on silence, which, so far, is more effective than anything else they've ever tried.

By the last evening, Hunter is limping, his posture twisted from dull pains in his neck and back, most of his muscles sore as they awake from atrophy and are tested for the first time in years. His fingers are locked into a claw from all the tugging and hammering and hauling. The next morning, he gets up in stages and his feet remain numb until he has already been walking for a few minutes. He is trying to grow a beard because he thinks it's the perfect look for this kind of work, but at the moment, all he has achieved are clumps of wispy hairs scattered about his mouth like the fuzz on a dandelion.

Every room is repainted, every surface cleaned. Light bulbs replaced, holes in drywall patched, furniture rearranged, stolen essentials replaced. The carpets in most rooms have been removed, exposing hardwood floors. The now-useless pieces of furniture—Kait's dresser and wardrobe, for example—have been donated to Goodwill, along with her remaining clothes. The few possessions of hers that weren't stolen by her family (her alarm clock, a couple pairs of shoes, the peridot earrings and necklace somehow untouched, maybe a gesture of forgiveness) are packed into a box labeled KAIT that is carried down to the basement and placed alongside the Christmas and Halloween decorations. Her photo albums are stacked neatly on a shelf in the spare bedroom closet, where he can find them if necessary but doesn't have to see them every day. The globe is set up in the living room, adjacent to the couch, where he can see it and spin it and envision the world from the comfort of his home. They rehang photos, Hunter standing on a stepstool above his television, placing a level on top of a portrait of him and Kait—hands clasped around her wedding bouquet, she's wide-mouthed with laughter as he looks into her eyes—while Willow stands beside him, waiting to catch him if he stumbles.

In the evening, the three of them sit on the couch, Jack sipping on scotch while Hunter and Willow smoke a few more joints. Willow asks Hunter again about his trip. He has told them nothing so far, but the combination of the sense of accomplishment and the pot are making him talkative, words machine-gunning out in a way they haven't in months. He describes the sights and the broken-down car. Does not mention Jessa or the Bad Bitches. Says he saw so many things he never thought he'd see, and finds himself scrolling through the photos on the phone, narrating the events and filling in details about Amber, Paul, and Austin. They allow him to sputter until he runs out of things to say, and the last thing he says about the trip is this: I'm glad it's over. When he's finished, Willow says he should write his story down, not to share with anyone, but to process his grief, to better understand himself and remember the person he was at the lowest points of his life. "There's value in remembering the negative," she says.

Their final act is to plant a bush in the backyard. Willow's idea, not his. The notion being that this land has been poisoned by an untimely death and the subsequent depression and wanton destruction, and he needs to make amends. He also needs to allow the land to make amends to him, she says. And although she wants him to plant an apple tree or something ostentatious like that, he talks her down to a hydrangea bush, which is placed in the far corner of his backyard, where Willow says it will bloom every summer.

That evening, Hunter falls asleep before sunset, and he does not wake until noon the next day.

By then, Jack is already gone—he had to get back to the office, couldn't wait any longer for Hunter to wake up—and Willow has set her suitcase near the front door. She says, "Don't worry, I'm not leaving yet," by which she means her flight isn't scheduled until the evening. He asks what's the rush, and she says, "We still have a day to enjoy together."

"What am I supposed to do when you're gone?"

"You're always welcome to stay with us."

"Did Jack tell you to come home?"

"Honey, your father doesn't *tell* me to do anything."

"You can't just stay another day?"

"Your father doesn't know how to be alone," she says.

THE FIRST SEVERAL HOURS Hunter spends alone in his resurrected home are consumed by browsing the Internet. Reading local news he doesn't particularly care about, researching famous widowers, skimming social networks for people's most inconsequential thoughts on every topic, finding nude pictures of just about any female celebrity he wants to see nude. Deep into the online binge, he receives an e-mail.

SUBJECT: Amber Lang has sent you a friend request.

Then another.

SUBJECT: Austin Winslow has sent you a friend request.

Of course they found him online. Everyone everywhere can find everyone else, there is no more hiding. He doesn't remember telling either of them his last name, although maybe they saw it on the urn. Or maybe he did tell them, subconsciously wanted them to track him down. So he clicks through and views their profiles, sees that Amber has posted over a thousand photos of herself online, ranging from posed shots in formal wear to drunken pictures of her passed out on a toilet, pants bunched around her ankles. She likes to use emoticons to express emotion. She looks strangely unlike the girl he remembers from the trip. Austin's profile is pared down and sanitized to protect the corporate job he probably starts next week. In his only picture, he is wearing a tie that fits him as comfortably as wings on an elephant.

Hunter's first impulse is to click a button accepting their friendship, to open up his online life to them too, to invite them to see his photos and know his favorite movies and books and to read his opinions on his neighbors and his pet peeves, and in exchange for their tolerating his every whim and thought, to listen to their beliefs and responses to everything that interests or annoys them. To inflate his number of friends—he's lost some since Kait's death, but there are still three hundred people in the world willing to call themselves his Internet friends. To trick himself into believing there is something more to social networking than vanity, in which everyone can position themselves as the most important person in their own little world and to have their vanity reinforced by the cadre of hangers-on that *every single person* has, regardless of their relative levels of popularity. He thinks about clicking that button to accept their friendship, but then he stops himself. He clicks the other button, the one that says IGNORE, and he closes his laptop, steps away from it like it's a rattlesnake coiled and ready to strike.

He denies their friendship because maybe it's best to leave that part of his life behind. He had some memorable times, and it was a pivotal moment in his life, but why does he need it to linger? The fallacy of these shallow online friendships is in the belief that it's possible to continue preserving every moment, to maintain all relationships and feelings and experiences from the entirety of one's life. Some things are meant to be temporal, he thinks, and there is a reason humans used to move on instead of clinging to every bond they'd ever formed. Nobody's hands are big enough to hang on to every moment for eternity. He shoves the laptop under a couch cushion so he can't see it, and then declares that today is the first day of the Month of No Internet.

HE SLEEPS RIGID ON the edge of his bed, only venturing toward her side to search for her scent in the pillow, or to gather her stray hairs from the sheets and drop them in the trash. Some days he finds himself clutching the emptiness against his body, the absence of the cube heavier than the cube itself ever was. He still talks to her, a continuous narration of the day's events.

In the car now, he is listening to music, his stations, not hers. He is driving through the city, sticking to back roads to avoid traffic; he wants to revive their old game, take them both on a guided tour of the past. The tattoo on his forearm is visible at all times when he is driving. Since he has been tattooed, nobody has asked him about the *R.I.P. Kait*, although he has caught a few stares in the grocery store, a middle-aged woman studying him sadly as he reaches for an apple and exposes his loss. Hunter pulls over alongside a strip mall, turns the radio down, engine still running, and says, "This Chinese restaurant here, that's where you and I went for our first meal after we bought the house. You remember? We went inside and there were no seats, but you'd been talking about Chinese all day so we said we were okay waiting a half hour, and then the half hour turned into an hour, but we'd been waiting so long it didn't make sense to leave then. So we waited and while we waited you

talked about all the work we had to do in the house, which I wasn't
happy about because you know how I hate painting, but you were
so excited about making it *our place*. And then the food—it was
the best Chinese food I've ever had. So good, like great-sex good.
And you liked it too, but you got sick before we even finished, ran
outside, right here by this pole and first you spit, which was funny
because for some reason you didn't know how to spit right. But
then you threw up. Everywhere. I remember the chunks of pork,
that's what I remember most. And the color—duck-sauce orange.
Like it was glowing. And then you were sick for a few days, but I
took care of you. Remember that homemade soup?"

The next stop is a post office outside of which Kait once found
a rubberbanded roll of twenty-dollar bills, and then spent the next
hour trying to find the money's rightful owner. The amazing thing
about that day was that nobody seemed to want the money; Hunter
had never imagined it would be so hard to give away free cash, but
everybody was honest, nobody lied and pretended it was theirs.
Eventually, Kait turned it in at the post office lost and found, and
even called the next day to see if someone had picked it up. Hunter
spent the rest of that night talking about what they could have
bought if they'd held on to it. The things they could have owned.
Just more things he would have had to throw out after her death.

He drives past Rittenhouse Square, points out a bench and reminds her of the time a stray cocker spaniel stole a sandwich right
out of her hand. Outside city hall, he narrates the story about the
group of teenagers pelting him with stale hot dog buns from a passing car. He drives through all of the city's neighborhoods, from
Northeast down to Southwest, stopping to tell her stories about
record stores he patronized during the Month of Owning Vinyl,

a country club they visited for a golfing date, bars where they met friends and he tried to talk to her while she got drunk, awnings they huddled under during thunderstorms, mailboxes they'd leaned on during casual conversation, patches of grass where she'd once stood, rays of sunlight that had reflected off of her skin, air molecules she'd exhaled and breezes that had rippled through her hair.

It's nearing fall, the air crisp like apples, wind cool but not biting, the sun setting soon after people return home from work. He drives through the dimming light, past the city limits, and parks on a tree-lined suburban street. Tells her, "We would have made friends here, in that house over there. I would meet this guy at work after I got a new job, and we would have had double dates and dinner parties, and sometimes we would come out here because it's so quiet and it smells like honeysuckle, which you loved because it reminded you of Christmas. Sometimes their neighbors would come over too, and we'd be like an unofficial part of the neighborhood. There are foods they would cook for us that we'd never had—eggplant and ceviche and butternut squash risotto. There are words they would use that we'd never heard: he used to be in the Navy, so he has these great stories about life at sea and being in battle, and his wife has lived all over the country because her mom was schizophrenic, and listening to her would be like traveling. They listen to us too, when we talk, they want to know things about us, where we're from and what we believe in and why, and you would be in there amazing them with your great job and your generosity, and I would do okay too. And later their kids and our kids would be out in the backyard chasing lightning bugs, and right here, here on the sidewalk where I'm parked is where you would come outside to catch some fresh air and to get away from the kids for just a few minutes, but you would always come back and I would never have to worry about you. We would have moved out here eventually, to be closer to our friends and so the kids could play together, and there would be school board meetings and graduations and fiftieth birthdays and arthritis and kids' weddings and grandkids, and one day I would trip on the curb over there and take a bad fall, break a couple of bones, and you would start to feel tired and irritable earlier in the day, and we would neither of us look like we used to, but we would be here together, that's where we would be. You can see it, through the windows. Me and you in the kitchen peeling carrots, not talking because we don't even need to talk anymore to know what the other is thinking."

Above the front door of the house he's staking out, a light flicks on, glares at him like an interrogation lamp, and he starts the engine before anyone confronts him or calls the police. On the drive back toward his house, the tour continues, pointing out places where he will one day stand, restaurants he will one day enter, jobs he will one day hold, people he will one day meet, friends he will one day make, and women he will one day date. "It's not that I want to get remarried," he says in the middle of detailing a date at an upscale steakhouse. "It's just, people need people around in order to stay normal. That's all." He tells her about selling the house and beginning again, but always carrying her with him. "You're the only reason I can imagine a better future," he says. "You loved me and taught me how to love someone else, and that saved my life." He rests his hand on the empty passenger seat, as if she's still sitting there, and tells her that whatever good comes of his life now, it's due to her. In the car, rumbling along quiet roads back toward his house, he promises to keep talking, because he still has stories he has to tell.